R
I
C
O
C
H
E
T

RICOCHET

KATHRYN BERLA

flux ®

Mendota Heights, Minnesota

First Edition
First Printing, 2019

Book design by Jake Nordby
Cover design by Jake Nordby
Cover images by Paradise studio/Shutterstock

Excerpt(s) from THE HIDDEN REALITY: PARALLEL UNIVERSES AND THE DEEP LAWS OF THE COSMOS by Brian Greene, copyright © 2011 by Brian Greene. Used by permission of Alfred A. Knopf, an imprint of the Knopf Doubleday Publishing Group, a division of Penguin Random House LLC. All rights reserved.

Flux, an imprint of North Star Editions, Inc.

This is a work of fiction. Names, characters, places, and incidents are either the product of the author's imagination or are used fictitiously, and any resemblance to actual persons living or dead, business establishments, events, or locales is entirely coincidental.

Library of Congress Cataloging-in-Publication Data
Names: Berla, Kathryn, 1952- author.
Title: Ricochet : a novel / by Kathryn Berla.
Description: First edition. | Mendota Heights, MN : Flux, an imprint of North Star Editions, Inc., [2019] | Summary: "When seventeen-year-old Tatiana discovers that she is living four different but parallel lives in the multiverse, she and her other selves must band together to stop a megalomaniac scientist: their father"— Provided by publisher. | Identifiers: LCCN 2019015456 (print) | LCCN 2019018168 (ebook) | ISBN 9781635830415 (ebook) | ISBN 9781635830408 (pbk.)
Subjects: | CYAC: Science fiction. | Fathers and daughters—Fiction. | Lesbians—Fiction.
Classification: LCC PZ7.1.B4578 (ebook) | LCC PZ7.1.B4578 Ric 2019 (print) | DDC [Fic]—dc23
LC record available at https://lccn.loc.gov/2019015456

Flux
North Star Editions, Inc.
2297 Waters Drive
Mendota Heights, MN 55120
www.fluxnow.com

Printed in the United States of America

To George, who holds my hand and my heart.

"If a quantum calculation predicts that a particle might be here, or it might be there, then in one universe it *is* here, and in another it *is* there. And in each such universe, there's a copy of you witnessing one or the other outcome, thinking—incorrectly—that your reality is the only reality."

"It's at once humbling and stirring to imagine just how expansive reality may be."

—Brian Greene, *The Hidden Reality: Parallel Universes and the Deep Laws of the Cosmos*

CHAPTER 1

A story starts like this and ends like that. But sometimes we can only guess when a story really starts and wonder if it ever really ends.

My story starts when Priya and I spit into our matching tiny plastic vials. We spit until they're full—mine, slightly yellow-tinged; Priya's, clear and frothy.

"You so have a sinus infection," she says. "That's gross."

It does make me wonder. I forgot to brush my teeth that morning, and I'm too embarrassed to admit it. I wonder if Priya is turned off by me now, repulsed enough to not want to kiss me later tonight. I blush.

"Shut up," I cap my vial and slide it into the precoded envelope. "People have different-colored saliva just like they have different shades of whiteness to their teeth."

I don't know whether that's true, but Priya usually believes me when it comes to science. Or math. Or anything related to school and academics, actually. We're both *academic achievers*, as our teachers like to say. Perhaps unhealthily so, but we're competitive and eager to excel so we're not about to change. We also have to

T
A
T
I

put up with the nicknames at school: Smart and Smarter (although it's unclear who's Smart and who's Smarter), the A-Team, and the Einstein Twins, to name a few. We don't mind; in fact, we welcome it. When it comes to the other stuff, like how to act around people; what not to say so I won't come off as the biggest nerd on earth; an approximation of what to wear; what music to listen to; and generally, how to transform myself into a person who can successfully disappear in school by blending in—well, then I rely on Priya. My parents are old hippies, so I can't count on them for suggestions on how to fit in. They normally only suggest things that make my situation worse, although that unconditional love thing is a decent enough trade-off.

"Aww . . . you're so cute when you blush." Priya comes up behind me and wraps her arms around my waist, one narrow brown hand still clasping her sealed vial. I feel the warmth of her cheek pressed against my shoulder. Her soft breasts pushing against my back. The touch of her hand on my belly stirring sleeping butterflies.

"I'm not cute," I blurt out in my typically clumsy, self-effacing manner. It isn't charming, and I know that, but can't help myself and don't feel I have to when I'm with Priya. She circles around to face me.

"Miss Tatiana Woodland, you're as cute as . . ."

"As?"

"As Hercules."

I scrunch my face in barely disguised disgust. "Hercules is a Pekinese."

"But not just *any* Pekinese. Hercules is *my* Pekinese."

"Well, since you put it that way."

"Okay, here's your spit." She pushes the vial into my hand.

"No, actually that's your spit. Mine's already in the envelope ready to go."

"*My* spit, okay, but your idea. Remind me again why we're wasting your parents' money and our precious bodily fluids."

"Remind me why we need to get an A in Ethnic Studies in a project that was originally your idea."

"Was it? A dumb idea in retrospect."

"Oh. Oh. Did I just hear an admission of weakness from Priya Gupta? Anyway, it's too late. Like you said, wasting my parents' money and all."

"I'm just messing with you. It's going to be a cool project. Although I'm pretty sure I already know what my results will be—one hundred percent Indian subcontinent. Zero percent everything else, although it would be fun to have a surprise. But you already know your birth parents were Ukrainian."

"Russian."

"Same difference."

"Don't tell them that."

"Okay, the next time I never meet them I won't. And don't tell them I said so when you never meet them."

I give her the glare—my goofy glare, she calls it.

"All right, let's go mail these. The sooner we get rid of them, the sooner I can erase the image of your gross yellow spit from my mind."

I flush warm again and she sees it. "Kidding!" She stands on tippy-toes to offer a soft, plushy kiss, something I rarely receive from her in her own home. Even with Priya's dad at work and her mom picking up her little brother, Nikky, from school, it's a huge deal—forbidden, and therefore all the more delicious. I slide my hands up her sides until they rest on her shoulders, and gently pull her closer to me.

The kiss ends and Priya's wet tongue darts across my face in one bold sweep. "There's a little more spit for good measure." She giggles.

When she lowers her heels to the ground, taking her kiss with her, I can still feel its ghost on my lips. I wipe the wetness away in an exaggerated motion of disgust with the back of my hand. Hercules watches us intently from the open doorway to her bedroom, his front paws splayed outward, his turquoise collar studded with rhinestones. Does Hercules know he's witnessing something rare in this household? A moment of pure, unguarded bliss. He slow-wags and then pads away down the hall toward the den where he spends most of his day lounging on a pillow by the fireplace.

"How come . . ." My eyes slide to my feet and my shoulders slump as the rest of the sentence catches in my throat.

"Tati, c'mon." Priya draws out the second word and her voice takes on that distant quality, the tone she uses when she's leading a group discussion or solving an equation on the board in front of the class. Her serious, problem-solving voice. Her absolutely-uninterested-in-indulging-the-petty-emotions-of-silly-children-like-me voice.

"C'mon, what? You don't even know what I was going to say."

The spark of fun that lit her eyes just seconds ago has

extinguished. "I know exactly what you were going to say," she says dolefully. "Sometimes I think I know you better than you know yourself. And you already know the answer, so why keep belaboring the point?"

"Do you even love me?" I ask in full self-pity mode. It's a train wreck I can't stop.

"Of course I love you." She steps forward to press against me again and tilts her face toward mine. I can feel her warm breath against my throat, and the tiny hairs on my body stand up. "Who loves you more?"

"My parents."

"Okay, maybe equal, but who loves you *more*?" She raises her hand to cradle the side of my face so gently that my fingertips actually tingle. Her eyes grow round with concern. The humorless schoolteacher voice is gone just as suddenly as it arrived. My Priya is back. "I love you, Tati. My parents are conservative, you know that. They wouldn't understand . . . us."

"It's getting harder and harder for *me* to understand us," I say stubbornly, apparently on a mission to sabotage our relationship. Sleepovers at my house are where happiness takes place—hugging, nuzzling, kissing. Sleepovers at Priya's are relegated to the friend zone—simple schoolgirl stuff like homework, binge-watching our favorite Netflix shows, and stuffing popcorn in our mouths. "When you sleep at my house everything's real. When I stay at your house . . . I don't even know what we are. I'm sorry but it's not right. What are we? Are we a couple? Are we really even in love?"

Priya's face darkens again, and she pulls away from me.

Her eyes latch on to mine. "*You're* sorry? You're the one with the cool parents who let you do anything you want. Maybe a little sympathy for me? You think I like living all confined like this? And, by the way, how many kids do you know whose parents would be cool with them sleeping with their lover? In their own bed? Under their parents' roof? Your parents are a little weird, Tati. Admit it."

I know she's mad. I've pushed too hard, but I couldn't help myself. It doesn't take a whole lot to trigger feelings of insecurity in me despite the best efforts of loving and supportive parents. The doubting voice that speaks to my darkest fears late at night tells me Priya *does* like living within the confines of her parents' narrow-minded social beliefs. It's her excuse for keeping us a secret at school, among our friends. Priya wants it both ways—all hers when she wants me, free as a bird when she doesn't. But then my rational self fights back—Priya loves me like no other. She's my soulmate. Who am I to accuse her of duplicity when she's suffering more than me? Do I really want to risk losing her over another confrontation? One day she'll have enough, and will I be prepared to go on without Priya in my life? I don't think so.

Hercules is back in the doorway, peering into Priya's room, most likely alarmed by the uncharacteristically loud and unhappy voices disturbing his tranquility. His ears are perked, and he angles his head for a better listen. His collar is silver, glistening. A small bell jangles under his chin. My knees suddenly feel loose, as if they might buckle if I shift my weight even one centimeter in either direction. A thrum starts low and grows louder, like a tuning fork hit against the side of my head.

"How did Hercules change his own collar?" I ask before sit-crashing to the ground. I pull my legs up and bury my face between my knees, drawing in great heaving gulps of air.

"Tati." Priya kneels and brings her lips close to my ear. "You okay?" she whispers.

"Hercules's collar was blue." Tears stream down my face. "Just ten minutes ago."

"No, it's silver," she says. "It's always been silver. Tati, is it happening again? Are you having a seizure? Have you been taking your meds?"

So many questions.

Priya unfastens the top button of my shirt, sits down, and pulls my head into her lap. She strokes my hair and coos to me, but what she's saying, I can no longer hear. The tunnel appears where it's always been before—just above me, gleaming with such intensity, a light so bright it seems white. Beckoning.

CHAPTER 2

ANA

They say I had another seizure although I don't remember it at all. But here I am in the nurse's office at school with Nurse Pat staring down at me, concern written all over his round face.

"Have you been taking your meds?" he asks. It's perhaps the question I've heard most often in my life; one I can usually answer with a *yes*.

"I may have skipped a bit lately," I reply guiltily. "They make me so tired I can't focus on anything."

"I called your mother," he says. "When she gets here we need to chat about getting with your doctor to prescribe something new with fewer side effects."

I stare at the faint wrinkles that splay from the outside corner of his eyes like a bird's footprint in the sand. *Crow's feet*, I remember the expression. Makes sense. It's the only evidence in his otherwise smooth, brown skin that betrays any sign of age—that and a few flecks of steel-gray hair near the temples. I wonder for a second how old Nurse Pat is and how I ever could have survived without him for the past three years of high school. My guardian angel, my safe harbor in the storm whenever the storm arrives.

"Are you listening to me, Tatiana? This is serious. This is your life. If you're going to skip doses because you don't like the side effects, you need to try something else. There are a lot of options, so it's just a matter of playing around with them until you and your doctor find the perfect fit."

Nurse Pat is the only one who calls me by my full name. Everyone else calls me Ana.

I've spent so much of my life trying to enter the magic rabbit hole, which is what I call the tunnel that appears at the end of my seizures. It's irresistible and yet always just out of reach. The way I would describe it, if there were anyone to describe it to, is I'm Alice chasing after the white rabbit—but when I get to the edge of the hole, there's a trapdoor preventing me from entering Wonderland.

There was a time when I did try to explain this feeling. To Mom. To Dad. To Nurse Pat. Even to Dr. Masterson. But there's a limited number of times you can explain magic rabbit holes to people before they seriously start to question your sanity. And my number was up a long time ago.

"What if I never find a perfect fit with my medication?" I ask. "I've been trying for a long time already, you know?"

"Of course I know, sweetie." He pats me on the back of my hand. Nurse Pat can get away with calling me sweetie even though it's probably not appropriate for a school official. All the kids would agree because we know how much Nurse Pat cares about us. "Now you just rest here until Mom comes."

That's another thing he does—he says "Mom" instead of "*your* mom." It's endearing.

"I'm feeling fine now. I'd like to go back to class, if it's okay. You and Mom can have *the talk* because I've had enough of it today."

He frowns and shakes his head slowly. "You're probably the only kid in school who begs to get back to class. You sure you're all right?"

"Yep."

School is the only thing that loves me back as much as I love it, except my parents, of course.

"Ana!" My ethnic studies teacher looks up when I walk in mid-class. "So glad you're here."

The teachers never question me when I'm late or my homework is late, which rarely happens anyway. They know I'm the girl with seizures, and if I were the type to take advantage, I could skate through school with minimal effort. But where would be the fun in that?

"We were just discussing our final projects. Have you given yours any thought? No worries if you haven't. You can talk it over with me after class if you need ideas."

More of that teacher leniency.

Priya side-eyes me when I slide into my seat. She smiles and wraps her long, glossy hair into a neck-bun, which she fixes with a pencil. A lustrous black lock escapes to frame her light-brown face. Priya's gorgeous, and the object of my mad desire ever since I first laid eyes on her in our freshman year. We share most classes, being the "smart girls" of our school (which is actually a pretty silly name for us since we're the smart *kids*—smartest of the girls *and boys*), trading first and second place back and forth like a tennis set that's gone on for three years. I know Priya respects me and she's always been really nice. She just never looks at me the way I look at her, or the way I think I must be looking at her. She never seems breathless in my presence. She never stammers when she speaks to me. I hope she doesn't notice what I try so hard to conceal.

"You okay?" she whispers, and I nod.

"That's okay, Mrs. Falco," I answer my teacher. "I already know what I'm going to do for my project."

"Care to share with the class? The others have already done so."

"Well, you know I'm adopted," I start, and Mrs. Falco nods me on. "And I know my birth parents were from Russia. So I talked it over with my parents and they're going to let me do one of those DNA tests that breaks down your ethnicity by percentages. I thought I would research the most surprising discovery I make. I mean . . . not the obvious, like Russian, but something I would never have guessed. And then write a paper about the forces and events in history that would have brought my ancestor of that ethnicity into contact with my Russian ancestor. A macro view that merges geography, history, science and statistics."

The class murmurs and I can tell it's from approval. Even Priya's impressed.

"Woah. Cool idea," she says, her mouth forming a small oval of approval.

"I would expect no less from Ana," Mrs. Falco says. "Wonderful idea, Ana. I'm looking forward to going on this adventure with you, as I'm sure your classmates are."

Priya nods her head in agreement. She's the only one whose opinion I care about at that moment although I hear more murmurs of approval. I'll miss Mrs. Falco when ethnic studies is over in December and we begin our next elective after the holidays. I already know (because I've already asked) that Priya and I will be in the next class together too—computer programming.

"Hold up," Priya says after class as she quickens her step behind me.

I stop in my tracks and turn to face her.

"You okay?" she asks with a real look of real concern. "I heard that you . . . that you . . ."

"I had a seizure in PE."

"Yeah, that's what I heard. You okay?"

"Yep, I'm fine. I can usually tell when it's about to happen, so I was sitting down. Supposedly, I need to be more rigorous about taking my medication."

"Why wouldn't you?" She seems surprised. "I mean, if I had . . ."

"Seizures." I know from experience it's uncomfortable for others to talk about it to my face because . . . well, I guess because it's an alien concept to most people, and it's not something people are accustomed to seeing. I think I must look strange when it's actually going down—checking out and staring into space, trembling, rigid. The first indication I have is that something's just plain off about the world. Then a weakness levels me like I'm suddenly transformed into a liquid state. After that, I disappear into my head and a tunnel appears, or at least its entrance. I have an overwhelming feeling that I need to climb into the tunnel and see where it leads, even though I never can. After that, I'm not sure, except eventually I open my eyes and see some worried face hovering over me. Once I peed my pants, but thankfully that was only once. The truth is, no one wants to lose control in public. I'm the girl who does, so my reality scares people, even people who know me.

"If I had seizures I would do anything I could to stop them. I'd take any medicine they told me to take. So why *wouldn't* you?" This line of questioning is a little invasive and, honestly, none of Priya's business, but I feel her sincerity and I know it's not just morbid curiosity.

"I do for the most part." The halls are crowded with kids rushing to their next class. A boy (probably a freshman) squeezes in between Priya and me in his hurry to pass us. You can always tell the freshmen by their anxiety about not being late to class. Priya and I, as seniors, saunter along at a much more leisurely pace. "But they mess with my head. The one I'm supposed to be taking dulls my thought process and creativity. Plus, I feel so tired all the time."

"Ohhh. I totally get that. That sucks. Maybe there's something else they could give you?"

"Hah! You sound just like Nurse Pat. To be honest, I

don't think the medication makes a difference one way or the other."

I love being this close to her. I love being the object of her undivided attention, even if it is sort of a pity thing.

"What causes them . . . your seizures?" she asks.

"They don't know. There's nothing obvious, so I guess I'm just one of the lucky ones. Or unlucky. At least it's nothing physical like a brain tumor."

I bite my lower lip and hope I don't sound too maudlin. I don't want Priya to associate me with being a downer.

"I read a book that said in some cultures they believe having a seizure is like having a holy experience," she says. "The seizure opens a pathway that's like a conduit straight to the spiritual world. That could have been a good subject for your project."

We're wading into uncomfortable territory. I don't want to be the girl whose identity is about her affliction. And I slightly resent that Priya would want to pin that on me like I couldn't just have a normal interest in some other normal topic that normal kids write about.

"Yeah, well it's too late," I say. "My mom's already ordered the kit and it cost a hundred bucks. But yeah . . . might have been a good idea." I try not to come off as too brusque but I'm bristling underneath.

"I'm sorry, I hope I didn't say anything to offend you," Priya says. Maybe it was obvious in my tone. Or maybe the hot flush I felt in my face was actually visible. Her phone buzzes and she takes it out of her pocket. Her home screen displays a little dog with a scrunched-up face wearing a rhinestone-studded turquoise collar. *Just like Mom's sweater,* I think. Priya swipes the face of her phone to open the message, then closes it without replying.

"No, not at all," I lie. Why do I do that when I simply could have told her the truth? I've known Priya for three years. We've had a lot of conversations, about school mostly, but we haven't broken down that wall yet: the barrier that separates friendly classmates from friends who just happen to be classmates. And, of course, my feelings for her could run much deeper if I ever got a sign from her that she felt the same way. "Is that your dog?" I ask.

"Yeah, that's Hercules. He can be so annoying," she says in a way that lets me know she thinks he's anything but. "We should totally do something sometime before the school year's over and we both go off to college and never see each other again."

"I'd love to," I blurt out, forgetting that, just a moment earlier, Priya was almost getting on my nerves. Almost. I doubt whether she could ever completely get on my nerves. And it makes me sad to think about the time when we go our separate ways and never see each other again. It's not that far off in the future.

"Okay, let's do something sometime," she says before ducking into a classroom, and I have a sinking feeling we'll never do anything anytime, and Priya was just trying to be nice.

When I walk through the door after school, Mom's standing there, hands on her hips.

"I missed you at Nurse Pat's office by less than five minutes. Why didn't you wait for me?"

"I was fine. I just didn't want to miss class and have to stay after school to talk to Mrs. Falco."

"Wouldn't have killed you, Tati. You drive yourself too hard and I don't think that's exactly good for you."

Mom and Dad are old hippies who don't believe people should drive themselves hard. Mom still wears long Indian-print skirts and peasant blouses. She doesn't wear a bra and her long curly hair hangs loose and unstructured. Because dying her hair would be unthinkable, she's almost completely gray. I walk into her outstretched arms and she folds me against her soft, ample breasts. I pull away and look into her twinkling blue eyes. Deep wrinkles radiate out like spokes, giving them the appearance of two tiny, blue suns. She's stubborn and often preachy, and at times she talks too loud and occasionally smells because she doesn't believe in deodorant. And I love the shit out of her. Dad too—he's her male equivalent. Mom and Dad are older than the other kids' parents because they tried for so long to have kids before they finally gave up trying and traveled to Russia to adopt the baby who eventually became the me I am today.

We walk into the living room, Mom's arm around my shoulder. Dad's sitting in his reclining chair, feet up. He folds his newspaper and sets it down on the small table to his side. He picks up a glass of wine on the table and takes a sip.

"Ana, baby girl. You doing okay?"

Most kids wouldn't come home to find their parents at home, sitting around drinking wine in the early afternoon, but my parents are already retired. Like I said, they're old. Dad also has issues with his legs swelling and probably shouldn't be drinking, especially this early in the day, but he says it's his life and we shouldn't worry because he's not about to check out until Mom and I don't need him anymore.

"I wish everyone would stop worrying about me," I say.

"Aww, honey, if we stopped worrying about you, what else would we do? Besides, your feelings would probably be hurt." Mom blinks her little blue suns.

"Mommy tells me you haven't been keeping up with your medication." Dad lowers his foot recliner and leans forward. This is as close to a serious tongue-lashing as I'll ever get.

"George . . ." Mom warns. "We've had this discussion already. I'm not so sure the medication isn't worse than the actual—"

"Okay, let's stop right now," Dad interrupts. "It's one thing to let Dr. Yang treat our fevers and colds and your . . . change of life, but Tati's seizures are something else. Banish the thought before you even speak it."

Dr. Yang is our family's Chinese herbalist.

Mom purses her lips and releases a loud stream of air from her nostrils. She plunks down on her own recliner adjacent to Dad's. In a normal house they'd be facing the TV, but we don't have a TV in our house.

I unfold my long torso into the giant, overstuffed bean bag chair facing them. Nirvana after what I've been through today.

"It just makes me sleepy and kind of depressed," I say. "I hate the feeling."

Mom shoots Dad a side glance, but he halts anything she's thinking of saying by jerkily lowering his flat palm, as though pressing against an invisible force field that's pushing up against him. Dad has a tremor, but it's a benign one, the doctor says. Nothing that will lead to anything scary. "We'll go see Dr. Masterson and get you something new to try," he says. "I've already made the appointment. But you need to communicate these things with us, honey. We had no idea."

"I know, sorry." And I am. I hate to stress my parents out because they mean so well and they care so much. Sometimes too much.

Mom's face brightens. "Guess what came in the mail today?" she says. She rises from her chair and disappears into the kitchen, reappearing a minute later with a small, brown package in her hand. "The DNA test kit. You want me to help you with it?"

And now my face brightens. "Yay! Just in time." It takes three weeks, so that'll give me two weeks to work on my final project once I have the results. I clamber out of the bean bag chair to retrieve the package from Mom. "I'm going to go do it now before the last pickup at the corner mailbox."

"I don't know who's more excited about this," Mom calls after me, "you, me, or Dad. Holler if I can help."

I lock the bathroom door for some reason, as though the collecting of DNA is a private affair that should have no witnesses. After reading the instructions, I remove the vial and prepare to spit. And spit. And spit. As the vial fills slowly with my spit, I wonder if I should have given my teeth a good brushing before collecting my sample. I was reluctant to ask for Mom's help. It would almost be like asking her to examine my feces, which she actually did once when I had the stomach flu. That led to Dr. Yang's medicinal tea, which was a nasty brew but worked pretty well.

But the unsavory act of spitting is soon replaced by thoughts of Priya's admiration when I explained my project to the class. And her almost-invitation to hang out sometime. Unrequited love really is a bitch. I have no idea what Priya's sexuality is. I've never gotten a vibe from her that she could be interested in me beyond just fellow super-nerd status. But I've never seen her with a guy, either—not in a cozy, flirtatious way—so I've allowed my fantasies to roam wild, which probably isn't the best idea. The strong pull I've felt toward her has been going on for two years now, which is more than a little pathetic. And like she said, in less than a year we'll be off to college and probably never see each other again. Unless we both get in to Stanford—but what are the odds of two kids from the same high school getting into Stanford? Maybe pretty good if the two kids are Priya and me.

I'm not bragging. It's just a fact.

I seal the vial according to the instructions and pack it in the supplied self-addressed envelope.

"Be right back," I tell my parents. "It's all ready to go."

"Oh, Ana," Mom says. "Almost forgot to tell you that

Anthony stopped by on his way home from school. Does he live nearby? I see him walking past our house every day."

"I think so." Anthony transferred to our school this year. He made friends with us easily, being a likeable and smart person.

"Did he say why?" I ask.

"I think he's sweet on you," Dad says.

"Dad!"

"Okay, okay, I know. Seems like a good kid, though. Nice. Knows his manners."

I know Dad's kidding, but part of me wonders if he secretly wishes I wasn't gay.

CHAPTER 3

Nordhaven is a dismal little town near the Baltic Sea in Germany. It's not home to me and never will be, but this is where I live for now. My German isn't perfect, but it's good—although nobody would be fooled by my accent. In any case, I don't venture far from home, and if my future is like my past, we won't be here much longer. Today is my birthday and I wonder if Mother will remember before bedtime.

"Tanya," she calls out from the cramped kitchen, and the weariness in her voice is unmistakable. "Please peel a few potatoes, would you?"

I'm not getting much done anyway. Mother expects me to study for six hours each day, but the wind slaps at our house like a cold, angry hand, and the draft and dampness make my bones ache. I unwrap the blanket twisted around my feet and set my book down on the table beside me. The room is weakly lit by one tottering lamp, which rattles distractingly whenever a particularly strong gust of wind rises up from the sea. Today I'm studying poetry and reading in English. Although Russian is my native language, I've learned six others.

T A N Y A

The kitchen is warmer from the boiling pot of water and the heat of the oven. We don't have an electric heater set up in the kitchen because we usually don't need it.

"What are you studying today?" Mother asks as she scales a rubbery, gray fish she brought home wrapped in newspaper tonight. It's an automatic question she asks every night when she gets home from her job cleaning rooms at an inn in the next village over. I know she wants an answer, but I also know she's too tired to truly care. Anything will please her. She just wants me to be safe and to keep my mind occupied.

"I'm studying poetry," I say. "American poets."

"Mmm," Mother says while she rinses the fish under the tap.

I decide to tell her. "Someone came by today," I say. "A man."

Mother drops the fish in the sink, and it stares up at me with a dead eye. "Who?" she asks, her own eyes as cold as the darkening gray outside the small, framed window, her mouth a tight, set line. I notice the deepening wrinkles around her lips, bringing a severity to her face that didn't exist when we left Russia just . . . has it already been seven years?

"A man . . . I don't know. I hid in the bedroom until he went away."

Mother doesn't say anything, and even though I hate this town, I don't want to move again. I'm afraid. Afraid of the man and afraid of another move.

"He probably was just a neighbor," I say quickly. The fish has been forgotten in the sink. Mother clutches the scaler in her raw, red hands. Her knuckles are white, as though she's tightening her grip in preparation for battle. "Or he could be a postman," I add.

"Was he wearing a uniform?" she asks.

"A suit," I say, hoping the idea of a man who cares enough to dress in a suit would put her mind at ease. Surely a man in a suit would bring no trouble to our door.

But this appears to make Mother even more tense. Her forehead blanches. "Did he speak?" she asks. "Did you hear him say anything?"

"No, he just knocked. And then he went away."

"How hard did he knock? How long before he went away?"

I scramble to recall any helpful detail. I almost didn't tell Mother about this because I knew what her reaction would be, and yet, at the time, I felt it was nothing. "Not long," I said. "He didn't knock more than once. And he left after a few minutes."

"He didn't see you look out the window," she states more than asks.

"No, of course not," I lie. I did look out the window after I heard his footsteps moving away from our house. Just before he got to the street, he turned his head quickly and I ducked behind the curtain, hoping, praying he didn't see me. I looked again a few seconds later and he was gone. I hadn't seen a car parked in front of our house, but most people don't drive cars in Nordhaven. They take the bus or walk or ride their bicycles. I put a half-peeled potato down and turn to face my mother. "Everything's okay," I say. "I'm sure he was just lost, asking for directions." I put my hands on her shoulders and feel the tension like an iron rod across her back.

"We've already been here a year," she says and those are the words I was most afraid to hear come out of her mouth. "Maybe it's time to move on."

"But why, Mother? Surely he's forgotten about us after all these years." The "he" to which I'm referring is, of course, my father. "He must have another family by now and probably never thinks of us anymore. And even if he does, what would this man have to do with my father?" I always call him *my* father, sensing that "Father" alone would wound Mother too deeply.

"He has resources to hire people." She picks up the fish and resumes the process of scaling and gutting. She pulls the slimy gray insides out with vengeance, as though it were Father she was gutting. She runs the back of her fingernail against the inside spine, releasing the trapped blood into the fish's cavity, and then rinses inside and out before setting the carcass on a clean, waiting plate.

My mother's moods, behavior, and statements have become increasingly erratic over the years. I worry about her emotional health. I worry about her physical health. I worry about her mental health. I worry what will happen if my mother loses her faculties and has no one but me to care for her. Me, Tanya, whom my father used to call Tatyana so many years ago before we ran away. Tanya, the afflicted girl, caring for a helpless mother? I'm helpless myself, with my seizures resistant to medication. Mother says that when I was young, the doctors explained that medication would be of no use to me because my seizure disorder was not the usual kind. So I'm not even allowed to have a normal seizure disorder. I'm not allowed to have a normal life at all, with all this running and hiding from people and being cut off from whatever family I have, except Mother, who doesn't seem to be holding up all that well. "What people are you talking about?"

"Tanya, I'm not keeping secrets from you," she says. But of course she is. What else would one call it? "It's my job to protect you, and the less you know, the better."

"How could that possibly be beneficial to me?" I slice the second potato, browned slightly from the cool air. I drop its four sections into the pot of boiling water and hold my hands above the hot steam to loosen my joints, stiff from cold. "If you want me to be safe, then I should know everything. And right now, all I know is that Father . . . *my* father . . . wasn't a kind man, although you've never even told me what he did to you."

"To *us*," she says, grinding a piece of stale toast with the back of a spoon in a large bowl. "To *us*," she repeats.

"He never did anything to me, so I don't know why you say that." I pull my hands from the steam and wipe away the moisture on the sides of my pants.

Mother looks at me like she wants to tell me something. "Whatever he does to me, he does to you," she hisses.

"Mother, please," I begin and know I'm going somewhere that won't end well. "I should be in school. I should be under the care of a qualified doctor. You shouldn't be working this hard. We should go home, back to Russia where we at least have family and friends who might still remember us."

I don't see it coming, it happens so quickly. Mother's open hand across my face, biting into my skin already tender from the relentlessly cold weather. But the insult of her slap is so much more bitter than the wind that howls outside. Tears spring from my eyes and I know a welt is blossoming on my cheek. I turn and walk into the other room. I sit on the chair where I had been reading before Mother came home. I wrap the blanket around my feet, squeeze my eyes shut, and take slow, controlled breaths to keep my emotions at bay. I'm so very scared, and it's not even clear to me what scares me the most. My own mother or the bogeyman she's created in my mind without ever bothering to define him? I've just turned seventeen, but I feel as helpless as if I were seven.

And then I think about Victor, my only friend. Mother doesn't know about Victor, of course. He showed up at our house one day, and since he was obviously a child, I opened the door. Small and scrawny, his clothes much too large, he asked in broken German if he could shovel the snow in front of our house. I immediately recognized the Russian cadence of his accent and switched to Russian. His face lit up and that smile has been the only radiance in my life since then. Victor is ten. His mother is Russian, and his father abandoned them once they moved to Nordhaven, Victor says. Victor's family lives in even more unfortunate circumstances than Mother and me. All of this and more, Victor has told me. He comes to visit from time to time when he knows Mother isn't home. He seems to miss more school than he attends. I share my lunch with him and read to him—fairy tales are his favorite. He doesn't read well but with my tutoring, he's coming along.

Maybe the man who knocked on my door today was a relative of Victor's family, although they don't live near us. Maybe he was looking for Victor—an uncle perhaps. Or coming to tell me something unfortunate has happened to Victor or his mother or younger sister. But how would he know I'm Victor's friend? I nervously long to tell Mother about my hunch to assuage her worries and have her do the same for me, but I know she would be angry if she knew about Victor. Even the friendship of a ten-year-old boy is forbidden to me.

Already the sting of Mother's slap is a memory. She calls out to me that dinner will be ready in twenty minutes. I smell the fish frying in the kitchen and the power of hunger and promise of its satisfaction replace my hurt feelings for now. The symphony of popping, hot oil and gurgling, boiling water take me back to happier times when I was much younger than Victor, though not as poor. I'll make Mother work at gaining my forgiveness. For a few minutes longer, at least.

I pick up the collection of *Great American Poets* and open to the bookmarked page. I start reading where I left off, Robert Frost's "The Road Not Taken."

I shall be telling this with a sigh
Somewhere ages and ages hence:
Two roads diverged in a wood, and I—
I took the one less traveled by,
And that has made all the difference.

Mother hasn't said a word about my birthday and I know she doesn't remember. But Victor will remember even if no one else does.

CHAPTER 4

"Are you feeling better, *dochka*?" Papa asks.

December in Moscow. A cold, steel-blue haze replaces the sky. Darkness is nearly complete and it's only 4:00 in the afternoon. Outside my window, I can see multiple sets of footprints have flattened a path to our front door. Papa's. The important men who come to visit Papa. My *tyotya*, who is my father's sister, Irina. Useless little footprints that will be gone by morning, buried in a shroud of soft powder—the cycle beginning anew each morning.

"Did I have a seizure?" I ask. Sometimes I know I've had one. This time I don't.

Outside, snowflakes appear to be suspended midair, traveling sideways instead of down. I extend my finger to touch the glass. The cold bites my skin, the conduit between outside and inside. Numbingly cold versus cheerily warm. An icicle dangles from the eaves and a fire blazes in the hearth. Something about the glass and the separation of the two worlds unnerves me. How easily that glass could break, and the outside world could tumble into everything that's safe and familiar to me.

"If you're feeling well enough, I need to take

TATYANA

a sample from you." He sidesteps my question. "I'll take it to the laboratory tomorrow."

How many samples has Papa taken over the years? Sometimes it's blood, but with more modern technology he's often able to accomplish the same thing with saliva, which is a huge relief for me. All the hours in the laboratory, all for nothing so far. Papa says he'll find a cure for me one day—my seizures. An answer for what's causing them. But he never discusses his findings with me and, when I probe for answers, he's vague. I assume it is his way of protecting me. Not getting my hopes up. There's been nothing encouraging to come out of it, and I'm beginning to feel like one of the rats he keeps locked away in the long cages that line the walls of his laboratory. I can't go there anymore. I can't bear to look at the rats. Their shifting eyes so desperate when they scurry to the fronts of their cages as I walk by, as though I had the power to deliver their freedom, which I suppose I do. Deliver them from whatever torment they're enduring in the name of science. It's why I can't go there anymore. The misplaced hope in their eyes turns me into a fraud.

"Okay, Papa." Depressed. His non-answer to my question confirms I've had another seizure. So many this year. Each time I feel more tired than the time before. Papa stands and walks to the console table. He pours water from the crystal pitcher into a matching tumbler. He shakes a pill from the dispenser and brings both the glass and the pill to me. I swallow the pill without thinking and without even wondering anymore. What does it contain? I have no idea. Papa is a famous scientist—a physician as well. My tyotya

Irina is too. They must know what's best for me, and if not them, then who?

The pill catches in my throat for a second, causing me to cough before I gulp it down. I'm glad I don't have to stand in line, wait in crowded lobbies to receive my medical care. I'm glad we have special privileges and access to material items and comforts that others aren't able to receive. I'm glad because it makes my life more comfortable, but I feel guilty too. Like with the rats. Why must some of God's creatures live out their lives in cramped cages, subject to who knows what kind of abuse, while others roam freely? Why do some struggle with hardship and poverty while others live in luxury? It's not that my life is free of hardship—in many ways, I feel that for much of my life, my condition has defined who I am. Tyotya and Papa never allow me the freedom other girls my age have. To socialize with others away from their homes. To grow into young women without fear as their constant companion—their parents' most reliable chaperone.

When we ride through the icy streets in our chauffeur-driven limousine, I sometimes see girls my age walking arm-in-arm along the sidewalks. I can tell from their dress and their manner that they don't have the financial resources of my family, and yet I would trade places with them in the blink of an eye. For their freedom. For their carelessness. For their friends.

Tyotya and Papa are my only friends. I know they love me as much as is possible for one person to love another, but not enough to set me free. The cage I'm in is one of dependence and anxiety. While many others my age will be attending college in a year, I'll continue to be schooled at home. And who can argue? Papa and Tyotya Irina are two of the most brilliant minds in the world. It's true, I know, because I've read it in scientific journals, their backgrounds in medicine and their advanced studies in theoretical physics. But their knowledge doesn't stop there. Literature, music, art. Nothing has been neglected in my education. Between the two of them, there seems to be nothing they haven't mastered, and I'm free to ask any questions. I just don't know what questions to ask anymore, or perhaps I don't care.

The door swings open and a blast of cold air crosses the threshold of our home as though Tyotya has invited it in. She's carrying a large, flat box, and I think I know what's in it. I've barely noticed the syringe that Papa has plunged into the meaty part of my upper arm and is now withdrawing. It's something I've learned to block out.

"Hello, my darlings," Tyotya twitters cheerfully. "I have such a delightful surprise. Can you imagine what it is?"

I can.

"A birthday cake?" I ask without true excitement.

"Yes, it is, my darling girl."

She sets it down and leans over to kiss my cheek. "Happy birthday, Tatyana. Such a grown girl, you are."

She steps toward my father and leans forward to kiss his cheek. "Can you believe our baby is seventeen?" she asks him.

My father sets his mouth in a thin, grim line. "Our baby has had another . . . episode," he says. "But she is fine. Fine enough to celebrate with some champagne tonight, I think.

What do you think, Tatyana?" He rises from his chair and winks at me.

I smile.

"Really? Alcohol with the medication?" Tyotya Irina's brows dip toward her nose.

"It's fine," Papa says. "Tonight, we celebrate and leave all the worrying for another day. But first . . ." He hands me a shot glass, my special spit-collector. I begin the nauseating process of expectorating into the cup. My father slips it from my hand before I open my eyes. He knows I don't like to see it. Tyotya replaces it with a champagne flute filled halfway; tiny bubbles float to the top, creating a layer of white, an inverse of the snowstorm outside.

"Thank you, Tyotya." I sip far too fast and the bubbles transform into butterflies fluttering helplessly inside my head.

"Careful, dochka," Tyotya Irina warns.

"Let Tatyana be, tonight," Papa says. "We only get our birthdays once a year, and this is the last time she'll celebrate as a child."

Tyotya beams at the two people she loves most. She slides the cake onto the table between us and proceeds to carve three slices from the perfect circle—a *Moskva* cake, my favorite.

"*Za tvoe zdorovje*," she says, raising her glass to my health. The golden brew sparkles under the light of our chandelier.

"Our little girl," Papa says. "Who no longer is so little anymore. Who one day will astound the world."

I don't know how I will ever astound the world or even

myself from within the confines of the gilded cage in which I live. "Cheers," I say, because good health is all I really want.

CHAPTER 5

Although it's been a while, Priya and I are still tiptoeing around each other since my last seizure, being extra careful not to say anything controversial and just be sweet to each other. She bought me a beautiful pink cashmere sweater for my birthday a few weeks ago, which is totally her and not at all me. But I've worn it three times since then just to please her. In central California there aren't many days when a cashmere sweater comes in handy, so I've taken advantage of every day when it did.

"It's so you," Priya had said the first time she saw me wearing it. It's really not. But I love her for still thinking, after a year of us being together, that I could pull off something that feminine, because honestly it doesn't come at all naturally to me.

There's something that's been bothering me since my last seizure. It isn't the first time it's happened and, given the increased frequency of my seizures, I'm sure it won't be the last. Priya brought it up the next day, but I pretended not to remember because . . . it's a little scary. The thing about Hercules's collar. I remember distinctly it was blue—turquoise studded with

TATI

rhinestones. There's a reason I remember. Mom has a turquoise sweater with a rhinestone pattern on the front. It's her *fancy* sweater she almost never wears, only when she goes to a special event. She wears it along with a pair of black jeans, which is dressy for Mom. And I remember thinking how it would make a cute picture if Mom and Hercules posed together in their matching "outfits." Then, minutes after Priya and I had the argument, Hercules shows up at the bedroom door wearing a shiny silver collar with a dangling bell. And Priya's telling me I'm crazy when I ask how Hercules managed to change his own collar because no one else was in the house. Well, not exactly telling me I'm crazy, but she must be thinking it, right? And now I'm wondering if I *am* crazy. Things just seem off lately. Memories of things being one way but then my eyes tell me something different. Last month it was the comforter on my bed. That's something no one would forget, right? You sleep with it every night and it's so ingrained in your memory. How could I have thought my comforter was navy blue and then wake up the morning after a seizure and discover it's actually pink with embroidered flowers? I hate pink.

My phone rings and the image of smiling Priya appears on the screen. She's so beautiful in this picture, my favorite of her. I'm in it too, but I cropped that part out because I looked more like I was baring my teeth than smiling.

"Hey, Priya." I turn over on my bed so I'm lying on my back and staring at the glow-in-the-dark stars Dad stuck to the ceiling when I was twelve and determined to be an astronaut. They're still magical at night, although every now and then one flutters down on top of me and I have to use glue to re-stick it. They're not quite as bright as they were when Dad first put them up. Or maybe they are but I'm just used to them.

"Guess what came in the mail today?"

"You got your results?" The DNA test, of course. It's been three weeks. "What'd it say?"

"I did have a little surprise. A big one, actually. I have Southeastern African DNA. At first I thought it was a mistake. But I did some digging and discovered that in the nineteenth century, the British sent tens of thousands of south Asians to Uganda as indentured laborers to build a railroad. When the project was over, some stayed, including one of my ancestors. They were all expelled in 1972 when the Ugandan president Idi Amin accused the Indian citizens of disloyalty, but I think my great-grandpa returned to India before the expulsion. So, you see! Amazing, huh? Great idea of yours to do this project. Oh wait, it was *my* idea . . . ha ha."

"And my money," I say.

"Your parents' money," Priya reminds me. "Thank your mom again for me, will you? It's been an exciting afternoon doing all the research."

"I wonder if Mom brought the mail in today." It's already dark and I didn't check.

"I got my results by email. Have you checked?"

I roll over on my stomach and turn on my laptop. Open my email. Nothing. "Nah. Dang! Now I'm excited to know. No fair."

"You'll probably get it tomorrow," she says. "Hey, I gotta go, but let's video chat later, okay?"

"Okay. I love you."

"Love you too," Priya says. She's been doing that lately—dropping the "I." But I need to get over it. Stop looking for trouble or something else to obsess over and worry about. She's telling me she loves me in her own way. Why am I so insecure? What's wrong with me?

And then I'm thinking about the other stuff—Hercules's collar. The comforter. There's more but nothing as drastic as those two. I wish I could quiet my mind every once in a while and relax. I have an appointment tomorrow to get yet another MRI, which makes me nervous. I hate sliding into that dark tunnel, forced to lie there for so long with all the loud banging and clanking. What are they going to see that they haven't seen before? It's almost as if they're hoping for something new to show up.

When I was younger, Mom went into the room with me and sat at the opening holding onto my foot, so I had a connection to the outside world. That reassured me I wasn't alone. Wouldn't disappear. But they don't do that anymore, although they give me a sedative and put a scarf over my eyes so I can't open them and see what's all around me—the darkness. The isolation. Nothing like the bright tunnel that shows up in my seizures.

I missed school this morning, which I hate doing, but I had my MRI and hopefully that's it for another year. I rush to the table where our group eats lunch and Priya scoots over on the bench to make room for me. I squeeze in between her and Anthony, who's obviously reluctant to move. I don't think Priya's aware how much he crushes on her.

"Did you check your email?" she asks once I'm seated. I was just doing that and had been doing it all morning, before and after my MRI. Truth be told, I checked once in the middle of the night when I got up to pee. Nothing.

"Nothing," I say. "I don't get it. We sent it in at the same time and got our confirmation emails at exactly the same time."

"Why don't you contact them?" Priya suggests. "We should get started on our project. I mean . . . I'm already way into it but we have to figure out the tie-in, the part where we link our two lives together."

"I could start doing that now, I guess. While I'm waiting for my results." I pluck a grape out of Priya's lunch bag. I pierce the thin skin with the sharp edges of my back teeth and allow the cool, sweet juice to drizzle down the back of my tongue. I take another one.

"That kind of defeats the purpose, doesn't it? Since you don't know what it's going to say."

"I can fake it. I mean . . . I know generally, and I can write something to fit the general scenario and we can revise it later on if we need to."

Anthony leans forward, and I know he's trying to listen in. Our voices are low although we're not discussing anything personal.

"Take it," Priya pushes the bag of grapes toward me. "You didn't bring lunch, did you?"

"Nah, I just wanted to get here and not waste any more time." It's only now that I realize how hungry I am. I haven't eaten anything today.

Priya leans in and whispers, "How'd the test go?"

"It was fine." I reach for her water bottle and gulp down half of it in one breath. "Same old same old."

"Jeez," Priya says. "Dehydrated and starving. Keep it." She slides the bottle over. "I have another one in my locker."

I wish it was just me and Priya, so I could tell her the truth. How stressful the whole thing was this morning, how it always is even though you'd think I'd be used to it by now. I'm still a little groggy from the sedative although it was light, but I took it on an empty stomach since I'm always too nervous to eat on my testing days. I pick up my phone and click on the email app again. Still nothing.

"Okay, I'll send a message asking what's up." I scroll through to find the original confirmation and reply to that, so all my information is right there for them to see. "Done."

Priya slides her hand over and puts it on top of mine underneath the edge of the table where no one can see. The soothing that small gesture brings to my soul is instantaneous and close to miraculous. I squeeze her hand gently and then let go. I've learned not to be too greedy.

"Take it easy the rest of the day, okay?" she says, and her eyes are soft and compassionate. "Don't push yourself too hard."

I glance over at Anthony, who's turned to speak to the

person on his other side. But Priya and I are practiced at speaking in subaudible tones. We almost don't even need words, we can read each other so well. A smile lifts the corners of my lips.

"Yes, Mom." I grin. "Later, alligator."

We both rise from the table at the same time, and I help her gather the trash remnants of her lunch. We say goodbye to the rest of the kids just as the bell rings. "Don't wait for me after school," she says. "I have to get Nikky. Video chat at 5:00, okay?" Our hands brush against each other, and then we're off to classes in different wings of the building.

By 4:30, I have my answer. Two, in fact, and neither one reassures me. My MRI results are back, and nothing has changed. Just a normal-looking brain, they say. They want to schedule me for another EEG, but I'll probably refuse. Sleep deprivation. Lights flashing in my eyes. Anything to induce a seizure so they can measure the electrical changes in my brain, but it often doesn't work. When it has worked, my brain waves are normal, which is highly *ab*normal. Nobody can figure out what's going on with me, so I refuse to put myself through that again, and I'm pretty sure Mom and Dad will back me up.

I have an email response from the DNA testing facility and they say there was an error so they're sending me another kit for free to run another test. But the test won't be done in time, spelling disaster for our project. I type out a response email asking if they can put a rush on the results, considering I did nothing wrong and it was their error. And could they please overnight the test kit to me.

CHAPTER 6

Anthony Vargas walks me home from school.
He's so sincere and thoughtful that it's hard
for me to be honest with him. I'm pretty sure
he likes me, and he's cute and smart, but I'm
not into guys and not into pretending I am.
Now, all I have to do is break it to him while
preserving our friendship. I'm just about to say
something when Anthony clears his throat like
an important announcement is about to come
out of there.

"You know, Ana, if there's ever anything
you need. I mean . . . if you're sick and ever need
me to bring homework for you or anything.
Ever. Just hit me up, okay? I mean it."

"Thanks," I say. "But I'm never sick, you
should know that." Anthony and I have a lot
of classes together.

"Yeah, but I mean . . . like your . . ."

"Seizures." I finish his sentence, resisting
the urge to roll my eyes. How many times have
I had to supply the word for the other person
who can't bring themselves to say it? "It's okay.
I get over those pretty quickly, and since I can
usually tell when they're coming, I get myself
to a safe place."

Anthony smiles and doesn't say anything more about it. Maybe he's working up to a prom invite. That would be fine with me, as long as he knows where we stand. I run through this scene one more time in my head, as I have so many times before.

Anthony, you've become a good friend and I feel I can trust you to stay that way with what I'm about to tell you. I'm into girls and, although I've never been in a relationship, I want to be and will be one day. But I also really want to be your friend, so I hope that never changes.

It better sound good after all the airtime I've given it in my brain.

Yup, the friend zone. I've been relegated to the friend zone with Priya, so I know how it feels, which makes it doubly hard for me to say. But I owe it to Anthony. He's too good a person to not deserve complete honesty. We've arrived at my house and I'm just about to say those words when the door swings open and Mom comes out, purse slung over her shoulder, her car keys in hand.

"Ana, we have to go right now. Dad drove himself to the hospital while I was out doing chores. He was having chest pains." She's pale. Visibly shaken. "Silly man," she mutters. "You don't drive yourself to the hospital if you're having chest pains."

For a second, I feel like *I'm* having chest pains. I glance over at Anthony who somehow knows just what to do and say.

"You okay to drive, Mrs. Woodland?" he asks. "I'll be happy to drive if you don't mind me taking your car."

Personally, I'd be relieved to have his company, and Mom doesn't look so hot. In fact, she looks awful, and I'm hesitant to get behind the wheel under this stressful of a circumstance. Mom looks relieved too.

"Thanks, Anthony." She hands him her keys. "I don't feel so well myself," she says.

Mom sits in the front seat and I'm in the back, asking every question I can think of just to keep me from derailing. Dad's health is so precarious that this is a constant background worry for our family. Mom answers my questions, which I know helps keep her calm too, but I don't think either of us are really listening to what the other is saying. My heart is pounding, and my stomach is dive-bombing. After ten minutes, Anthony pulls up in front of the hospital and drops us off.

"I'll go park," he says. "Meet you inside."

Mom and I track Dad down in the emergency room. He's in his own little cubicle with curtains half-drawn around him. He's already hooked up to a bunch of wires that connect to the digital display of his heartbeat. The beeping noise and wave-like pattern are reassuring. An IV is dripping fluids into his arm.

"The doctor will be back in a minute," a nurse says as she leaves his side and draws the curtains against prying eyes. I think about Anthony out in the waiting room, but I know he'll be fine and I know he'll wait as long as it takes.

"You look okay," Mom tells Dad, even though he doesn't. His face is puffy, almost doughy, and he looks . . . sad. "I brought you some lozenges with echinacea and vitamin C.

Make sure to take one every few hours to boost your immunity." She tucks a bag of the natural-remedy lozenges under Dad's arm and then retrieves a blue, plastic molded chair from the corner and drags it next to Dad's bed. She scoops up his hand and presses it to her cheek. "You gave me such a worry, and don't you dare ever drive yourself to the hospital if you feel anything like this again." It's not the first time Dad has been to the hospital for angina, which I assume is what brings him here again.

"Don't fret, Mommy," he says. "They're taking good care of me here."

The curtains part and the doctor walks in holding a computer printout. Her dark hair is blunt-cut and falls to her shoulders. Her eyes are steely blue. She's pretty for an older lady—younger than my parents but much older than me. Somehow her face is familiar, although I know she hasn't treated either Dad or me before. Maybe I've seen her walking through the halls—God knows I've been in this hospital more than a few times in the past. Sometimes it feels like we live here.

"Hello, Mr. Woodland. I'm Dr. Sokol," she says. She has a detectable accent, but it's not super noticeable. "I've had a chance to go over your chart and I see you've been with us a few times before. Anything I need to know? You're taking all your meds as prescribed?"

"He sure is," Mom says. "I give them to him myself and watch him take them every day. He can be forgetful."

The doctor smiles without looking at Mom. "We'll keep you overnight for observation," she says. "Your cardiologist will stop by once you've been checked into a room. It will probably be early evening before he makes his rounds. I'll have the admissions clerk come down to go over some paperwork with you, so we can get you out of the ER and into a more comfortable bed."

"Mrs. Woodland?" she finally turns to look at Mom. "Keep up the good work—your husband obviously has a valuable ally in you." Then she turns to me. "And you're the daughter."

"Yes, I say. Ana." I reach out to shake her hand.

"Ana," she says, staring intently into my eyes for what feels like too long. I wonder if she's trying to relay a message to me about Dad. My mind veers off into all kinds of paranoid territory. What if he's really not okay and he's dying, and she doesn't think Mom and Dad can handle it? I look back just as intently, trying to read an answer in her eyes if there is one. But there isn't. A smile flashes across her face, revealing even, white teeth, and she grips my hand before letting it go. "Your parents are lucky," she says before turning to leave, and drawing the curtain behind her.

Lucky for what? For me? For each other? For Dad surviving another scare? I want to call her back to clarify what she meant, but I don't.

When the admissions clerk arrives, I leave Mom with Dad and go off to find Anthony. I know we have two midterms tomorrow and I feel guilty for holding him up when he could be home studying. The ER nurse directs me to the waiting room for family and friends, where I find Anthony typing away on his laptop, precariously balanced on his knees. He leans forward with his shoulders hunched, his neck craned in an unnatural position. I know he can't be comfortable. My heart softens at the sight of him—almost too much. The emotions I've been holding back are right there on the verge of where they might transform me into an embarrassing, sobbing mess. He looks up at me and I slide into the seat next to him.

"Thanks for doing this," I say. "I feel bad you're not home studying." I know he takes school every bit as seriously as Priya and I do. His glasses have slipped to near the bottom of his nose and he pushes them up with one finger.

"No problem," he says. "Nowhere else I'd rather be. How's your dad?"

And for some reason this makes me cry. I lean over, cupping my face inside my open palms and only my posture and the shuddering of my shoulders give me away. Anthony puts an arm across my shoulders.

"He's okay," I say once I've composed myself enough to straighten up. "Sorry. I'm just losing it a little, I guess, but I'm okay now." He withdraws his arm after a few gentle and reassuring pats on my back and I wipe my nose with the back of my hand since I don't have any Kleenex on me. I hand him a twenty-dollar bill. "My mom said to give this to you, so you can grab a taxi or an Uber. She says thank you so, so much." He smiles kindly. "And I say it too," I add.

"It's okay." He folds the bill back into my hand and closes my fingers over it. "I already called my dad and he'll come get me. I was just waiting to make sure you were okay and to give you the keys."

Anthony's such a great guy and I pour my heart out to him right here, right now. Unfortunately, the careful script I'd planned (and memorized) doesn't come out the way I thought it would. I mostly bumble my way through.

"This is probably the most inappropriate time for me to tell you this," I say. "And I'm not even sure why I'm telling you right now. But I feel really close to you."

Anthony looks a little taken aback like I'm about to propose marriage or something. "What's wrong?" he asks.

"I know that you . . . I mean, I feel like you're one of the best friends I have in school even though we've just gotten to know each other this year. But I want to be honest with you about something." Is it possible I've made a major miscalculation about Anthony's feelings and he isn't even interested in me that way? But I started, so I need to finish. I want to get back to my parents and let Anthony be on his way too. "I'm gay," I say. "I mean . . . well, you know what I mean."

It's not that I'm ashamed of what I just told him, but the way I said it makes it seem like I'm embarrassed. And I'm not embarrassed about being gay, it's just uncomfortable having to reject him before he's even given me anything to reject. I visualize kicking myself about five times in a row. I'm not the smooth and unflappable type, and being here with Dad in his current condition isn't helping a bit.

"Wow." Anthony flips his laptop shut and slides it into his backpack. "I guess I'm honored you told me," he says.

"Thanks." There's not a trace of sarcasm or bitterness in his voice.

"I wasn't sure if we were heading somewhere, other than just friends, that is," I say. "So, I wanted to be honest about everything, you know?"

I'm dying inside. Poor Anthony. He's giving up an important night of midterm studying just to hear this from me?

"Hey." He puts his hand on my shoulder to tilt me toward him because I'm doing everything I can to disappear right now. "*I'm* not even sure where we were going, to be honest. Yeah, I probably would've brought it up at some point . . . you and me . . . so I'm glad you told me because who knows how long it would've taken me to work up the nerve. But I'd rather have a friend at this stage of my life than a girlfriend, so don't feel bad. I just really like you and enjoy your company, and besides, you're incredibly brilliant. Now go see your dad and tell your parents I said goodbye."

"Thanks, Anthony." I lean over to give him a hug, hoping I'll get one in return because I could really use it right now. I do. Afterward, he hands me Mom's keys.

"I haven't been making you feel uncomfortable or anything, have I?" he asks, and his eyes are so earnest and sincere.

"Oh my God, no, never. And I'm sorry if I made you uncomfortable."

He flashes just the right kind of smile to let me know we're all good.

I'm about to go looking for Dad's room, but first I take out my phone and scroll through my texts, messages, and emails. There's an email from the place where I ordered the ancestry test. It's been three weeks so I'm excited the results have come back. I can share with my parents and take their minds off this rotten, horrible day. But instead I see a message from a woman named Cynthia Purdue who's in customer relations. She asks me to call her and has left the number for her direct line. There's still a chance she hasn't left the office, so I dial her number.

"Hello, this is Cindy," a voice on the other end says.

"This is Ana Woodland," I say. "I got an email asking me to call about my test results. I was supposed to ask for a Cynthia—"

"That's me," she cuts me off, rather rudely in my opinion. "Ana, we'll be refunding your testing fee although we're not obligated to do so. Please don't resubmit with us because your name has been flagged."

What the . . . ?

"What are you talking about? I haven't received my results yet." Nothing goes through my head because nothing about what she just said makes any sense.

"Don't think people haven't tried this before," Cindy says. "We get this more often than you'd realize."

"Get what?"

Maybe my confusion is getting through to her. Maybe she pauses just long enough to consider that I might not be guilty of whatever she thinks I'm guilty of. Or maybe she has me mixed up with someone else?

"Ana Woodland?" she asks, cautiously.

"Yes."

"Do you have your confirmation number?"

I scroll back through my emails and find the original confirmation. I read the numbers to her slowly, carefully enunciating each one. I hear the click of keyboard keys and Cindy's breath while she's looking for something.

"Non-human DNA, Ms. Woodland. Go see your vet if you want your pet tested."

CHAPTER 7

I wake up this morning to a girl's cries. She sounds so forlorn that my only thought is to reach out to her and comfort her in my arms. I cast aside my woolen blanket and slip my feet into the leather mules I keep bedside to avoid walking on the icy-cold floor. I go to each window of the house and peer out but see no one close enough to make such a loud sound to wake me. I see no one who gives any indication of being in distress. Only the elderly man who lives across the street, sweeping the dead leaves from his walkway. Only a young mother carrying an infant, the mother's neck swaddled with a thick, gray scarf, the infant bundled in multiple layers so as to appear without human form. The sky is thick and gray like the mother's scarf. It must have been a dream and yet seems so real. The pain of the crying girl feels like my own. I've experienced this before, a blurring between what's real and what exists in my imagination, but only after a seizure. Perhaps I've had one in my sleep.

I take the mug of tea I've made to my seat near the lamp. A picture looks across the room at me: Mother and me, long ago when Mother's

T
A
N
Y
A

gray hair was black. Before she stopped coloring it after it started to go gray. I was very young, two years old perhaps. And on the other side of Mother, Father has been snipped cleanly out of the picture. Out of our lives. I know this for a fact because one day I removed the picture from the frame to get a closer look behind the scratched glass. I saw a partial arm pressed against Mother's and it was a man's arm, bigger and clothed in what looked like a dark suit. I feel it must have been Father. I know it must have been Father. I long to connect the arm to his body, his face—to see him again and remember what he looked like. What he sounded like. I don't know if I ever saw Father after this picture was taken because I have no memory of him.

In the picture we're standing under a tree and in the background a glimpse of a house can be seen, and it looks like a nice tree and a nice house. I wonder if we were rich back then because Mother is wearing a beautiful dress and looks stylish with her dark hair cut short. She's wearing make-up and pointed shoes with heels. I have a smile on my face and am also wearing a pretty dress with buckled shoes. I'm holding a toy purse, crooked in the angle of my elbow, just as though I were an adult myself.

Mother says she was a doctor before but can't practice medicine or Father will be able to track us down. I don't know whether this is true or one of the fanciful creations of her paranoia, but I tend to think it's true because she's smart and understands everything the doctors have told us about my seizures. And yet, at the same time she's skeptical of what they say. Always skeptical. I don't think I've seen

Mother smile once since that picture was taken, right before we disappeared, which is why the picture is so special to me.

I wrap the blanket around my legs and feet and reach for the book I'm reading. I'm so cold all the time. Victor says it is because I'm weak from lack of physical activity.

"Come shovel snow with me," he says. "You'll be strong in no time. A person needs fresh air."

The muscles of my legs and arms are flabby. Even my belly is flabby, and I know that's not what other girls my age look like. I keep my weight down, but my skin is dull and my hair is limp. I need fresh air. I need to blow in the wind and be free and strong like the tree in the picture. Mother agrees, so she takes me on walks sometimes in the evenings when she isn't so exhausted from a day of work. But we don't walk far because my muscles aren't accustomed to it and tire easily. Mother's muscles are developed from her work, but they get tired too, from overuse. Mother has convinced me it's not safe for me to be out on my own. Whether she's right or wrong, it seems wise to believe her, because I've come this far in life with no harm coming to me. She says a strong mind and body are essential, so she's given me a set of calisthenics to perform every day. But I often skip them, finding the cramped interior of our home not at all conducive to the freedom my body craves.

To make up for it, I exercise my mind by studying hard. I must make myself the best person I can be to prepare for whatever might happen. That's what Mother says. Today, I am studying Vulgar Latin, the basis of the Romance languages. Of those, I have mastered Spanish, French, Italian, and Romanian. I have also taught myself English, though I'm far from perfect. Of course, I can only guess at the pronunciation since I have no occasion to speak with another person. German is more difficult for me, but I could speak with anyone in this town, if only there was someone to speak to. Occasionally, I encourage Victor to speak with me in German, but his German is so poor that I eventually take pity and switch to his native tongue. Mother is no help. She hates everyone but Russians so that's the only permissible spoken language in our home. And yet we can never return to Russia.

There's a rap on the kitchen window, which is Victor's usual sign. I check to see it's him before going around to open the back door.

"You're not in school again," I state the obvious fact.

He rubs his hands together. His coat is thin, and his cheeks are red from the cold.

"Do you know why your cheeks are so red?" I ask. He presses his open palms against his cheeks and shakes his head. "It's because your blood vessels dilate to allow the blood to flow into the parts of your body that are most important to keep warm. Like your head. And your internal organs."

"Then why are my hands so cold and white?" he asks. "They're important too."

"Not to your survival," I say.

"To *my* survival they are. If I can't work to help my mother, we can't eat, and I need my hands to work."

I can't argue with that.

"Why do you read so many books?" he asks. "I can go to the library and look up anything I want to know on a computer, and I can do it in any language, even Russian if I want. A book is already outdated long before it gets to the bookstore."

"Pfft." I shake my head slowly and with dramatic emphasis even though I wonder about what he's said. Mother won't let me go to the library to use a computer. I wouldn't even know how to use one. Every week I make a list of the kind of books I'd like to read, and she brings them home from the library. "The really important things in life are never outdated," I tell Victor. "True knowledge is timeless."

"If you say so." Victor plops down on the floor by my feet. "I can make a fire if you like," he says, although the electric heater is running and it's relatively warm in my house.

"Better not." I don't want to explain anything to Mother, and burned logs in the fireplace would require an explanation, and therefore a lie.

"Okay, then read me a story, please," he says. "*The Snow Queen.*" It's his favorite tale, one he requests frequently, and one we both enjoy. Although Victor knows the story well, he often interrupts to ask questions or just to reflect on what he's hearing. "The Snow Queen," he says. "Is she bad?"

"I don't really know. I suppose she's neither bad nor good."

"But she keeps the boy as her prisoner," he says. "How can that be good?"

"It's a story, like in life . . . sometimes there are no answers for why people act in ways that are both good and bad."

But I'm troubled all the same. In the story, an evil troll has made a mirror that reflects only the ugliness of the world and none of its splendor. Splinters from this terrible mirror pierce the heart and eye of the boy, Kai, rendering him unable to see or feel beauty and goodness. In my mind's eye, I visualize Kai, alone and friendless, his heart numbed to the frozen landscape of beauty that surrounds him. As a prisoner of the Snow Queen, Kai lives in a cloistered world, a dazzling snow palace that gleams under the sun, the beauty of which Kai cannot see. A frozen lake glitters like a diamond in the background.

But then it's no longer the boy, Kai, that I see. I remember a girl.

A girl who looks like me.

CHAPTER 8

Papa and I have come to spend a week at our country estate. Tyotya must stay in the city to work this time, so it's just the two of us plus Magda, the housekeeper who lives here permanently, and Igor, our driver. Each time we drive up the lane and I have the first glimpse of our home, it makes my breath catch and tightens my chest. The beauty is overwhelming, especially today when the snow has frosted the grounds like an enormous wedding cake. Only tiny paw prints here and there mar the surface that shimmers under the sun, so blindingly beautiful I have to squint in order to see. Even the lake is covered with snow, invisible to anyone unaware of its existence.

I love this place for many reasons, not the least of which is Magda's dog, Pepper. I'm not allowed to have a dog in our city home because of Tyotya Irina's allergies to their fur and general disgust with the uncleanliness of animals in a house where people live. But in the country, she tolerates Pepper, probably because she's so reliant on Magda to keep things in order and ready to receive us on a moment's notice. She knows Magda can't be expected to live on her

TATYANA

own without companionship of any kind, more than five kilometers away from the nearest village, and many more miles than that from her home country of Hungary. I think Tyotya Irina also tolerates Pepper for the smile he brings to my face. Papa is fond of him as well.

Magda is old and moves slowly. Her hands have large knuckles and her fingers are perpetually curled. Her back curves in a camel's hump, which pushes her head forward in a way I imagine to be painful. Papa keeps Magda's workload light. She's been with us for about ten years, but I generally try to stay out of her way. She frightens me a little, but I think it's just her appearance and general taciturn nature. Ten years ago, when I was a little girl, her appearance brought to mind the crones and witches of Grimm's Fairy Tales. I no longer think that way, but there's a residual unease that lingers even to this day.

Igor is Papa's driver and bodyguard. He's an enormous man who doesn't say much, but I've always felt safe in his presence. He opens the car door for me, and no sooner do I step out of the sedan than the front door opens and Pepper bounds from the house, runs to me, and stands on hind legs to lick me sloppily across my face. He's a large dog, and the weight of him tips me over onto my back, where he covers me in kisses while I laugh helplessly, protecting my face with both arms and turning my face first this way and then that. Papa strolls over and offers me his hand, pulling me up and helping to brush the snow from my hair and the back of my coat.

"Pepper," Magda finally calls out, giving him just enough

time to perform the ritual both Pepper and I look forward to before she pretends to scold him. "Leave *Tanyusha* be! Back in the house, you rascal!" Her voice is thin and crackles.

Papa laughs heartily, and Igor retrieves our suitcases from the trunk of the car and carries them inside. If Tyotya Irina had been with us, Magda would have held onto Pepper's collar when she greeted us at the door.

Everything is prepared for us, so after settling into our rooms, we come down for a late lunch. A fire burns in the huge hearth, and delicious smells waft from the kitchen. Dinner cooking. The dining table is long, but Magda sets a place for Papa in his usual position at the head, with a place for me on his right-hand side. We eat cold meats and cheese. And we've brought fresh fruit with us for dessert, which we don't always have if Magda hasn't organized a delivery from town.

After every meal, it's our custom to relax and talk no matter which home we're in. Magda brings a hot cocoa for me, and for Papa, a snifter of brandy. She sets the bottle of brandy on the small table near Papa's chair. I know from experience he'll drink most of the bottle before the night is through. We sit in two overstuffed velvet armchairs and watch the flames of the fire twist eerily inside their dancing cave. It's at moments like this I catch Papa stealing glances at me that appear more sorrowful than fond. This generally happens when he's tired and thinks I'm not paying attention.

But I'm always paying attention to Tyotya Irina and Papa. They are my lifeline. My happiness is dependent on theirs.

Later, I'll take a walk with Pepper and then go up to my room and continue what I started weeks ago—researching various universities and the requirements for attending. I know this won't ever be my reality because a university would never agree to have me—the liability for them would be too great if I was to have a seizure and be in a precarious situation with no one watching over me. Tyotya Irina and Papa have explained this to me over and over again, and I know it's true, but I can't help but dream. On my laptop, I can pretend I'm just like any other girl my age with a promising future ahead of her. A college education. A career. Perhaps even children. Pretending is what keeps me going. And here, in our country home, a modicum of freedom. I can walk outside for a mile or more with Pepper by my side. Igor follows, far enough behind to give me a sense of independence but close enough to watch over me.

But right now, I am with Papa and he is with me. We sit by the fire and talk about a variety of subjects, as is our custom. Papa is happy tonight and has already refilled his glass several times. Eventually our conversation leads to religion, which is something we only consider in terms of historic or cultural significance because we aren't a family of believers. Papa believes Karl Marx was correct when he said, "Religion is the sigh of the oppressed creature, the heart of a heartless world, and the soul of the soulless conditions. It is the opium of the people." Papa says that people without hope need religion the way that a dying patient needs opium to ease their pain. The way primitive man needed religion to explain away occurrences, such as a solar eclipse, that are now explained by science.

"We are scientists," Papa says, taking another sip of brandy before he continues speaking. "And science is the highest order of the universe. Science is the pinnacle toward which all should strive. Science is . . . well, science is God," he concludes.

"I'm confused," I say. "When you state that science is God, you're implying there's something greater than us. Something omniscient." My father has always said there's nothing greater or more powerful than our own minds.

"Tatyana," Papa turns abruptly to face me. "What if there was something so great, a scientific discovery so astonishing, it would render the very idea of God obsolete even to the most ardent believers?" Father's eyes shine, and I know it's from more than the glow of the fire's reflection on their surface. He pours himself another glass from the bottle of brandy that Magda has left.

I don't know what to say so I wait for him to speak again.

"What if the person who made this discovery . . . who dedicated his life to it . . . Why wouldn't that person be Godlike? Why wouldn't that person be God, himself? Or herself," he quickly adds.

"What do you mean, Papa? What are you describing?" I lean closer to him, excited and yet somehow unsettled at where this discussion is leading. Why is Papa bringing God into the subject of science when I was always taught the two don't mix?

He takes another thoughtful sip of his brandy as though trying to collect his thoughts. I know this elixir, as Papa is fond of calling it, loosens his tongue, relaxing him into truths he wouldn't otherwise come forth with—but it has never caused him to depart from the truth. And I have no reason to believe otherwise right now.

"You're familiar with the multiverse, Tanyusha," he says. This is not a question. We've discussed it on many occasions. We've discussed many scientific theories in detail that would be denied any other person my age, simply because they wouldn't have access to a scientist with the caliber of knowledge my father possesses.

"Of course." Pepper wanders in, his clicking toenails on the hardwood floors heralding his entrance. He sidles up to my chair, insistently placing his head under my hand, knowing I'll reciprocate with the behind-the-ear scratching he craves.

"And the difficulty that scientists have had in proving its existence."

"Yes," I say. "Because if parallel universes exist, we're unable to see them, much like a person who lived out their life in a soundproofed room would never know that another person could be living in a similar room on the other side of the wall."

"We know, or have surmised, that an electron can exist in more than one state simultaneously, but when viewed by an observer, the theory doesn't hold."

I love these discussions with Papa. I've forgotten about Pepper, and he nudges my hand to remind me he's still there.

"Because when something that exists in a wavelike state is observed it becomes a particle. Schrodinger's cat," I say proudly, hoping Papa is pleased I've learned my lessons well and can think of an example to illustrate his point.

Quantum mechanics is not something I understand well; however, I have a general idea of the theory that supposes the mythical cat could be both alive and dead at the same time and, only upon observation, would it settle into its particle and observable state of one or the other. I also understand people use the science behind Schrodinger's cat to support the theory of parallel universes, the multiverse, where different versions of oneself could be living out entirely different lives just millimeters or perhaps light years apart—an infinite number of versions, based on every decision one makes and its consequences. But these are just theories and I don't understand what it has to do with God. I'm waiting for Papa to explain, but he doesn't, and that's typical of Papa. He loves to present me with an idea or concept, often quite farfetched, just to see where it will lead. Mind exercises, he calls them, and I suppose this is another mind exercise.

"Do you believe in reincarnation, Tatyana?" Papa asks. Strange that he asks, because he must know the answer. I believe what he and Tyotya Irina believe, and I assume that doesn't include reincarnation. But suddenly I'm not so sure about anything.

"I don't know," I say. "I suppose there could be a life force . . . an energy that doesn't dissipate with death. And if that's true, then I suppose that energy would have to go somewhere because energy doesn't just disappear. But it can't be proven . . . at least not yet. Can it?"

I know Papa prefers me to answer my own questions even if I have to grapple with them in silence. But I'm not feeling confident. I have an odd feeling, and suddenly I'm fearful. Cold and yet sweating. Weak. A little dizzy. A loud buzz bounces around the inside of my skull.

But Papa is lost in his thoughts and doesn't seem to notice the change in me. "What if people who believe they've been reincarnated are actually just experiencing the vestiges of traveling to a parallel universe?" he asks. "And what if I could prove it? Would that make me God? Would that make me greater than God?" He chuckles as though just now realizing he's speaking to someone and not thinking out loud. But his voice has become a muddle. The smirk on his face seems more sinister than embarrassed.

My vision fades to black right before the bright tunnel opens before me. It's white like the snow. Blinding me if I dare to look into it and yet entreating me to enter.

And this time I do.

CHAPTER 9

The doctor recommended another EEG, which measures brain wave activity, unlike the MRI, which only allows them to get a visual of my brain. I've had two in the past and the results weren't conclusive, in fact quite the opposite. I thought my parents would back me up when I said I didn't want to be put through that again. But I was wrong.

"It's been a few years, Tati," Mom said. "It might give the doctor some important information. Maybe we'll see changes." And Dad backed *her* up instead of me. So, ten days after my MRI, I was back at the neurologist for an EEG. He did everything he could to induce a seizure—sleep deprivation for twenty-four hours before I went in, shining strobe lights in my eyes. Nothing happened, so I got sent home with an appointment for yet another EEG today.

This time it does happen, but it doesn't seem like it happens because of what they did. It seems like it happens just because it was going to happen anyway.

Afterward, the doctor calls us into his office and delivers the same bullshit lines as before. *No electrical changes. Normal brain waves.*

T
A
T
I

"Dr. Browning," Mom says. "I've been listening to you tell us the same thing for years. So now I'm going to put you on the spot and ask you a tough question I hope you'll answer honestly." I hear the hopelessness in Mom's voice. "You say there's no evidence of a seizure having occurred and yet you can see with your own eyes that it happened. Are you trying to tell us that our daughter is making this up? Acting out a seizure? Lying to all of us? *Performing?*" She draws out the last word. Incredulous.

I know Mom doesn't believe it herself; she's trying to force something out of Dr. Browning. She wants him to defend his test results or maybe embark on a different path. They say the definition of insanity is doing the same thing over and over and expecting different results. I'm not expecting different results anymore, but I can't help but feel everyone else is. Like me, Mom and Dad are at the end of their rope. Dad sits quietly in a seat off in the corner of the office since there are only two in front of the doctor's desk.

"That's not at all what I'm telling you, Mrs. Woodland." The doctor keeps his voice even, calm.

"Then exactly what *are* you telling us, Doctor?" Dad being Dad usually does a lot of listening and then moves in for the close. That's the way it is with Mom and Dad. The one-two punch, I call it.

I bite the inside of my cheek so hard I can taste blood. Whatever Dr. Browning is going to say is something I know I don't want to hear.

"It's a medical mystery," he says. "Sometimes we don't

have an answer to every question. I'm just as perplexed as you, and I want an explanation every bit as much as you do."

"No, you don't," I say without thinking. Even though I know it's not fair, it comes out anyway. Dr. Browning's a good and caring man, but he can't possibly come close to wanting an explanation as much as I do.

He looks straight at me and, compassionately, doesn't respond. I get up and walk out of his office, slamming the door behind me, and go out to the lobby to wait. I wonder if Dr. Browning will drop me as a patient for my rudeness. I guess that's the sucky part of being a doctor. When there are no answers, people take their rage out on you because it's easier than taking it out on their failing bodies.

A few minutes later my parents walk out, and we go to our car where I completely lose it.

"I told you they wouldn't find anything, but you made me do it anyhow. Why. Do. You. Keep. Making. Me. Do. This? It's always the same result!" I've never yelled at my parents, and Mom gets out of the front seat and comes around to the back where she pulls me close with a hand across my shoulder. I try to twist out of her grasp, but Mom's too strong even though she's smaller than me. Dad turns around to face us.

"Dr. Browning probably *does* think I'm faking. You probably think so too. Do *you* think I'm faking?" I start to cry. A big, ugly, slobbering cry.

"Of course not." Mom hugs me tight, reaching her other arm across my chest and clasping her hands together, locking me into her arms. "Of course we believe you." And now Mom is crying and I'm feeling like a piece of shit. This is my first real fight with my parents. Or at least my first confrontation and I'm already feeling guilty about it.

"Don't worry, honey." Dad is the only one in the car not crying, although he looks like he's about to. "This is it, the last time. We're never putting you through this again."

Mom releases me to dab around her eyes and nose with a Kleenex. "Why don't you see if Priya can spend the night tonight?" It does sound like a pretty good idea at this moment. I feel low, lower than I've ever felt before, and I could use some Priya time. "I'll make cookies and you can rent a movie," she adds. It's sweet that my parents accept Priya unconditionally into my life, knowing what we have is real love. Adult love. And yet Mom can't help but pamper us like the two schoolgirls I guess we still technically are. My heart swells with love for her.

I call Priya, who says she'll be over in an hour. When we get home, I hover over Mom in the kitchen while she sets to work making her famous double-chocolate-chip cookies. Dad's settled into the other room watching some of his favorite cooking shows, which are clogging our DVR almost to ninety percent.

"Come watch. Calgerian cooking," he calls out. "California cuisine with a North African flavor." I roll my eyes at Mom and she smiles sympathetically but neither of us makes a move to join him. "I'll make it for dinner tomorrow," he says but we both know he won't. He intends to cook all of these dishes, but in reality, he would rather watch someone else cook, even if it's on TV, and leave the cooking to Mom—who prefers it that way also.

"Mom, tell me again what you know about how my birth mother died. Even something that might seem totally meaningless. Even if you've told me before."

If there was something about her death that has anything to do with what's going on with me now, I want to know. I *need* to know.

Mom stops and stares at the ball of cookie dough in her hands as if it will present the answers I need. Then she looks up at me. "I've honestly told you everything I know. You can look at the paperwork anytime you like. It's in the file cabinet in your adoption folder."

"So . . . she may have committed suicide. She may have been murdered. Nobody knows anything more than that?"

"She was a Jane Doe," Mom says. "And you were a tiny, helpless baby who obviously couldn't say what you saw. They never identified her."

"How could that even happen? That a woman, holding her baby, would shoot herself through the head? And they found the gun a few feet out of her reach. With no fingerprints."

Mom shakes her head slowly and goes back to rolling out the dough. "It could have been the recoil of the gun that drove it out of her hand. And she was wearing gloves. It was cold. Thank God you weren't there long before someone found you."

"Who found me?" I ask, although I've asked this question before.

"They don't know. Just a random man who dropped you off and was never seen again. A good Samaritan. Just a tiny, helpless baby wrapped in a blanket with your name embroidered in Russian on it."

"And the gun?"

"Untraceable," Mom says grimly. "Which I understand is not difficult to obtain on the black market in Russia."

"But . . ." I don't know what else to ask. I wish there was more—there must be more. I never wanted to know about my birth mom as much as I do right now. "What did she look like?"

Mom takes a deep breath and exhales. "Tati, you know that when someone is shot in the head, we're going to have a skewed picture of what she looked like."

To put it mildly.

"But . . . did they say anything about her?"

I know it's painful for Mom to talk about this. She wants to spare me and, anyway, it's not the easiest thing to discuss when you're in a warm kitchen making delicious cookies, trying to cheer your daughter up.

"They offered to let us look at the autopsy photos, but your father and I declined. They said she was on the short side. A little stocky. Blonde hair. Late twenties to early thirties. That's all I know."

Short, stocky, and blonde sounds nothing like me so I guess I take after my birth father.

"Nothing else, Mom? Nothing at all you can think of?"

"Tati, I wish I could help you. You know I'd do anything to give you everything you want. I wish I knew more, but all I know is that when Dad and I first laid eyes on you, we knew we'd do anything to bring you home and give you all the love you deserve. We were bursting with love for you after just five seconds in your presence."

I reach over and hold the non-sticky back of her wrist that isn't covered in dough and flour. "And I know I'm the luckiest person alive to have you and Dad. But isn't there anything else you can remember, no matter how insignificant it might seem? Something one of the nurses at the orphanage might have told you?"

"Tati, please. Do you really think I'd hold back on you? It's been seventeen years, but I remember it like it was yesterday," Mom says.

I release Mom's wrist and she goes back to her cookie dough. "When did I have my first seizure?"

"Before we even got on the plane to take you home."

Priya arrives while the cookies are in the oven. We haven't spent the night at her house since our argument. I think we both realize that not allowing ourselves to be ourselves only creates stress and tension that we take out on each other. But at my house it's all good. I answer the door and we fold ourselves into each other's arms with a lingering kiss I know Dad is giving us time to finish before he calls out to us through the door to the TV room.

"Would you two care to join me for an episode of *Spice of Life*?" Another of his cooking shows.

"No thanks, Dad," I say. "We're going to work on our ethnic studies project."

"Thanks anyway, George." My parents insist Priya call them by their first names.

Once in my room, all I really want to do is unburden myself to Priya.

"The EEG was awful," I say. "And there's never any proof I'm actually having a seizure so I kind of freaked out today because we thought the doctor was implying I was faking it."

"*Was* he?" Priya's eyes go wide. "Implying, I mean."

"Probably not," I say. "I mean, he said he believes me but just doesn't understand why my brain waves look normal. I don't know, maybe he *does* think I'm faking it and was just trying to be nice about it."

"But you're not." Priya flops down by my side on the bed. She wraps my arm around her. "I know you're not."

"Priya, there's something else that's really bothering me, and I need to tell you about it."

"What?" She twists her neck to look at me, but I continue to stare at the ceiling because eye contact will make me less brave and I really do need to tell her. "*What?*" She sits up and looks down at me, lining her face up with mine so I can't look away. She's inches away from me and I smell cinnamon on her breath, which I know she adds to her tea. I'm guessing she stopped at the Tea Cozy on her way over. "*Say it.*"

"It's nothing bad . . . about us, I mean. It's just that . . . remember the whole thing about Hercules's collar being silver and I thought it was blue?"

"Yeah, so, that doesn't mean anything. Like you're

supposed to memorize the color of Hercules's collars? He's got about twenty different ones."

"It's not just that." I stare at the glow-in-the-dark ceiling stars. "Once I woke up and almost had a heart attack because I was sure my comforter was navy blue, but it wasn't. It was . . . this." I pluck at the fabric of my comforter and then let it drop with disgust.

"But you've always had this comforter ever since I've known you."

"Yeah? Well you could have fooled me. I hate pink. Why would I have chosen pink?"

"I didn't know you hated pink," Priya says, probably thinking of the pink cashmere sweater she gave me for Christmas.

I'm such an idiot.

"I mean . . . there's other stuff. The towel rack in my bathroom was always on the left side of the sink and then one day it's suddenly on the right. Like that. A lot of other things too. Little things."

She lies down beside me again and snuggles against me, stroking my hair, smoothing it away from my face.

"Hey," she says. "That happens to me all the time. I'm always forgetting where I put things and . . . I mean, your seizures must be doing a number on your memory. Of course they are. Big deal. And why didn't you tell me before? Have you told the doctor?"

But isn't it a big deal? After all, forgetting where you put your car keys isn't the same thing as forgetting where you put your towel rack. Or forgetting the color of your comforter.

"Nope."

"Your parents?"

"Double nope."

"Why not?"

"I don't know." I've relaxed a little and am willing to believe Priya that maybe it isn't a big deal. Maybe it *is* just my seizures affecting my memory here and there. And how bad can that be? I'm still at the top of my class. They say even Einstein forgot where he lived sometimes and would walk into the wrong house. "It was hard enough telling *you*. I don't want everyone to think I'm crazy."

"Let's not worry about it right now. Let's just see if it happens again, okay?" she says.

"Okay."

"And if it does, you'll tell your parents. Okay?"

I nod.

"Priya, do you remember the day we first met?" She's lying in a curled C-position facing me. One of Hercules's silky hairs clings to her black yoga pants. I pluck it between my thumb and forefinger and hold it up to the light.

"Of course. Sophomore PE, second period."

"But when we *really* first met." I bring the silky strand of Hercules's hair to within inches of my lips and blow, releasing it to ride the current of my breath.

"What're you doing?" Priya asks.

"Making a wish."

"On Hercules's hair?"

"It's as good as anything."

"What did you wish for?" she asks.

"I can't tell, or it won't come true." But I wished for health and answers and Priya's continuing love. Probably too much to expect from the hair of a dog, even one so beloved by Priya.

"So?" I look at Priya, raising my eyebrows.

"So . . . when did we *really* meet? I guess last year in Calculus."

"Do you remember how you dropped your pencil and we both leaned over to pick it up at the same time and our hands touched and you smiled at me?" I ask.

Priya smiles again. Just like she did that day. "I do."

"That's what gave me the courage to ask you to come over. That smile. Just the way you smiled right now."

Priya takes my hand in hers and strokes it gently with her thumb.

"What if I hadn't asked you to come over? What do you think would have happened to us?"

"I think we would have gotten together somehow on a different day."

"I don't think so, Priya. I think the stars were aligned on that day. The pencil dropping. Our hands touching. Your smile. That's what gave me the courage I wouldn't have had on another day. Would you ever have approached me if it had only been up to you?"

"Honestly?" Priya asks, and I appreciate that she never lies to me. Still, I know what's coming and part of me doesn't want to hear it. But I asked so she'll answer.

"Honestly."

"I probably wouldn't have," she says. "I was scared to

admit my attraction to you and I never would have had the courage to initiate it. My parents . . ." she drifts off. She must notice the disappointment on my face. She runs her hand through my hair, down the back of my neck, leaving a trail of tingling goosebumps in her wake. "But lucky for me, you didn't have my same hang-ups. Remember our first kiss?"

"Mmm. I didn't feel particularly courageous at that moment. Wasn't sure if you would slap my face or jump my bones."

"Liar, liar, pants on fire." Priya's eyes crinkle cutely and her lips part into the slightly crooked smile that still reminds me of that day. "I couldn't have vibed more nonverbal cues if I'd written down actual instructions."

I laughed. "I've never been great at nonverbal cues, but I suppose I did pick up on one or two. Like when you retied my scarf because, supposedly, I'd done it all wrong."

"You still do it wrong," Priya scrunched her face in fashion disapproval.

"Is this one of those annoyingly cute stories we'll tell our kids one day, like my parents do? And they'll hate us for making them listen to it over and over again?"

"I hope so."

"But seriously, Priya. One little thing. One decision I made that day, and everything changed for us. Do you ever wonder what our lives would be like right now if we hadn't gotten together?"

"I don't wonder because I don't want to know," Priya says. "And I believe in fate and that we were meant to be."

For Priya, life isn't messy and confusing the way it is for me. I envy that about her.

"So, when's your DNA result supposed to be ready?" she asks.

"Today, actually. I forgot all about that, but they overnighted the second test to me and I overnighted back to them and then they put a rush on the results when I explained the problem. Today's the deadline."

"Well, let's just see then." Priya hops off the bed and walks over to my desk where I've left my phone. "Here." She tosses it to me.

There's a knock on the door. "Come in," I call out while I'm opening my email app. Mom walks in with a plate of warm cookies, which smell divine.

"I can get you girls some milk if you like," she says.

"None for me, Maggie, thanks," Priya says. "You want some milk, Tati?"

But I've already found the emailed results and I'm opening the attached report. I scan through all the boiler plate information to get to the part where it breaks down my results. My heart's pounding just as though I was getting ready to meet my birth parents for the first time. My birth grandparents and great-grandparents. They're somehow about to reveal everything about me I never knew before.

We regret to inform you that your results are inconclusive. We were unable to get an accurate reading and will be issuing a credit to the card that was originally charged.

I throw my phone across the room while Mom and Priya stand by in stunned silence.

CHAPTER 10

ANA

Dad has had a small heart attack, it turns out, which is worse than what they originally thought. Mom spent the night at the hospital, which means I spent the night home alone. My parents don't like me to be alone in case of a seizure, but I insist. Dad needs her more than I do, and I need to be able to trust in myself or fate or karma or whatever's going to determine my life going forward. Mom suggested I invite a friend to stay with me, and there were a few I could have called. I even played with the idea of calling Priya, who said she wanted to hang out sometime. In the end, I didn't. Time alone seems to be part of growing up and becoming independent, which I have to do someday. And I'm finally at the point where being alone doesn't cause me anxiety. Mom knows all of this too, so she doesn't insist.

After school I call Mom, who says Dad's doing well, all things considered. She talked to the nurses about moving Dad's bed because the feng shui was totally wrong, but not surprisingly the nurses answered her with blank, over-worked stares, probably wondering whether she was serious or just seriously insane. She's going to come home, shower, and rest up. Dad should be released tomorrow if all goes well, so I walk to the Tea Cozy with a group of friends. It's our favorite hangout, and we spend an hour talking about classes and school and each other. Anthony walks there with us but then splits off and makes an excuse about having to get home for something he has to do. He's never joined us at the Tea Cozy, even though we always ask him to. I sometimes wonder if he feels excluded because the rest of us are girls.

"One of these days, we're going to convince you." Priya laughs.

"Just not a big fan of tea," Anthony says, and his face turns pink. He's only been at our school for a year, so I think we're still a little intimidating.

"They have coffee too," I suggest helpfully.

"I'm not a huge fan of any products that grow out of the ground and are used primarily as a caffeine-delivery system," he says.

"They have herbal tea." I giggle. Anthony's cute when he's uncomfortable but only when it's because he knows we all love him. He pushes his glasses up the bridge of his nose and rolls his eyes.

"No hot drinks period," he says in a fake angry tone. "And no iced tea if you were even thinking about suggesting it."

Everyone else is in line ordering, so I give him a quick hug and we make plans to chat about homework later tonight.

After the Tea Cozy I walk home by myself, and a few blocks from my house I notice a man walking behind me. It always creeps me out to have anyone walk behind me for too long, especially a man by himself, so first I slow down, then I speed up. I look behind me but he's still there, the same distance away. There's a bench at the bus stop, so I stop and prop my foot on the bench, pretending to tie my shoe. He catches up to me but instead of walking on, he stops.

"Is this yours? I think you dropped it." He's holding something in his hand but I don't want to make eye contact, so I just shake my head.

"Are you certain?" he asks, catching me off-guard, so I glance up to see what he's holding. It's a plastic baggy of grapes left over from lunch that was in the pocket of my hoodie. It must have fallen out somehow.

"Thanks," I reach out for it without looking him in the eye. "I guess I did drop it." He's a generic-looking type of guy whose features don't stand out for any particular reason. He's white and his hair is sandy-colored and cut short. He's wearing those aviator-type sunglasses that cops go for, but he doesn't look anything like a cop. He stands there for a second but when I don't say anything else he walks away.

I toss the bag into a nearby garbage can and wonder why he followed me for so long before giving me the bag of grapes. I let him get about half a block in front of me before I start walking again. He turns the corner and, by the time I get to that side street, there's no sign of him. For some reason this bothers me, because now I have no conclusive evidence he's not following me again. In another half block I pass my house, but I keep walking. Mom's car isn't out front and, besides, if he's watching me, I don't want him to know where I live. I walk on to Anthony's house.

"*Qué sorpresa*," Anthony says when he opens the door. "*¿Quieres entrar?*"

"*Sí, gracias, amable señor*," I say. Anthony and I are in AP Spanish class together.

"How's your dad?" he asks.

"According to Mom, as good as can be expected and worse than we'd like."

Anthony's smile turns upside down. "Sorry." He steps to the side and I go inside. I know where Anthony lives, but I've never actually been to his house before. Everything is neat and tidy, unlike our house, but it's basically the same type of design since all these houses were built at the same time by the same developer.

"Anthony, who is it?" I hear a female voice call out from what seems like upstairs.

"S'okay, Ma. It's for me." He looks at me. "My mother works from home. She's an accountant."

"I hope I'm not disturbing anything."

"No, not at all. Let's go to the kitchen, I'll get you something to drink."

But after three cups of tea, I'm not really looking for liquid refreshment. "No thanks, but actually, can I use your bathroom?"

He points down the hallway. "I'll be in here." He gestures to the room off to the side where Dad would be reclining in his La-Z-Boy chair, a glass of wine by his side, a mystery novel in his hand, if this were my house and if my dad weren't in the hospital.

When I join him, he motions to the spot on the sofa beside him. He has a controller in one hand and has obviously been playing video games. "You play?" he asks, and I nod *yes*. I sit down and Anthony hands me a controller.

We don't say much for the next fifteen minutes other than the occasional vocal outburst when something goes either very right or very wrong. It's fun. I haven't just kicked back and relaxed with someone over a video game in a long time. When I was younger, my parents read somewhere that certain games could trigger epileptic seizures, so they wouldn't let me play. But soon it was obvious that had nothing to do with it, so out came the game system from the closet where it had been stashed for a few months.

Anthony pauses the game and looks over at me. "Don't get me wrong. I'm really glad you're here, but is there a reason you came? I mean, I thought we were going to chat later tonight. Something to do with your dad you want to talk about? School?"

I feel a little guilty I'm not there on my own with no other reason than to seek out his company. Just because I want to strengthen our friendship by hanging out. And I do. But I'm straight up with him because he's Anthony and I know he'll understand.

"Actually . . . I was walking home and some creepster was walking behind me the whole way. Then when I stopped to tie my shoe at the bus stop he came up to me and asked me if I dropped a bag of grapes."

"Did you?"

"Yeah, but . . ."

"But what?"

"Okay. If you just happened to be walking behind someone and they dropped something, would you just keep walking behind them until they came to a stop? Wouldn't you jog after them and say something like, *Hey, you dropped this bag of grapes*?"

Anthony considers this. "Fair enough," he says. "Anything else? I mean, creepster is a pretty strong word."

"Nah, but . . . I just had a feeling."

"Fair enough," Anthony says again. "You want me to walk you home?"

"Hell, no," I say, putting the finishing moves on Anthony's guy in the game. "I'm not a damsel in distress. I can handle this myself. I just didn't want him to know where I live."

"Well, you totally just led him to my house." Anthony puts his controller down, puts his feet up on the coffee table, and looks over at me all exasperated, more likely from losing the game. "So now he thinks you live here."

"Oh my God, I did, didn't I? I'm so sorry. I'm such an idiot."

"It's okay," he says. "I was mainly just kidding."

"I better be going home now, though, because my mom's coming home soon. And thank you again a million times for yesterday. It means a lot to me. All of it, really." Just saying that makes me want to start crying all over again, but I don't.

"Well, I'm going to at least walk outside with you and check the premises to make sure the creepster isn't lurking."

We both laugh but he does walk outside and look around. There's no sight of the man.

Mom's home and unloading groceries when I get there. She catches me up on everything the doctor said and everything that's happened to Dad since last night, including his bowel movement.

"Mom, please. I don't need to hear that." I continue to unload the bags onto the counter while Mom puts things away. She seems upbeat, but I know her—she's stressed and trying to hold it all together. I don't mention the man or the fact that I stopped at Anthony's for that reason. But I do tell her about the DNA results and how I was accused of swapping my nonexistent dog's saliva with my own.

"Animal DNA." She chuckles. "Well, you are a little bit of a beast."

"It's not funny, Mom. I have a deadline, and this is going to mess up my ethnic studies project. It's sixty percent of our grade."

"Just make something up," Mom says. "We know you're Russian. Just throw in some German and Polish or whatever. Ukrainian, you know. Somewhere geographically not too far away. Or make it more interesting and pick somewhere far away like Africa or Greece."

"Mom!" My parents' moral code is a bit looser than mine when it comes to school. "I could never do that. That would be . . ." I leave it unsaid because I don't want to insinuate that my mom's a liar or a cheater.

She pours herself a glass of water from the fridge and leans back against the counter while she sips it. "The DNA company has competitors, don't they? Use one of them."

"I don't know if they can get it to me fast enough. I've already wasted three weeks."

"See if they have rush orders. Explain the situation. I'll pay whatever it costs."

"Maybe," I say. "I'll check online." I think about Priya's idea—the way some cultures equate seizures with holiness. That would be easier to do. I could ask Priya for the name of the book, which I'd probably want to read anyway. But then my stubbornness sets in. I'm not going to be *that* girl, the girl who makes everything about her affliction. Why shouldn't I be like everyone else?

"Ana," Mom comes over and puts an arm around me. "It's been a really tough twenty-four hours, but don't worry. Dad's going to be fine and we're all going to get through this together, I promise."

CHAPTER 11

TANYA

I'm by myself when the girl in the ice castle comes to me again. I've caught glimpses of her before, but now she appears before me as clear and real as the book by my side. Her skin is pale, the color of ivory, so pale I can see faint blue veins meandering along the undersides of her arms, and yet a blush of rose blooms in her cheeks. In contrast, my skin is sallow, a yellow-tinged, unhealthy pallor. Her dark-brown hair is lustrous and hangs silkily down her back and across her shoulders. My own hair is flat and sticks to my skull. She's a better version of myself.

She seems surprised to see me, but I'm not at all surprised to see her. Perhaps because she's seeing me for the first time, whereas I've known of her existence for a while, even if I can't explain it to myself or anyone else.

I'm in my chair and she's standing before me. We gaze at each other for what feels like a very long time. I want to speak to her, but at first, I don't have the ability, words won't come. When they finally do, they sound garbled to my ears, and I wonder if they sound the same to her. I try every language I know but she only shakes her head, opening and closing her mouth as if she's trying to say something but possesses no vocal chords. Perhaps this is what I look like to her.

Now she reaches forward with both hands and I reach toward her. We press the flat of our palms together, but I have no sense of human touch, no sensory feeling at all. In that moment, I see a vision of a large room, a huge hearth with a fire blazing in the background. An ornately carved round table is visible behind her. A crystal goblet stands alone in its center, half-filled with what appears to be wine. An intricate oil painting hangs on one wall—a man from long ago mounted on a white horse. A river is before him, and on the opposite bank a young woman sits on a large stone, her bare feet visible in waves beneath the surface of the water. It must be springtime in the painting because wildflowers are plentiful, speckling the grass with vibrant color. Who are they? Lovers? Strangers? The rushing current of the river separates them. I doubt they could hear or understand if one called out to the other.

I wonder what the girl before me is seeing right now. Does she see the small, cramped room where I sit with the blanket wrapped tightly around my feet?

As if we're commanded by the same inner voice, we pull our hands away from each other at the same time. And then she's gone, and I'm left as I was before. But I *am* awake. I know for certain I'm not in a dream nor in the throes of a seizure. And I feel the deep and inexplicable pain of loss.

I rise from my chair and go to the small room I share with Mother. Two narrow beds take up nearly all the space. I crouch down and pull out a small wooden box, inlaid with mother-of-pearl, from where it's stashed under Mother's bed. The design on the lid of the box kept me enthralled for hours when I was younger: a mermaid perched on a rock jutting out of the sea, a tall ship in the background. I open the lid and see the remainder of Mother's treasure. All the jewels she once possessed have slowly dwindled over the years to what I see before me. A gold ring with a gleaming ruby surrounded by tiny diamonds. A pearl necklace with matching drop earrings. This is our emergency trust. Over the years, Mother has sold off all the other pieces. Slowly they've disappeared from the box I once thought was magical. I once believed it had the power to restore the missing jewels, which would reappear when I next opened the lid. For years I never opened it, not wanting to test the potency of its magic. Now I see nearly everything is gone. There's a sharp knock on the front door and I close the box quickly, sliding it under the bed and placing Mother's slippers in front just as they were before.

I tiptoe out the door into the small room where I've left my book. I'm not permitted to light a fire during the day, so as not to arouse suspicion should someone see smoke rising from the chimney. There's a small window at the front of the house, but I avoid it, being careful not to betray myself with the cast of my shadow. I stay close to the darker parts of the room. The walls. A corner. Places I know well. Another rap on the door, which feels angry, as though sounds can convey emotion. Whenever Victor comes, he knocks on the kitchen window, a friendly and thoughtful knock. I know the person on the other side of this door is nothing like Victor. And I instinctively know it's a man, the same man who came before. I only have to hear his knuckles striking the hard wood to know that.

A few minutes longer. Even my breath is so quiet it practically disappears. Although I don't make a sound, I think he feels my presence during the long silence. I feel his. Heavy. Opaque. I feel his dark thoughts and I'm afraid. Now I know he's not a friend of Victor's, nor a relative. I know he's not a stranger who needs directions. He's looking for us—Mother and me. When he leaves, I know that as well, and only then do I allow myself to peek through the curtains to make sure he's gone. He turns right where the pathway to our house meets the street, and after he's walked about twenty meters, I lose sight of him.

When Mother comes home, I wait to tell her, and I don't care if she says we have to pack and move tonight. I sense the danger this man is introducing into our lives, loosing it like a pack of wolves into the sanctity of our quiet refuge. But when I see her tired face as she walks through the door, I begin to doubt myself.

"That overactive imagination of yours will be the death of you," Mother always says. But what else do I have left if not the world I create in my mind? Still, it does make me reconsider if another move is worth it for just a feeling I had.

I'll wait until we've eaten dinner and Mother's had time to relax. After that, we'll both have clearer minds with which to judge the situation—me, in terms of how I relay my story; Mother, in terms of how she reacts to it. The part about the girl, my elegant twin . . . that part is better left unsaid.

Mother has brought mutton home tonight, which is a rare treat for us. Normally we eat fish and boiled potatoes. Sometimes just the boiled potatoes. But tonight, we have mutton and Swiss chard with our potatoes. I savor every bite, chewing fifteen times before I swallow just to keep the taste inside my mouth for a few minutes longer. Mother even pours a small bit of wine from the only bottle in our cabinet. Just a few centimeters in each mismatched glass. She opened the bottle months ago and doles it out a few sips at a time. It's beginning to taste like vinegar, but I don't complain and I don't tell her.

"The man came again today," I say at last.

Mother puts down her fork and knife and stares at me in disbelief. "And you chose to keep this from me until now," she says. "How is it I gave birth to such a stupid girl?"

"Then leave me," I say, the anger in me rising quickly. "If I'm so stupid and awful, leave me, and I'll take care of myself." Somehow the girl, my twin, has given me the courage to speak to Mother this way. I feel stronger, as though she has become the other half to make me whole.

"Hah," Mother snorts. "*You* take care of yourself? A sick

girl like you who knows nothing about the world. How will you take care of yourself?"

I shouldn't put up with Mother's cruelty anymore. How will I know if I'm weak or if I'm strong if I never test myself? "Who made me this way?" I ask, wondering how it is I'm speaking to her like this. "This life, if it even *is* a life, was never my choice."

"Your father saw to that," she says cryptically. "And I was left to pick up the pieces." She swallows the remaining blood-red liquid in her glass in one gulp and then reaches over to take what's left of mine, which she swallows in a second gulp.

"My father never did anything to me. Why didn't you leave me with him if I was such a burden? I would rather have taken my chances with Father than live the kind of life you've given me."

I brace for the slap I know is coming. I can already feel its sting. But instead Mother just looks at me and slowly shakes her head. "Why didn't I leave you with him? I'm still a mother, after all, and you're still my flesh and blood." The tangy odor of turned wine adds a bitterness to her words. "You have no idea what he did to you," she says. The small amount of alcohol fuels the rage she normally guards with the severe line of her thin lips. "You have no idea what evil truly is. Your seizures . . . have you ever wondered why no medicine can minimize them? No test can detect them?"

A loud *bang*. The door crashes open, and large splinters of wood fly like missiles through the air. Oddly, my only thought at the initial moment of impact is *Now I shall never know the truth.* The man storms into our house with malevolence yapping at his heels. He's larger than I thought, and a thick, dark growth of stubble gives him a look of menace, as if even the sharpest blade couldn't clean that face. His eyes are blank. Dead. He grabs me by the hair and pulls me up from my chair. Mother recovers quickly and throws herself at him, beating with her fists, a puny effort against his massive presence. He pulls my hair harder, and the radiating pain forces unwilling tears from my eyes.

"Leave her!" Mother yells, her fists pounding against him over and over. He stops and turns to look at her. An insect. "My ex-husband is a monster, but you're just a pig," she says and spits a thick glob of phlegm, which lands on his stubble and slides like a slug down the side of his face.

While holding the hank of my hair with one hand, he reaches behind his back with the other and produces a gun. He points it at my mother and shoots just as I grasp the mutton knife I slid into my pocket the moment he invaded our home. And then, as if another person has entered my body, giving me strength I didn't know I possessed, I plunge the knife between his shoulder blades and the gun crashes to the ground. Blood is everywhere, bright red and slick. I smell it like rusted iron. I feel it wet and hot on my face, my hands, down the side of my neck. I did not see my badly bleeding mother scoop up the gun, but now I see her pointing and then shooting. A gaping hole appears like a third eye in the man's forehead, and he teeters like a felled tree before falling backward with a booming *thud.* His dead eyes are open and now they are truly dead. I hear moaning and Mother is on the floor, laying on her side, clutching her knees to her chest as though suffering from a terrible stomachache. I kneel by her side and there's so much blood I can't see where it's coming from. I take her hand and beg her to tell me what to do.

"Run," she says, her voice already a ghost.

"Where?" I ask.

"Anywhere," she says as I watch the life drain from her eyes.

CHAPTER 12

TATYANA

Papa leans back in the chair, his neck at an awkward angle, his hand still loosely clutching the almost-empty brandy snifter balanced precariously on his lap. A fierce snore escapes from his open mouth and his lips flutter slightly with each exhaled breath. It takes me a moment to ground myself to reality. I've had a seizure. I voluntarily entered the tunnel. Somehow, I've made my way back, and Papa has slept through the entire event. I recall that Papa was talking before I lost consciousness. In his state of drunkenness, he must have thought I'd fallen asleep first.

The moist film of cocoa on the bottom of my cup tells me not much time has elapsed, although it seems like hours have gone by. Then I remember what just happened. The girl, my twin despite the shabby clothing and general unkempt appearance. I wanted to ask her so many questions—Who is she? What is her name? Where are her parents? These and so many more. In her eyes and her surroundings I sensed desperation.

I want to wake Papa and tell him everything so he can help me make sense of it. If it was a hallucinatory dream, then what does it mean? Why is this happening to me? What is the significance of the white tunnel that has appeared in every one of my seizures, and why was I able to enter this time?

From Papa's loud snores, I know I'll have to wait for my answers. Magda comes in to let me know she has turned down our beds and is retiring for the evening. I'm so anxious to share my experience, I almost confide in her, but she looks tired and I know she'd never understand. I take the glass from Papa's half-closed fist and set it on the table beside him, and then climb the stairs to my bedroom although I'm certain I won't be able to sleep.

As it turns out, I do sleep, and when I come downstairs the next morning, Papa is already at the breakfast table, his hair slightly disheveled, thin folds of skin cradling his eyes like eggcups. I stop for a minute before entering the room and allow my heart to fill with fondness for him. On a morning like this one, he no longer appears to me as the larger-than-life man who halts all conversation when he enters a room. He's just my father, and this morning, as in others, he looks sad and—dare I say it—defeated. I enter the room and encircle his neck with my arms, kissing him on a cheek that feels as rough as sandpaper.

"Good morning, Papa. Did you sleep well?"

"Tatyana," he drapes an arm around my shoulder and squeezes lightly. "You should have woken me before going to bed. I opened my eyes and you were gone," he says. "The fire was left burning as well."

"Sorry, Papa." I don't want to tell him he was too far gone to wake. Too full of drink and regrets. Papa is still a man among men who commands enormous respect, but over the past few years I've seen a change in him. Lately, he speaks longingly of the days when he had nothing to prove and everything in front of him. When anything was possible, and he could create a legacy which would make his name a household word. The young scientists, who now see him as a mentor rather than a colleague, frequently visit our home to pay homage but don't ask him to collaborate on their projects. Often Papa is reduced to moments like last night when, encouraged by the alcohol, he betrays pitiful hints of the achievements he once aspired to.

Godlike. If Papa knew what he'd said last night, he'd be ashamed and embarrassed.

But today I'm thinking only of me. I need Papa for myself because I must speak of what happened, but not when Magda and Igor are close by.

"It's beautiful outside," I say. And it is. From my bedroom window I saw a brilliant sun against a blue sky. Its reflection off the snow was near blinding. "Can we walk after breakfast?"

Papa looks at me curiously. Normally I enjoy walking with only Pepper and my own thoughts. "Of course, dochka," he says, sliding a plate of buttered rolls toward me. "Eat first, then we'll walk."

The power of the sun is no match for the arctic winds, so I arm myself with fur hat, parka, boots, and a woolen scarf, which loosely covers my nose and mouth. Papa is dressed lightly in comparison, and he still doesn't seem like himself. Pepper bounds out of the house after us and Igor follows at a distance, although his presence isn't necessary for my protection when Papa's with me. Igor's loyalty touches my father, who would never turn him away.

"Is there something . . ." Papa begins but trails off, allowing me to insert either an answer or a denial.

Each step I take breaks through the thin crust of ice that glazes the snow like a crème brûlée. "Last night," I say, "when you were sleeping, I had an episode."

"Tanyusha." Papa stops walking and positions himself to look at me face on. I glance back and see that Igor has also stopped, some fifty meters behind us. "Are you well?" His hands rest lightly on my shoulders. His eyes fill with concern.

"I've told you about the tunnel," I say, and Papa nods his head eagerly, needing no further explanation. "Last night, I entered . . . and crossed through."

"Crossed through?" I think I can feel my father's hands trembling through the thick layers that cover my shoulders. "Explain, Tanyusha. Choose your words carefully, please."

"I mean exactly what I said, Papa." His obvious excitement encourages me. I was hoping for a reassuring chat, but Papa's eyes say I can expect more than that. What more, I can't yet imagine. "I entered the tunnel and . . . and I saw a girl who was just like me. Nearly like me but different in many ways. She was poorly dressed, and it was obvious no attention had been paid to her grooming, but she was me. I have no doubt."

Almost at the same time we both turn to look back at Igor, who's smoking a cigarette, his gaze averted from us at that moment. He exhales smoke, which coils around the frost of his breath. Papa pauses until Igor glances in our direction, then waves him off. "We'll see you at the house shortly," Papa calls out to him. Igor looks puzzled for a moment, then shrugs his shoulders, stuffs his huge hands in the pockets of his wool coat, and trudges back along the white footprints we made in the snow.

Papa takes my hand in his. "Let's walk," he says, and we continue our slow weave through the slender trunks of cedar trees. "Tell me everything. Every detail you can remember."

I describe the appearance of the room, the girl's appearance, the feelings I experienced, and my complete inability to communicate verbally with her. I tell him it was as though I was looking at the girl through a windowpane of thick glass. I tell him how wonderful I felt during and after, as though encountering a long-lost friend or meeting a sister I never knew I had. I've never had a friend in the real sense, and certainly no siblings. Only Papa and Tyotya Irina. "What does it mean?" I ask. "Was it a hallucination? Some type of response to a change in my brain chemistry?"

At first it doesn't seem as though Papa is listening to me, he appears so lost in thought. But then he squeezes my hand to let me know he's still with me. We've traveled much farther into the forest where the light is dim. I see tracks in the snow that I worry are wolf tracks, but I know Papa carries a small pistol with him at all times.

"The time has come for you to learn the truth," he says, but he doesn't seem sad or resigned—quite the opposite; his voice is strong and clear. "I wasn't sure this day would ever arrive."

"What is it, Papa?" A warning signal has gone off inside me. The truth suddenly seems like wolf tracks in the snow, a sign of something better left unseen.

We trudge forward, the crunch of our boots against the snow somehow reassuring.

"I've told you the story of the time before you were born, when your mother and I were newly wed and barely able to support ourselves." I nod to urge him on. "It was during that time I applied for and was granted government funding to do limited research on a very controversial project," he says. "But this next part I've never told you because only two others besides myself knew of it: my superior and my assistant, neither of whom are still alive. The project was eventually deemed too risky and was abandoned, the thinking being there wasn't enough obvious benefit to justify the cost or the potential danger."

The wolf tracks veer off into the underbrush and disappear from sight. In front of us, a dead tree has toppled, most likely unable to bear the weight of so much snow for so many years, or perhaps struck down in a lightning storm. "Sit with me," Papa says and pulls me next to him on the log. We sit close to fend off the chill and better hear each other. We've lowered our voices to near whispers in the event we come across a woodsman or a hunter. "Back then, I believed I was the only one who understood the science of human germline modification," he says. "The only one who believed it possible. Now that knowledge is commonplace in the scientific community."

I dare not look at Papa or utter another word for fear he'll have a change of heart and not share what comes next.

"Scientists possess the ability to genetically alter embryos by snipping out the DNA segments we wish to replace in order to achieve the desired genetic results. For instance, a genetic mutation that would lead to a specific disease at some point in a child's life could be snipped away and replaced with normal genetic material."

"How could that be a bad thing?" I ask. "I'd give anything if someone could have snipped away the part of me that led to my seizure disorder, and especially if they could have done that before I was born."

Papa shakes his head slowly. "People are afraid to eat genetically altered vegetables. It will be some time before the public readily accepts this . . . *gift* . . . we're able to offer them now. But my project's focus was unrelated to disease, and I'm afraid you may have been an unwilling participant with an unexpected outcome."

"*Me?*" I snap my head to the side to stare in disbelief at Papa, who leans forward to avoid my gaze.

"I didn't suspect at first," he says. "Your mother had had many miscarriages, and it was obvious she couldn't hold a pregnancy. Surrogacy was the only option to have children who were genetically ours. A pregnancy surrogate from the laboratory staff was arranged for us—a volunteer. We harvested twenty of your mother's eggs, which were fertilized in a lab by my sperm. The unused blastocysts—the earliest form of an embryo—were meant to be used for my research and then destroyed in seven days." He looks at me and his eyes are moist and soft, but I'm horrified at what hasn't yet been said. "We could never have paid the costs of fertility treatments on our own. This was a gift to us from our country in exchange for my research."

Unused blastocysts. Just a collection of cells. I know that's how life begins, and yet the detached way in which Papa speaks of it chills me more than the arctic wind.

"Later, when I had doubts, I began to suspect the wrong embryo . . . blastocyst . . . was implanted in the surrogate."

"I'm . . . the *wrong* embryo?"

"Tanyusha, you were everything to your mother and me."

He hasn't answered.

"How did you alter the blastocysts? What were you trying to achieve?"

"Alterations were made to introduce an oscillation to the strings of the genetic material. Do you understand what I'm telling you? I, your Papa, discovered a means of causing the strings that make up our cells to vibrate at different frequencies, exciting a resonance I suspected could open a wormhole to a parallel universe . . . to the counterpart of the person the blastocyst would eventually become."

"Me?"

"Yes, you." The forest seems to close in on me, yanking the breath from my lungs. "Tatyana, it's not what we wanted, but if it's true—and I believe it is—you must try to take it as far as you can. Do you understand the significance of what I've achieved? What *we've* achieved together?"

But I don't feel I've achieved anything. "You said *alterations*. How many alterations?"

"Three alterations were made in each embryo in case one or two failed. I swear they were meant to be destroyed. Seven days, no more."

"Is this the cause of my seizures?" I'm crying, and my tears are thick with cold, like sludge oozing down my cheeks.

"Your episodes aren't seizures, Tatyana. I've always known you weren't having seizures. I believe they're your body's attempt to cross through the membrane into the other worlds . . . the ones where you exist but under different circumstances depending on decisions you made or decisions that were made by others. I suspect your physical maturity is now turning that dream into a reality."

Papa's eyes glitter with undisguised excitement, which triggers a flash of rage within me.

"I never asked to be born. I never wanted to be someone's failed science experiment. I just want to be a normal girl with a normal life."

"You'll never lead a normal life, Tatyana, because you're a special person with great gifts."

And then I remember the conversation we had just last night.

What if the person who made this discovery . . . dedicated his life to it . . . why wouldn't that person be Godlike? Why wouldn't that person be God himself?

"It wasn't a mistake, was it?" I say. "This was your plan all along."

The truth in my eyes reflects back at him. He doesn't want to pretend anymore. He wants me on his side, where he's always wanted me. His Tatyana, totally within his control. I am a science experiment. Not a failed experiment. I'm a success. Papa's greatest success.

"Tanyusha," Papa says ever so gently, cautiously patting the back of my hand. "What if a person who loves you very much . . . more than anything in the world . . . what if that person did a very bad thing but did it for a very good reason? For love?"

CHAPTER 13

TATI

I wake with a start, struggling to take a breath, and sit up in bed, panting. I know for sure I'm awake, but it doesn't make sense that the tunnel is brightly lit and right in front of my face. It's not the usual view I have where it's smaller and somehow more mystical. This time it's smack-dab hovering in midair just above my bed, and it's big. Big enough for the real me, not the knocked-out version of me when I'm having one of my me-zures, which is what I've taken to calling them recently since no one, not even the doctor, can prove they're true seizures.

I take a minute to look around in order to orient myself. Yep, it's still dark outside my window—the red LED clock on my dresser says 2:41 a.m. Nobody here but me. I wait for my heart to slow a few beats per minute before I look back at the golden circle, which is still hovering and giving off enough light to turn my dark room into the equivalent of a sunroom. It's hard to look for too long, like staring at the sun, so I glance down at my rumpled pink comforter. I want to reach for my phone and call Priya, but my arm won't move. I think about yelling for Mom or Dad, but when I try, only a feeble croak escapes my lips and there's no way anyone would hear that. All in all, my body's betraying me at every turn.

I stand up on my bed and peer into the tunnel, which swallows me whole, like a popcorn kernel left an inch or two away from the hose of a vacuum cleaner. It happens so quickly, I don't have time to panic or even consider the feeling of being whisked away. I try to stand and grab onto something but it's futile because there's nothing around me except light, and you can't hold on to light.

When it feels like my eardrums might burst and my retinas might permanently be seared to the backs of my eyeballs, I exit somewhere cool, dark, and quiet. For a moment, I'm sure I've gone blind because I can't see a thing. My body shakes as fiercely as if I were having a me-zure, but I stand as still as possible, breathing in a slow and controlled way, at least slow and controlled considering the circumstances. Gradually my vision returns, or most likely my vision was always there but my eyes finally adjust to the dark.

I'm in a small bathroom that I recognize but also don't. The towel rack is to the left of the sink, and I grab the hand towel and pat away the sweat from my hairline, the sweat smelling of fear to me. I bury my face in the towel for a few seconds, deeply breathing in a lavender scent that has a calming effect. The lid of the toilet is lowered and covered with one of those plushy toilet-seat covers that gross me out because they seem unsanitary, like natural pee collectors. But sitting on top of it right now, I'm grateful for the soft seat while I wait for my knees to stop knocking together. In the meantime, I survey my surroundings. There's a toothbrush on the side of the sink, along with a crumpled tube of tooth-paste—my brand. It's squeezed just the way I squeeze mine—in the middle, without any finesse whatsoever, unlike Priya, who carefully folds her toothpaste from the bottom up. On the wall is a painting of a horse. I love horses and always have, so it catches my eye and gives me something to focus on while I catch my breath. I contemplate whether it's a stylized photograph or a print of an original painting—I decide the latter. There's a bathtub-shower and a small bath mat that matches the toilet-seat cover. Inside the shower, I see my favorite shampoo and conditioner in the rack. There are other sundries scattered around the sink—hair brush, hair bands. Some things look familiar and some not at all.

Once I've stopped shaking, I stand and walk to the open door, where I peer down a dark hallway. I vaguely hear snoring coming from a room that's all the way down on the other end of the hall. Another room is almost opposite from where I'm standing, and the door is slightly ajar. A soft, red light leaks through the crack and onto my foot. I nudge it open and walk inside the room, where I can see the silhouette of a bed, an extra-long twin like mine because I'm way too tall for a regular twin. An enormous silver moon is perfectly centered in the window frame. A red LED clock on the bedside table says 2:41 a.m. How can it be that no time has passed?

I stand by the side of the bed and am alarmed to see the shape of a person beneath a dark comforter, which is either black or blue—hard to tell in this light. Thick brown hair highlighted by moonbeams spills across the pillow. Although she's large, her shoulders are feminine, and she wears a silky chemise. Her arm, which is draped over a second pillow, rises and falls with her breath in a slow but steady rhythm. I should run from this room that appears to be mine, but I can't. Instead, I walk to her dresser, above which is a mirror, but my image looks distorted in the pale mixture of light. There's a framed photograph on the dresser, one of those hinged three-part frames. The pictures on either side are too small and too dark to make out but the one in the middle is a larger family photograph—a family of three. I lean over to make sure I'm seeing what I think I'm seeing: Mom. Dad. And me. There's a tall mountain peak in the background and it's covered in snow. The three of us are wearing parkas and scarves. Dad is wearing a knit hat to cover his bald head. The logo of his favorite baseball team is visible on the front of the hat. The only mountains I've ever seen are the Sierras, but I've only been in the summer because Mom and Dad hate the snow and I don't think I'd be a fan either. I've never seen this photo before. I've never been to this place.

I walk to the other side of the bed, closer to the window so I can see the face of the sleeping girl. The floor creaks beneath my foot, and she opens her eyes, slowly blinks, and then rolls halfway onto her back, props herself on one elbow, and looks up at me. She squeezes her eyes shut and then opens them again. *I'm still here,* I want to say, but I don't say anything. Surely she recognizes me, because I recognize her. Neither one of us seems surprised. My initial anxiety has vanished and I see no trace of fear or doubt on her face either.

"Tati?" I whisper but she shakes her head. She sits up and swings her long legs over the side of the bed. She pushes the covers to the side and she's wearing boys' boxer shorts along with the ivory silk chemise. The cheap buy-three-get-one-free type of boxers, which is just the kind of fashion mismatch I'd come up with that would earn me an affectionate rebuke from Priya.

A sly smile spreads across her face. "Sit," she pats the space on the bed by her side and I don't need any more invitation than that.

Side by side we gaze at the framed silver moon through the open window. A cool night breeze carries the scent of gardenias on its back. We look at each other and giggle as though we've just been caught in an embarrassing but not unpleasant act.

"Where are you—" we both start to say at the same time and then laugh.

"How did you—" we try again at the same time, and I have to resist the urge to call out *jinx*, which would have been funny if this were Priya and me. But it's not. It's *me* and me.

I'm not afraid, nor am I surprised. It's as if I knew I was here all along . . . wherever *here* is.

It's as if she knew I would come.

"What's happening to me . . . to *us*?" she asks, and I shrug my shoulders.

"I'm not sure. Some of this looks familiar to me and some of it doesn't. I mean, I think I've seen it before . . . your bathroom." I run my hand over the comforter. "This bedspread." All of a sudden everything falls into place. I wonder if there's a Priya in this Tati's world and if she has a dog with a turquoise collar. I wonder if I've visited here before or at least glimpsed it from afar.

"How are you here?" she asks.

"I don't really know that either. I get these seizures." She nods her head as if she understands. "And a tunnel opens up for me, but I've never been able to enter. This time I did."

"What do you think it means?" she asks, and I wonder why she's doing all the asking and I'm doing all the answering even though I have no clue. But since I'm the visitor and she's where she belongs, I guess it makes sense *she'd* be asking *me*.

"You're me, right?" My turn to ask a question.

"Yes." There's no doubt in her response and I'm relieved because I have no doubt either. "I'm sure of it."

"Maybe we're like . . . living parallel lives? Like you hear about . . . parallel universes. And somehow, something got messed up, some wires got crossed, so I'm here in your universe where I probably don't belong. I'm not even sure if it's safe for me to be here. Or safe for you."

"But . . . don't leave," she stammers. "I mean, I don't want you to leave, at least not right away. Do you think you even *can* leave?"

"I sure as shit hope so," I say. "Or your parents . . . *our* parents . . . are going to have joint heart attacks when they wake up in the morning."

She does that snort-laugh thing that Priya always teases me about and I want to wrap my arms around her and say *welcome home* or some foolish phrase that couldn't even begin to encompass the feelings I'm having right now. Instead, I look at the back of her hand and it seems like if I touch it, I'd feel it myself.

"The moon is so awesome tonight," I say.

CHAPTER 14

My life is officially out of control. And whereas that might have been a good thing this morning, right now (Saturday afternoon) it couldn't be worse.

I wasn't surprised when the girl appeared last night. Or I guess I should say I wasn't surprised to see myself at the opposite end of the magic rabbit hole. To me, it was validation of what I've always believed. It really does exist. It can be traversed. There *is* a miracle on the other side and somehow that miracle has everything to do with me.

She called me Tati, which was odd but not completely unexpected. Although most people call me Ana, Nurse Pat calls me by my full name of Tatiana. So why not Tati if I'm looking through the rabbit hole at my mirror opposite? Or is it something else entirely? I've spent most of the morning researching wormholes, but nothing makes sense and I haven't come any closer to understanding what happened last night and what's been happening for the past seventeen years.

Last night, I was tormented by jealousy when Tati (which is what I now call her) freely

A
N
A

entered the rabbit hole, leaving me behind and alone. Where did she go?

Am I Alice and is this my Wonderland?

As if things weren't hectic enough, in the middle of my research, Priya texted and suggested getting together tonight. Hanging out. Any other time, I would've been over the moon about it, but today I'm torn between going out or staying home and continuing my research. There's also the caveat that Priya mentioned inviting Anthony too, so it wasn't quite what I was hoping for. I accepted, guiltily hoping Anthony would have other plans.

That was all before Dad felt sick, probably a reaction to one of his meds, but when we called Dr. Masterson, he told us to get Dad over to the emergency room ASAP as an abundance of caution. And here I am in the hospital cafeteria taking a break because Dad's been waiting to see a doctor in the ER for two hours now. Two hours. I canceled with Priya and my life is officially out of control.

The cafeteria is busy right now, even if the fries are the soggiest I've had anywhere and the atmosphere couldn't be more depressing. About ten packets of ketchup and an extra helping of salt puts the fries on life support to the point where they're almost edible.

The Wi-Fi's decent so I can at least get back to my research. Google search: bright tunnel + seizure. Google search: doppelganger + counterpart + alternate universe. Google search: wormhole + parallel universe. Google search: seizure + hallucination. Scratch that last one—I refuse to believe what I experienced last night was a hallucination. I'm here now, aren't I? Totally present and aware of my surroundings. There's no difference between who I was last night and who I am right now. Last night, I was one hundred percent awake, even going so far as to get up and make myself a sandwich after the magic rabbit hole reappeared (bigger and brighter than I'd ever seen it before) and swallowed Tati whole before vanishing into thin air. If that was a hallucination, then I'm in trouble because my entire life must be one big hallucination.

On second thought, I'd better stop overthinking this.

I check my email, and there's one from the DNA testing company—the second place I've tried, which hopefully won't accuse me of being an animal like the first one did. When they said *rush order*, they weren't kidding. It's only been four days. I click to open, surprising myself by how excited I am to learn the results. Dear Ms. Woodland . . . blah blah blah . . . most sensitive test . . . blah . . . world-renowned . . . blah blah . . . there's been an error . . . resubmit or we will gladly refund . . . What the?

The *whoop* sound announces a text from Priya. *Sorry, let's reschedule. Hope your dad's better soon.*

Ugh and double ugh. Why can't I catch a break? And who's making all that noise? I turn in my seat to look behind me, and I'm beyond shocked at what I see. A huge man, fierce and bearlike, has a girl by the hair. He's dragging her toward the exit and the girl is crying, screaming. A woman pounds him with her fists but he doesn't let go of the girl. He reaches under his jacket and produces a gun.

"Help her!" I yell. "Somebody help her!"

Nobody makes a move toward them, but everyone turns

to look at me as if *I* was the one creating the problem. *Someone will come*, I think. There must be security guards all over this hospital. I've seen them in the past, but where are they now? My heart's so thick with adrenaline it doesn't seem possible it will survive one more beat.

But nobody comes before the man points and shoots. The woman falls into a devastating pool of slick, red blood. Nobody makes a move. Nobody even looks at them. I've heard about people not wanting to get involved but *really*? Why aren't they running? Why isn't help on the way? I stand so abruptly, my chair tumbles backward to the ground, and the man sitting closest to me gives me a startled look. Like he's scared of *me*. Me! In less than four strides I'm at the girl's side. She passes me a knife, and without thinking, I plunge it into the man's back as though I've rehearsed this action many times before. His gun clatters to the ground and the dying woman scoops it up, aims, and fires straight into the man's skull.

"Tatiana," someone is saying as my surroundings come back into focus. It's the doctor who helped Dad last time. Dr. Sokol. "Ana," she corrects herself. "Can you hear me?"

I nod. I must have fallen because the back of my head is sore. There's a small crowd gathered around, but they back up as Dr. Sokol waves them away. After a few more seconds of staring, they leave, and I see the man who was sitting next to me has resumed eating. How is everyone so calm and concerned only about me? And how am I still right next to the table where I was sitting, instead of near the exit where I swore I just stabbed a man, if not to death, at least to bring him to his knees?

"What happened?" I ask. "Did they get him?"

Dr. Sokol sits cross-legged on the ground next to me. She sighs deeply and is just about to answer me.

"Everything under control?" a male doctor wearing scrubs looks down at us. A stethoscope hangs from his neck like a good-luck charm.

"Fine, fine," Dr. Sokol says. "I'll stay with her. A mild seizure."

Mild seizure? What the hell?

"Ana, I'm going to stand you up, okay? You can lean on me because you may have suffered a concussion from your fall. Let's get you to a room where you can lie down. Can you make it?"

"Yes, of course."

"Sit up slowly," she cautions. "Let's make sure you're not dizzy."

I sit up halfway and feel fine. I sit up the rest of the way and still feel fine. Only the back of my head is tender. Dr. Sokol is on her feet extending a hand down. She's shorter than me but she's strong. I stand up and glance over at the spot where I remember murder and mayhem just minutes earlier, but there's no sign of a struggle. No blood, no nothing. Only my chair was knocked over, and a cafeteria employee is setting it right.

"I—"

"Let's find you a room," she interrupts, and I wonder why

she doesn't want to hear what I have to say. But I follow her dutifully, feeling I probably don't have a choice. We exit the cafeteria and I can feel everyone's eyes on me. It's a terrible feeling but not unfamiliar.

We walk down the hallway, making a few turns here and there. I focus on the colored stripes on the ground: yellow, red, blue. They come together and split off, leading to different wings of the hospital.

"Right here," she says finally. She turns the handle of an unmarked door and leads me into a small room about the size of an examination room. There's a single bed and an attached bathroom. "Do you need to use the restroom?" she asks but I shake my head and sit on the side of the bed. "This is a doctor's sleeping space for on-call physicians. I was just about to take a nap, but you can stay here as long as you like. Are you here because your father's back in the hospital?"

I nod my head. "What just happened?" I look up at her and her eyes tell me more than anything she could say. She knows what just happened to me. Now, I want to know too.

"You've had a seizure. I assume you've had them before," she says.

"Why would you assume that? And how do you even remember my name?"

"Ana," she says and sits on the bed beside me. She takes my hand in hers, which I find very strange. I've known lots of doctors in my life and most of them were really nice. None of them sat next to me and held my hand. "It wasn't that long ago we met," she says. "I remember my patients and their families. Especially the ones who make an impression on me."

I pull my hand away from her. She's lying.

"What happened to me and who *are* you?"

She looks away and then looks back at me with those keen, brown eyes filled with intelligence and mystery. "Why don't you tell *me* what happened first," she says. "Doctor's orders. Then I'd like to perform a few quick tests to rule out a concussion."

She asks me about any nausea or dizziness, and peers at my pupils with a tiny light. She listens to my heart, just for good measure, she says. And then she asks me a few questions.

"Tell me everything you remember, beginning when you started to feel something was off until you opened your eyes and saw me."

I think about not telling her anything other than the obvious—my seizure, which everyone in the cafeteria witnessed. Not about the visit from my doppelganger, or other self. The magic rabbit holes that materialize at the end of my seizures, how they tempt me to enter. The man, who I'm now pretty sure didn't exist. How he dragged a girl by the hair. How he shot the older woman who then shot him. But who else can I tell? Mom? Dad? They're barely coping these days with Dad's health being so precarious. On the other hand, Dr. Sokol is smart and doesn't seem judgmental. She also happens to be a doctor, so if anyone can help me, maybe she can. There's something about her that makes me want to confide in her. She knows things about me and I have to find out what they are. She doesn't just remember me as the polite and loving daughter of one of her hundreds of patients in the ER. Of that, I'm one hundred percent sure.

"It started last night," I begin. "I woke up in the middle of the night . . ." I stop. It didn't start last night, it started so long ago I can't even remember. I try again. "My whole life I've had these seizures," I say, and go on from there.

I dump everything on her and she doesn't seem to mind. Things I've never told anyone, even Mom and Dad. Dr. Sokol doesn't interrupt and she never breaks eye contact. She doesn't have to urge me on because, honestly, I don't think I could stop talking even if I wanted to. It feels like a much-needed purge. I've never been this truthful with Dr. Masterson—never revealed even a tenth of the information I've just shared with Dr. Sokol.

"And so here I am," I say once I've divulged as much as I can bear to share.

"This woman," she says, surprising me with her interest in what I'm now convinced must have been a hallucination. "The one who shot the man. Can you describe her appearance?"

The fluorescent light above flickers and sputters. Dr. Sokol gets up and flips the switch so only the light flowing in through the bathroom door staves off total darkness in this windowless room. In the dim light, Dr. Sokol looks older. A shadow falls across one cheek, giving her a gaunt appearance.

"I need to have them replace that bulb," she apologizes. "But for now, it's probably not the best thing for you in the event you did have a concussion." I wonder if she's just saying that to make me feel better but is actually worried about triggering a seizure. She shouldn't be, though, because flickering lights have never been an issue for me. "I'm sorry, go on," she says. "You were about to tell me what the woman looked like."

She turns her head in such a way that a fleck of light catches the strand of her hair which frames her face, turning it silver in contrast to the surrounding dark locks. In my mind's eye, I can see an image of the woman throwing her slight body against the bulk of the bear-like man. Pounding him with her fists, fearless in the face of unthinkable terror. She looked worn. Beaten down by life. She looked like a woman who had already lost everything and had nothing left to lose.

"She looked like you," I say, glancing up at Dr. Sokol.

CHAPTER 15

TANYA

Everything that was ever my life is hurtling toward me, memories traveling at supersonic speed set to collide with the present my mind refuses to accept. And then, just before impact, this life of mine—what has masqueraded for too long as a normal life—all the moments, like tiny building blocks set one atop the other, swerve sharply around my mother's corpse, still warm and sticky with blood, and rush off into the future, leaving me in danger of never being able to catch up.

I drop Mother's hand and stand up, gazing in horror as I back away from her, as if she has done this horrible thing to herself. The bad man . . . I can't bear to look at him. I toss two white napkins from our dinner table onto his wicked face and its vacant third eye. The cotton napkins drink greedily from his wound until they're satiated and transformed into red warning flags of danger from which I must flee.

I stumble backward in my stocking feet, cutting them on small shards of dinner plates and wine glasses, which now litter the floor. I lurch toward the kitchen sink where I run cold water over my face and hands, purging myself of the blood of everyone in this house. I rinse and rinse until my hands are numb from cold and the water runs clear. Then I stagger to the bedroom and sit on the edge of my bed, picking glass splinters from the soles of my feet before squeezing them into a pair of Mother's warm boots, several sizes too small. In the closet hangs her one good coat and since it's warmer than anything I own, I slip into it and pull Mother's knit hat over my head. I search frantically for her gloves before finding them in her coat pocket. The last thing I reach for is the wool scarf on the dresser. I wrap it twice around my neck—a noose that chafes and chokes.

Run, Mother said. *Anywhere.*

I have no doubt others will follow. People will come looking for the man, and since he was looking for me, they'll come looking for me. If I leave through the front door, someone will notice, so I'll go out the back. But where? It's so dark and cold and I know nothing about this town or its people. I only know Victor.

I try to remember everything Victor has ever told me about where he lives. What streets he walks down when he comes to my house, the sights he sees along the way. I try to imagine the distance and the time he says it takes. I have no other choice and no time to think about an alternative, if one even exists

Run. Anywhere.

I clutch the handle of the kitchen door, which opens to a path leading to a narrow alley. Everything that was my life is in this house—my books; my journals, which I've filled with poetry over many years; a porcelain doll that was Mother's when she was a girl. I've never thought I had any sort of life to leave behind, but now it breaks my heart to leave just these few precious mementos. Mother's scent wafts upward from the woolen scarf, and for a moment it overpowers the rusty smell of blood I don't think I can ever be rid of. For a moment, I think of Mother with a tenderness I never felt when she was alive.

And then I remember the box and turn back to the bed-room. I kneel down and peer under the bed, my hands trem-bling when I push Mother's slippers to the side as if half-ex-pecting the box to be gone. Once it's safely in my hands, I take a few seconds to say goodbye to the tiny mother-of-pearl mermaid forlornly perched on her rock as though waiting for a miracle to happen. The smooth, polished box is the only hint that material beauty and bounty were once my birthright. Now I'll never know why they were taken from me and so cruelly replaced with despair and deceit. I grasp the ruby ring, pearl necklace, and earrings in my fist before dropping them into the coat pocket.

A noisy motorcycle roars down the street, stopping in front of my house. Its engine idles for a moment before go-ing silent. My heart lurches at the unfamiliar and unlikely sound. I slip through the dark kitchen and pull the door ever so carefully behind me as I exit into the cold damp. I hug the outside walls of my house and its shadows until I reach the dark alley, which smells of refuse because it's where the garbage bins are kept. I trace its path until it spills out onto Nordhaven's quiet main street, now barely lit by ancient street lamps.

Where am I? Where are you, Victor?

I sit on a crumbling stone wall and ponder the steps Victor would have taken to reach my house. A bakery. Yes, he often says he passes a bakery on the way, tempted by its sweet smells. Occasionally, the owner leaves the prior day's unsold goods on the back steps—stale but free if his timing is right. More than once, Victor has arrived at my house proudly carrying a loaf of day-old bread that he'll take back to his family. Once or twice he's presented me with a strudel, sticky and delightful, a surprising indulgence. I know the bakery must be on this street, so I stick to the shadows, keeping my eye out for any sign of it.

This street isn't entirely deserted, although it's quite late and all the shops are closed. When I do encounter someone, I'm tempted to ask for directions to the bakery, but I can't risk calling attention to myself. I don't know who might be on their way to my house, looking for the man who lies on the floor with a knife in his back and a bullet in his head. I imagine each person I pass has a sinister intent, although they, like me, are most likely just bundled against the cold, hurrying toward their own homes, loving families, and warm hearths.

When I reach the end of what looks like Nordhaven's town center I take a chance and ask a young woman for directions to the bakery. Her cheeks are red as apples under the flickering gaslight. The wind causes loose strands of her pale hair to twist in front of her face like sea snakes.

"The bakery is closed," she says, startled by my question.

"If you could tell me where it is, I could be there first thing in the morning when it opens."

I hope she doesn't sense the fear in me and doubt the absurdity of my inquiry. But she seems to accept it and gives me detailed directions that require me to double back and take a side street, and then another.

"Is it the only bakery in Nordhaven?" I can't risk being sent on a wild goose chase.

"The only independent bakery," she says. "The food market has a baked goods section if you'd like me to give you directions. They're open one hour earlier in the morning."

But no, I remember that Victor specifically mentioned the bakery as a separate entity. He spoke of its owners, a considerate older man and his wife. "Thank you," I say. "That will be fine." Before she has time to think of her own response, I turn and walk quickly in the opposite direction.

Once I'm standing in front of the bakery, I'm not sure what to do next. Large gold letters spell out the name of the establishment on the plate-glass window. I wish I could go inside, curl up in a corner that surely must smell like freshly baked bread, and close my eyes to the images of everything I've seen tonight. If I stand here much longer, I'll attract attention. Someone might think I'm planning to rob the store. But I do close my eyes, only for a few seconds. I see the girl—my better self—and remember the strength I gained from our encounter. Was it just today? Was it only hours ago? In the distance, I hear a dog barking. A very large dog from the sounds of it. I recall that Victor spoke of a dog who scared him witless the first time he passed by the house and was caught off guard. I step out into the street and follow the deep, hollow sound of the dog.

After a few minutes the dog is quiet, and although I know I'm close, I have no idea which way to turn next. I'm lost in a maze of narrow, twisting streets, neighborhoods that encircle the town's center. I could no sooner find my own home than find the bakery at this point. I pause and pray the dog's barking will start up again soon. It's mind-numbingly cold out here and the wind has picked up, indicating I'm closer to the sea, or perhaps just more in the path of its wind for whatever reason. Victor has never mentioned his proximity to the sea, and wouldn't a person mention a thing like that?

Fear and doubt have once again seized control of me, and I can't decide what to do next. Then, a low rumbling sound—a motorcycle coming down the street toward me at a slow speed. It could be an entirely separate vehicle than the one I heard earlier on my own street, but a motorcycle isn't a common thing in Nordhaven, or at least I've never heard one near my house before today. I see its single headlight approaching like an unblinking eye and I duck down behind a hedge and will myself to be small. It continues, slowing when it's only meters away from me, and for a moment I think it's going to stop. Then the engine grows louder, and the motorcycle moves quickly away from me, turning right at the next intersection. And, as if I'm blessed at that very moment, I hear the dog barking again. I've overshot the source of the sound, so I pull the knit hat down lower until it reaches just above my eyes and take off at a brisk pace, trying to cover as much ground as possible before the barking stops again.

I'm standing in front of a house that looks a little nicer than the other houses in the neighborhood. It's surrounded by a wire-link fence, and a tall dog, pure black except for a splash of white on its massive chest, strains against the fence to get a better look at me. I can see how a dog like this could have terrified Victor the first time he passed by if he was caught unaware. I can also see the dog means me no harm and his grumbling and snuffling seem almost friendly. He barks one last time and then sits on his haunches and whines mournfully. The front window of the house lights up and a hand pulls back the curtain. A man's face peers out for a few seconds before the curtain falls back and the room returns to darkness. Seconds later, the front door opens, and the same man is standing there.

"Come Rudi," he commands, and the dog gives me one last longing look before bounding into the house.

I dare not even breathe. I'm here, so now what?

This is the closest I've come to tears. I have no idea what to do next and imagine curling up in a bush or under a tree and being found the next morning half-frozen to death. And if I am found, then what? It's just a matter of time before Mother's absence from work will be noticed. Her employer will send someone around to check on her. But even before that, someone will come looking for the man, won't they? Why can't I feel sorrow over Mother's brutal murder? Why don't I feel anything except confusion and fear? And what of the motorcycle—is someone already looking for me? What was Mother about to reveal before the man broke into our home?

You have no idea what he did to you, she said about my father. *You have no idea what evil truly is. Your seizures . . . have you ever wondered why no medicine can minimize them? No test can detect them?*

But now I do know what evil is, and how could anything be worse than what happened tonight?

My shoulders shudder involuntarily as though I were crying, but no tears come. No tears and no relief. To my left, there's a street lined with more houses like all the others— battered by the wind, paint thinned by the salt air, exposed patches of raw wood spreading like rust. To my right I see a narrower, darker street where pavement gives way to gravel and dirt. There are no gaslights down this street. I don't even see parked cars. Off in the distance, I hear the buzzing motorcycle, still roaming like a prowling wolf. Its drone is drawing closer. For a moment I think of the American poem I've committed to memory and, with a prayer, I choose the less-traveled road.

I have nowhere else to go.

CHAPTER 16

TATYANA

Papa and I now eat our meals in silence. I can't bear to look at him and imagine a man who could have done what he did to his unborn daughter. He follows me around the house pathetically attempting to engage in conversation, when I know all he really wants is my forgiveness and total cooperation. I don't allow him to draw blood or collect saliva samples. All medication has stopped—in one of our worst arguments, Papa breaks down and admits the pills he's been giving me for years are only sugar pills. Placebos designed to give me peace of mind, as though such a thing was possible. This admission only makes me despise him more.

"And Tyotya Irina? Does she know everything?" These are the first words I've spoken to him all day and I don't know if I want to hear the answer. If she knows, then all is lost. I'm friendless and no more significant than one of the rats in Papa's laboratories. And just as helplessly dependent.

Instead of answering, he gazes at me with that maddening mixture of phony empathy and affection. That's my answer; I don't need to hear him speak it.

"So, she knows too!" I spit the words at him as though they were venomous and capable of traveling straight to his heart to poison him just as he's poisoned me. But Papa has no heart, it seems. "I hate you both!" I push away from the dinner table and run up the stairs, barely able to contain my tears until my bedroom door slams shut behind me. I throw myself on my bed in a tangle of tears for the third time today.

Through my gloom I hear a soft knock on the door. The knock of someone still testing the limits of his new standing in our new life.

"Go away!" I yell at Papa. "Go away, you make me sick!"

"Tatyana," comes his muffled response through the solid wood door. "Please open the door. I must speak with you now."

"I said go away!" I repeat forcefully enough for him to hear and have no doubt left in his mind.

"Tatyana," he says. "If you don't open the door I'll have to ask Igor to come and take it off its hinges."

Would he really do this? There's no question Igor will do whatever Papa asks of him, and I now know Papa can and will do whatever suits him.

I rise from my canopied bed and open the door a crack, barricading the entrance with my body. "What do you want?"

"I have to return to Moscow for a meeting," he says. "And I'd like you to come with me."

"Hah!" I say. "Not a chance."

"Very well," Papa says. I can feel his breath on me—that's how close we're standing. I keep my hand on the doorknob although I know Papa would never force his way in. That's not his way. He'd have Igor do it, perhaps, but never do it himself. Papa, the refined gentleman. Noble aristocrat. Butcher of his own daughter. "Very well," he repeats. "That's what I thought you'd say. And perhaps it's best you stay here and have time to collect your thoughts." His breath stinks of brandy and cigars. "Naturally, Magda will stay with you. And Irina will come to collect you tomorrow or the next day. Does this give you enough time?" he asks magnanimously as though he's granting me a great favor.

"Enough time? Enough time for what? Enough time to accept the fact that I'm nothing more than a failed science experiment . . . I'm sorry, a *successful* science experiment . . . to the two people who are supposed to love and protect me? There's not ever going to be enough time for that, Papa. Not even if I live for a thousand years. So just go."

I push the door shut and Papa doesn't resist. I'll wait until he's gone and it's safe to come out. Nothing can distract me from my dark mood—not the computer, not my book, not even thoughts of attending university one day, a laughable fantasy now. Father will never let me go. Not his walking, talking, living, breathing laboratory—the key to his immortality. Even if I could escape from here, where would I go? What would I do? I'm a victim of my own body. A prisoner of my own mind.

Only the girl brings me relief. The memory of the girl, who is me. She's suffering too, I can feel it. At least as much as me and perhaps even more. I wish I could get back to her, but I don't know how to get there on my own.

I hear a car door open and I go to the window overlooking

the front of the house. Igor has brought the limousine around and is waiting for Papa. He stands by the front door, a huge bear of a man. I used to look at Igor with fondness. He was my protector in the woods, a solid presence in my life. But now I remember Papa's words, *I'll have Igor take the door off the hinges.* Igor is not my friend or my protector. Igor belongs to Papa and I can't trust him anymore. Probably I can't trust Magda, either—after all, it's Papa who pays her wages. These are people I have depended on, but no more. Pepper scratches at my door and I quickly open the door to let him in. Pepper I can trust, but I fear he's the only one.

How quickly my life has turned.

Some time after Papa leaves, Pepper gets up and scratches at my door. He can hear Magda calling him from downstairs. I open the door and Pepper's nails click on the wooden floor as he flies down the stairs. My stomach is hollow, and the sky is turning black, so I reluctantly follow him to the kitchen. I don't want to talk to Magda, or anyone else. I'm not sure what instructions Papa has given her, but I imagine she's been told to keep a close eye on me and I don't welcome the scrutiny.

"Sit down," Magda motions to the kitchen table, dispensing with formality by not serving in the dining room. She speaks brusquely, but this is her way. She tosses a piece of suet in the air and Pepper lunges to catch it before it hits the ground. "Soup and cold meat is what I've prepared. Would you like me to make a dessert?"

I shake my head, no. Dessert is happiness at the end of a meal. Dessert is frivolous. Tonight is not a dessert night.

Neither of us speaks but this is also her way. There's an awkwardness because I've never stayed alone with her before, and our silence is heavy. But I don't feel like talking tonight and silence seems the preferable alternative to saying the wrong thing. I'm also illogically angry at Magda for having this job—anyone controlled by my father is suspect and can't possibly be my friend. To be fair, *I'm* controlled by my father. All of us are dependent on him: Igor, Magda, the staff at our home in Moscow, and even Tyotya Irina, who lives in a separate wing in our city home. *Even Pepper*, I think mournfully, as I toss him a slice of roast beef when Magda's back is turned. For a moment, I regret not having returned to the city with Papa.

"Why did you stay?" Magda asks, and I wonder if she resents having to watch over me when normally she'd be free to do as she pleases.

I shrug my shoulders and blow lightly on the thick soup in my spoon in order to cool it.

"You fight with your Papa?" she asks.

I brace myself for the inevitable lecture that must be coming and vow to control my anger. She couldn't possibly understand what I've been through—what my life has been about. "A disagreement," I say. I wouldn't even admit this much, but she must have heard our raised voices. How could she not? And she must be wondering why I'm here at all.

"Hmmph," she grunts. Her back is turned to me as she

tidies up in the sink and around the counters. I rise from the table and gather my dishes to bring to the sink.

"Leave!" she orders me, and I set the dishes back down on the table. I want to go to my room and shut the door behind me. Be alone with my thoughts.

"Can I help you with anything?" I ask, but she shakes her head, a simple act that looks like it must take tremendous effort.

"Just sit," she says. "Make company for me."

For the first time I consider that maybe this isn't the ideal life for Magda. Maybe a dog isn't enough company for the long winter nights. Maybe Magda isn't the recluse I always assumed she was. I sit down while Magda takes up a broom. It makes me uncomfortable to witness the physical struggle it takes for her simply to clean the floor, but I don't offer to help after being commanded to sit.

"I wish your mother could see you," she says at last. "A beautiful and smart girl . . . she would be proud. It's not right." She clucks. "A girl should have her mother."

Mention of my mother stirs unfamiliar feelings—a make-believe character who would save me if only she existed. But she's just an idea, a concept of a mother totally separate from my reality. I wonder what she was like, and for the first time, I profoundly feel her loss. Papa keeps pictures of her on his desk and, as far as I know, he's never loved another woman since my mother died from pneumonia before my first birthday. Papa doesn't speak much of her and I've never pressed him for details because the memories seemed difficult for him and irrelevant to my life. But now

I wish I knew more about her than just the image I have of a slender, dark-haired woman with a mysterious Mona Lisa smile. I know she was smart and that she and Papa met in medical school. Tyotya Irina was there as well—a year behind them. Now, after what my father told me about the surrogate, I understand why there are no pictures of Mother with a swollen belly while she was expecting me.

"I don't know much about her," I say.

Magda pauses her sweeping to take a breath. I see the dustpan in the corner, so I fetch it and bring it to where she's standing, a tiny pile of crumbs and dust by her left foot. I kneel, lining the dustpan up with the pile of dirt. Magda pushes it in with a flick of the broom, nodding her gratitude.

"She was smart and pretty like you," she says.

I almost forget to take my next breath. Has she heard the same stories I've heard, as scant as they've been? Seen the same pictures? Or does she know more?

"How do you know, Magda?" This is the most we've spoken in ten years, and I try to keep my tone nonchalant, instinctively feeling it's the best way to keep her talking. As if I didn't care what she had to say. "Has Papa told you about my mother?"

"Pff," she exhales dismissively, and I wonder how I've offended her. She returns the dustpan and broom to the corner and turns her attention to drying my dishes, which have been draining in the rack. "I don't need your Papa to tell me about your mother. I took care of her in this house," she says. My soup bowl slips from her hands and clatters to the counter. She curses under her breath while examining it for breakage, but when she sees none, she places it on the shelf.

"But you've only worked here since I was seven, and my mother was dead long before that."

Because her back is turned to me and she makes no effort to speak louder, I strain to hear her response. Finally, I get up and stand near her while she finishes her work. Seeing me move from my seat, Pepper comes to join us, but Magda points a crooked finger and he slinks back to his pillow by the wood-burning stove. I wonder how long I have before Magda points her crooked finger at my chair.

"My *second* time," she says. "My *first* time I work here twenty years."

"Your first time . . . working *here*?" I don't want to annoy her. Magda isn't exactly a paragon of patience, but I don't understand what she's saying.

"Yes, *here*." Her frustration is so loud and clear, I feel it in the space between us. "Your mother's house. Your grand-parents' house. I take care of your mother when she was a little girl. She play with my daughter."

"This was my *mother's* house?"

"So many questions," she hisses through thin, fleshless lips.

"Please, Magda. I'm sorry if I'm bothering you, but I need to understand. Are you saying this was my *mother's* house and you knew my *mother*? Is that what you're saying? Is that the truth?"

She turns her entire body to look at me which, I assume,

is less painful than swiveling her neck. "You think I lie?" she asks. She narrows her eyes, which makes me cringe inwardly.

"No. No, not at all. I just want to make sure I heard you correctly. I just . . . had no idea."

"Now you know," she says resuming her work. The cupboards in this kitchen are built at a level she can easily reach. There are higher cupboards, but Magda has a system where she keeps the dishes we use most often on the lowest shelves. I've often wondered why Papa never hired a younger housekeeper who could get around better and faster, up and down the stairs to clean more often. I asked him once, and he said Magda was loyal to us and we must be loyal to her in return. I suggested he could give her enough money to move back to her country where she could retire comfortably in her village. We could hire someone younger and stronger, but Papa said Magda deserved her dignity and didn't wish to live on handouts. Now, looking back, it seems particularly ironic to think of Papa talking about dignity and loyalty—a man like him. But even bad people can do good things and use those good deeds to present a noble face to the unsuspecting and gullible. To people like me.

So, my grandparents were wealthy enough to live in a house like this with hired help? That means my mother must have been wealthy as well. But Papa said he and my mother were poor when they were newly wed. That only through the benevolence of the government could they afford in vitro fertilization. I'd been told my grandparents died shortly after my parents were married. A car accident. Why hadn't my mother, their only child, received an inheritance? I didn't know they were wealthy. That this had once been their house. Nothing makes sense. My entire life is unraveling in a spool of lies. And if Papa was trying to keep this from me, why did he leave me alone with Magda? Did he think we would never speak? Or is Magda simply senile and spouting nonsense?

"Now you know," she says again, bringing me back to reality. I find it curious she's repeated herself this way, as though it was her purpose all along to tell me these things. Without another word, she shuffles off in the direction of her bedroom, which is just down a small hallway behind the kitchen. Pepper follows on her heels.

I toss and turn all night. Sleep eludes me, rest an impossibility in my current state of mind. I long for my twin, as I've come to think of her, although I now know she's much more than that. I wish I knew how to get back to her, because something tells me her life contains answers to mine. When sunbeams break through the tops of the trees in the distance I give up on the idea of sleep and shrug into my plush, lavender-colored robe. I slide my feet into matching slippers and pad down the stairs to find Magda. Papa said Tyotya will come to fetch me either today or tomorrow. I pray it's tomorrow to give me one more day alone with Magda and my questions. I know she's awake because she always rises before dawn, makes tea, and bakes rolls for our breakfast.

But I don't smell cooking as I descend the stairs, which might mean I'm not going to get the same royal treatment she gives Papa and Tyotya. Perhaps she's annoyed with me and my questions after last night. Perhaps she regrets what she's revealed. I call out for Pepper, but hear no clicking nails on the hardwood floor. In the kitchen, there's no sign of them. It's still early, although not for Magda and Pepper, but maybe they sleep late when Papa's not around. Maybe Magda doesn't feel the same responsibilities with only me in the house.

I heat up a kettle of water for tea, carefully removing it from the stove before it whistles, so as not to wake them. I rummage through the refrigerator, pulling out cheese, a sliced apple, and yogurt. In the cupboard I locate a box of muesli, a bowl and a spoon. I'll fix my own breakfast and clean up after myself, which hopefully will make Magda think more kindly of me. Perhaps she'll tell me more stories, so I can decide if she's speaking the truth or if it's simply the ramblings of an old woman's addled mind.

An hour later and she still hasn't risen. I'm beginning to wonder if she died in her sleep. But where's Pepper? Surely, he'd be scratching on the door to be let out or perhaps even barking in terror. I chastise myself for letting my mind wander to such a dark place. It's Papa who's done this to me. Nothing feels secure anymore.

But then I realize Magda has probably taken Pepper outside. He needs to be let out to relieve himself and stretch his legs after waking. All the doors are locked, but I check out front anyway. It snowed last night and there are no tracks in the snow. I call out Magda's name but there's no response. Finally, I go to Magda's room and knock loudly on her door. No answer and no sign of Pepper. I knock again and call out her name while I open the door. I scan her empty room. The bed is made up or hasn't been slept in. All of her possessions are gone.

Magda is gone, and Pepper with her.

I recall the last thing she said to me before disappearing into her room.

Now you know, she said.

I have a moment of panic before composing myself. During that time, I'm close to calling Tyotya Irina to come fetch me straight away, but something stops me. Here I am for the first time in my life with no one around, no one to tell me what to do or what not to do. For now, I can pretend I answer to no one and make all my own decisions. I need to think carefully about whether I'm willing to sacrifice this gift for the sake of a false sense of security. I decide I'm not. I must sit down and come up with a plan, and I must write it down to help me think it through.

It's always been understood that I should stay out of Papa's office, except when he's working and I need to ask a question about schoolwork or want to sit quietly on one of the leather upholstered armchairs where I can read while he works. Even then, I'm expected to knock before entering. Otherwise, Papa's office is considered to be a serious place of work which everyone understands is his realm. Even Magda asks permission before she comes in to clean. Even Irina, like me, knocks before entering. But I'm feeling emboldened, so I enter the spacious room lined with built-in bookshelves, original oil paintings, and buttery-soft leather furniture. It smells like cigars, leather, and old books. It feels strange to be in here without Papa, as though this room has a soul that departs when Papa isn't breathing life into it. I sit on the massive chair behind his great mahogany desk—the king's throne. I pull a sheet of his personal stationery from a monogrammed leather container and retrieve a Montblanc pen from the top middle drawer. I draw a line down the middle of the stationery. On the left side, I write *Things I Want*. On the right side, I write *Things I Must Do*.

I begin on the left. *Things I want* include: find the girl again; find Magda; find the truth about my mother and her parents. Then I turn my attention to the right side. *Things I must do* include: possibly exposing myself to more seizures in order to find the girl (how do I do that?); walk to the closest village, where Magda may have lived (a distance of five kilometers in the snow, and I'm not even certain she ever lived there); call Tyotya to delay her another day. It's a beautiful day and it's quite early, so I think the possibility of walking to the village is realistic, although dangerous if I have a seizure on the way. But the easiest thing on the list that I can do right now is to delay Tyotya's arrival, so I pick up the phone on Papa's desk. I'm giddy with my first real sense of independence. Anything seems possible.

I reach Tyotya Irina in her office and, I'm in luck, she's at her desk and has a minute to talk.

"Were you planning to come today?" I ask innocently. I hope she hasn't gotten too many details from Papa regarding our fight or she might feel more inclined to come sooner rather than later. I hear someone in the background asking a question about a scheduled afternoon meeting, but Irina asks them to wait until she's off the phone.

"How are you doing, Tanyusha? Everything okay?"

"I'm fine," I say. "I could use the extra day to relax if you're busy."

She pauses, and I know she's thinking it over. Weighing whether or not I'll be all right without making it seem like she doesn't trust me. "Magda's not much company, is she?"

"She's fine," I say, and this is not a direct lie. She's asked me a question about Magda, but I haven't overtly implied that Magda is here. Anyway, why should I care about a lie? Papa's lie supersedes all, and now I have reason to believe his lie is also Tyotya's lie. But how much does she know? How much is just misplaced loyalty to her brother?

"If you're sure you're okay, then . . ." she trails off.

"I'm fine. I'll see you tomorrow." And then I decide to be bold. "Or the next day if you're busy tomorrow."

"I'll see you tomorrow, dochka," she says firmly.

I have twenty-four hours to do what I need to do. Twenty-four hours isn't much and may not be enough, but I feel strong for once in my life. And determined.

I slide open Papa's top drawer to replace the pen and notice a tiny envelope in the back, remarkable for its small size. I put my hand on top of it and feel the outline of a key. The envelope is sealed but I'm suddenly consumed with curiosity for what this key can unlock. I go about Papa's office testing each drawer of each wooden cabinet until I come across one that won't budge. The size of the key I can feel through the envelope seems to generally match the size of the lock on the drawer. All the other drawers in all of the other file cabinets are equipped with locks, but only this drawer doesn't open. If I try the key, Papa will know what I've done.

I hesitate only for a moment. *Twenty-four hours.*

The key slides easily into the lock and I open the drawer, both afraid and excited by what I might find. But there are just a few non-descript manila folders, the same type that fill the other cabinets where he stores notes from conferences, research papers, and personal documents that have to do with his finances. On occasion, Papa has asked me to pull a file for him when he's in the middle of a work project and I'm reading nearby. So why is this drawer locked?

I lift the files out of the drawer and take them back to the chair where I sit down and turn on the nearby reading lamp. The files are clearly marked S.P.I.T. 1, S.P.I.T. 2, and S.P.I.T. 3. Each one has a range of dates, by year. The last one is most recent, with a beginning date of five years ago and no end date yet.

I open the first file and flip through the pages, which are highly technical and mostly incomprehensible to my layperson's eyes. The first page of typewritten notes is dated eighteen years ago, and at the top of the page, I have the answer to my question about the acronym S.P.I.T.

STRING PULSATION IN INTERUNIVERSE TRAVEL

So, this is Papa's project, the discovery of which has upended my world. Nothing about me has changed physically since my conception, but everything has changed in terms of how I look at the world. Papa's been honest with me, so there's no reason to look through these notes that I wouldn't understand anyway. But then again, why is there a folder leading up to the present day, if that's what it is, when the project ended before my birth? I open the last file and thumb through the contents. As I suspected, much of it I can't understand, but I see a spreadsheet with current dates, the last of which is only a month old. The dates are at fairly regular intervals, and it seems they must be test results. I think of all the times Papa has collected saliva and blood samples. I wish I knew what he was looking at or looking for.

The morning is slipping away, and I need to get started if I'm going to make it to the village and back before dark. I hope the road has been plowed so if I walk along the edge, I'll avoid traipsing through snow, although the drifts will force me to keep to the pavement. I'm just about to replace the file when I take one last peek at the oldest file, thumbing through the pages looking for something I might under-stand. Am I the entire S.P.I.T. project? Is everything in this file about me? Just as I'm about to put it away, something falls on the floor. I lean over to pick it up and see it's an old photograph. I bring it under the light to examine the three people standing side by side, arms around each other. On either end are Papa and my mother, smiling cheerfully into the camera. In the middle is Tyotya, her belly so swollen it appears she's about to pop. Tyotya, who has no children and has never been married, was pregnant.

CHAPTER 17

T
A
T
I

One piece of the puzzle is solved. I now know where I belong. I belong with my parents. I belong with Priya. And I belong to the girl with the blue bedspread. I made a promise to Priya that I'd report anything unusual to my parents, but I can't keep that promise. The girl, whose name is Ana, has transformed me. She's replaced my fear and frustration with confidence and curiosity. Even Priya's noticed, although she doesn't know the reason why.

This *has* to be real, because I don't want to go back to the old Tati with all her insecurities and clinginess. At the same time, I have sympathy for her. For *me*. And that's something new because, before Ana, it seemed like I spent a lot of time wanting to kick my own ass. Now I can stand outside of myself and see things more clearly—literally outside of myself. I've given up on my need for control over the me-zures because, after all, I had no control to begin with, so what was the use of pretending I did? I've given in to the unknowable and cast aside my doubts about Priya. Then a surprising thing happened. By giving up my need for control,

I suddenly had control—over myself, at least, and how I respond to a situation.

People are afraid of the unknown, so why should Priya be different? She has to deal with her own unknowns—the fear of rejection when she finally lets her parents see what's inside her heart, *who's* inside her heart. And if I can get past my fear, I hope, one day when she's ready, Priya can get past hers too. In the meantime, I can only support her with unconditional love and acceptance, the same way she supports me. The same way my parents support me. And Ana.

I have no idea why, but there has to be a reason Ana is happening to me.

I'm able to visit her at will. I can't describe how I do it—I simply think it and the tunnel appears before me. A few years ago, Mom signed me up for a series of biofeedback classes to help me deal with the stress of what I then thought were seizures. After about ten classes, I could *think* my hands into warming up a few degrees. At the time, it seemed like a huge accomplishment. Now, using the same technique—focused concentration—I can think my way into the tunnel that whooshes me into Ana's life and Ana's world, which isn't so different from mine. I visit her nearly every night and she's always waiting for me. For some reason, she can't come to me, even though we see the same tunnel and have the same *episodes*, as she used to call them. After I told her about me-zures, she started referring to them the same way. She tries to climb into the tunnel when it appears, but she hasn't been able to make it inside. She doesn't understand when I explain how I do it, but in fairness I can barely explain it to myself.

"Just think it and feel it," I say. "Imagine your body melting into the light. Becoming whole with it. Letting it flow through you. Imagine you *are* the light."

And she tells me she's trying but it doesn't work. She's also admitted she's afraid. Afraid that if she's successful, she would never make it back home. And although I tell her my parents are her parents, she doesn't see how that can be true.

"They must be different somehow," she says. "You and I . . . we're the same, but we're different too."

She says she wants it more than anything. "One of these days, I'll surprise you," she says. But she's still afraid.

And here's the strangest thing of all. Ana loves Priya, but Priya doesn't know. Yes, there's a Priya in Ana's world too. An Anthony. A Nurse Pat, who was the school nurse at our school but left the year before I started high school. In Ana's world, Nurse Pat is still there, and she'd be lost without him.

"I can't believe you're with Priya," she says.

"Why not?"

"It's just . . . I was never even sure if she was gay. And I'm positive she's not into me. But maybe she isn't gay in my world," she says.

"I'm confident that kind of thing can't change," I say. "No matter which world. But why not talk to her? If it hadn't been for the day when our hands accidentally touched picking up a pencil at the same time, I never would've seen her special smile. And if I'd never seen her special smile, I'd never have had the courage to be honest about my feelings. It happened just like that . . . trusting her, knowing she wouldn't laugh or push me away. It's a scary thing to put yourself out there," I say. "But where would I be if I hadn't done that?"

"I'm not sure," Ana says. "It's not the same. You don't know my Priya."

But I think I do know her. I must. She's my Priya too, and what makes her who she is must be the same at its core no matter what world she inhabits. "You're right that we're different, that's obvious. But how much are we the same? Weird, huh?" I look around the room and in a single visual sweep, I take in everything that tells the story of my life, from the type of books on her bookshelf to the style of clothes in her closet. But there are differences too. Our hairstyles—hers long and mine shoulder-length. The pictures on our walls. The color of our bedspreads.

"All change starts with a single decision," I say. "Everything. Even my decision to climb into the tunnel, although it felt more inevitable than a decision at the time."

Tonight, Ana has something to tell me that could change everything, although neither one of us knows how or why. Ana has had an episode, a me-zure, she quickly corrects herself. But this time there was no glorious tunnel inviting her to climb in. This time something awful happened right in front of her eyes—a double homicide played out in the hospital cafeteria where she was eating. Only in hindsight could she call it a me-zure. It started with a huge, bearlike man, dragging a girl by her hair to a fate, Ana instinctively felt, that could only be death. Nobody but Ana reacted or even seemed to notice what was happening. Only one woman fought to free the girl from the man—pounding his massive chest with her fists. Everything that happened next happened so fast that Ana has no recollection of the order of events: the man shooting the woman, who fell to the ground but didn't die; Ana taking a knife slipped into her hands by the girl and plunging its blade into the monster's back; and then a final shot when his gun clattered to the ground and the dying woman took aim and brought him down. That's all Ana remembers until she came to her senses with a crowd gathered around. But one final thing—the girl, she's certain, was us.

Ana and I have decided to solve the mystery of our lives and to do it together. We don't have much time because I'm afraid to stay too long or to visit more than once a night. In fact, relatively speaking we have no time at all because the clock doesn't change from when I'm first swept into the tunnel to when I'm finally spit back out into my world. And yet it seems there's a huge passage of time. But just knowing someone else is equally invested in discovering the truth is like carrying a huge backpack filled with every book from every class, and then having a friend come along and offer to carry it for a while. Of course, Priya and my parents would do anything to help me, if they actually believed me and wouldn't think I was certifiably insane, but it's not the same. They're not *me*. Ana is.

It's clear that one key to unlocking the mystery is my birth mother—the blonde, stocky woman who put a gun to her head while cradling her tiny baby (me) in her arms. It's a road I can't help but go down. Mom and Dad—guilt-ridden they didn't request more information while they were in Russia, never imagining their daughter would be asking questions seventeen years later for which they had no answers—have hired a graduate student from the University of California to help with my investigation. Olga is pursuing a doctorate in political science. She studied Russian at Moscow State University and, although she's American-born, she has extended family and important contacts in Russia, not to mention fluency in the language. Because she's a student, Mom and Dad can afford to pay her a reasonable wage for the hours she spends basically doing whatever I ask. What started as a way to salvage our ethnic studies project has turned into a full-out assault on the facts of who my mother was and why she chose to end her life in a way that could have ended badly for me as well.

Tonight, Ana's excited about Olga and what we can hopefully learn from her research. She has more to tell me, too, but we've been talking a long time, so I think I should go. I do that thing where I imagine blending into the opening of the tunnel and it appears. I don't even have to think about entering anymore. It's like muscle memory, but I guess it's more like muscle, nerve, blood and everything else I'm made of memory. I can feel it right before I enter, and it feels amazing. It's as though all the molecules in my body detach from each other, floating freely while staying vaguely in my shape. Next comes the irresistible craving to blend with the light. Like stirring cream in your coffee as the white gets darker and the dark gets lighter until they're one thing, one color. The feeling is almost literally electric. On the other side, I'll be reorganized again and miss this sensation until next time.

But just before I'm about to leave, I remember Ana said she was eating in a hospital cafeteria and I wonder why she was there.

"Are you okay?" I ask her. "The hospital . . . why were you there?"

But it's too late to stay now that the tunnel has opened. There's no delaying and no going back.

"Dad's sick," she says. "Our father has a bad heart."

That's the last thing I hear as I'm swept away. Dad. Nothing can happen to Dad. Please let Ana's father be different from mine, at least in that one respect.

Once I'm back in my room in my home, I take the few minutes I need to adjust. This is the worst part because I always feel as if something's missing. Ana's missing, but it's more than that. I was a feather but now I'm a rock. I think it must be like this for astronauts who spend so much time being weightless and then return to Earth and its gravitational force. I'm Dorothy in the *Wizard of Oz* going from color to black-and-white. I empty the contents of a bottled water in about five gulps. Traveling to see Ana always leaves me feeling dehydrated when I return.

I tiptoe down the hallway and open the door to the guest bedroom where Dad will be sleeping. My parents still share a bed in the master bedroom, but Dad usually gets up and moves in the middle of the night because Mom's snoring keeps him awake. I turn the doorknob as quietly as I can and wait for my eyes to adjust to the darkness of the room because Dad prefers to sleep with blackout shades and not even a nightlight. He's sleeping peacefully, and I can hear his even breathing. He definitely could stand to lose a few pounds and maybe get out and walk around the block once a day. I don't know what I'd do without my parents, and I promise myself I'm going to work on Dad to get him healthier. Starting tomorrow.

CHAPTER 18

ANA

"Wait up," Priya calls after me in the hallway after school. "What's going on with your project?"

"Things aren't going according to plan," I say. "So, what was the name of the book you mentioned, the one about cultures where seizures are a spiritual experience?"

Two fails with two different DNA testing facilities—there's no time to try a third.

Priya tells me the name of the book and asks if I'm coming to the Tea Cozy with everyone.

"Nah, I think I'll go home. I have a lot of work to catch up on."

"I think we've finally convinced Anthony to join us." She smiles slyly. "You should've come out with us Saturday. We did sushi for dinner, then went to see Argentina's entry for Best Foreign Film, which was amazing. We missed you. In fact, all we did was talk about you." She nudges me with her elbow. "What's up with you and Anthony?"

"Umm . . . nothing." My heart jolts a few bumps while I consider why she's asking.

"You sure about that? I think he likes you."

It's a majorly awkward, uncomfortable

moment that makes me inexplicably sad and slightly angry at the same time. I remember what Tati said about being honest with Priya, but I could never be. If there was any chance she was into me, she sure wouldn't be pushing me off onto Anthony like this.

"I'm sure," I say. "I like Anthony *as a friend* and ditto for him. We've already discussed it in detail."

"Really? Guess I misjudged, and I guess I'll shut up about it. Sorry." It's hard for me to stay angry while looking into those genuinely doleful eyes.

"That's okay," I say. We've arrived at my locker, and Priya waits for me. "If anything, *you guys* would probably make the great couple," I say unenthusiastically, wondering why I'm falling into the same dumb trap of mindless matchmaking, especially when I don't even mean it.

"Hah," she says. "Nope. Anthony's a cool guy and fun to hang out with but . . . What's wrong? You seem really sad today."

And here I thought I was keeping it pretty well together given the circumstances.

"That transparent, huh?" I say.

"All day today, every time I've seen you, your face looks like it's on the verge of . . . crumbling."

I pull the last book I need out of my locker and spin the dial on my lock. "Crumbling?" I don't even try to laugh it off or reach for a witty response.

"You look like you're two steps away from bursting into tears," she says softly.

I stare at her wordlessly and feel my eyes sting, but I trap my tears like a pro.

"One step," she says.

Make that zero steps. I lower my face and burst into tears.

"Hey, I'm gonna skip the Tea Cozy today." She gently places her hand on my arm. "Let's go to Starbucks, okay? Just you and me," she leans forward to fold me into a stiff but still comforting hug. Hugs aren't a thing between us and there's never been a reason for one before. She pats my back awkwardly a few times before drawing away and ducking her head to look into my eyes. "You okay?"

I nod, not wishing to speak until I can do so without a sob in my voice. I reach into the pocket of my jacket and pull out a fairly disgusting old paper napkin and dab at my eyes before burying my nose in it for a big honking, snot-clearing blow. Oh, I'm so charming.

"I'd like that," I say. "The Starbucks idea. I could use someone to talk to right now."

I think about Tati and how I can tell her anything. But our meetings always feel rushed and seem too important to waste on me whining about how unfair life can be. And for the first time, I'm not even thinking of Priya as fantasy potential girlfriend material. I'm just thinking of her as potentially a really good friend.

"It's my dad," I say once we've gotten our drinks and are seated in a tiny round corner table that boasts the most privacy of any table in the place. "He's been sick for a while, but now he's *really* sick and they won't let him leave the hospital. My mom's always there with him and I wish I could be too, but she makes me come to school." I think guiltily about taking just this time away from being with Dad, but I feel like a pressure cooker that needs the valve opened for a minute before I face the hospital again.

"Actually, I should be at the hospital right now. Actually, I should be at Math Club right now because that's where I'm technically supposed to be." I sound like an ungrateful idiot and a bad daughter. "Do I sound like an ungrateful idiot and a bad daughter?"

"Whoa!" Priya says. "You just finished saying you wish you could be there, so the answer to that is, no, you don't sound like either . . . whatever those insults were you just hurled at yourself. You sound like you need a hug and a good night's sleep and possibly a day at the spa. But since you're unlikely to get the last two . . ." She leans across the table and gives me an arm-around-the-neck, feather-light hug.

"Thanks," I say. "Last night the doctor told Mom that my dad needs to be put on the heart transplant waiting list. And I don't know about his chances of getting one or even surviving the surgery because he's older." I begin another round of sobbing and Priya hands me a few napkins off the pile we've brought to the table.

"Oh, wow, that's pretty intense," she says. "I can't even imagine what you're going through. Do you have any siblings for support?"

I realize how little we know about the other's life even after all these years of being friendly school competitors.

"Nope, I'm adopted. I mean . . . not that that means I couldn't have siblings, but I don't." I'm not making much sense right now. Obviously, Priya knows I'm adopted because I've never kept it a secret and even talked about it recently in our ethnic studies class. I miss Mom and Dad so much right now and suddenly I can't wait a minute longer to see them. "I need to go," I say standing from my chair, leaving a half-finished white chocolate mocha on the table. "My mom probably needs me."

Priya stands too, but she's holding onto the rest of her drink. "Hey," she says, and her voice is so compassionate and true and real. "Reach out to me anytime, I mean it. Middle of the night if you need someone to talk to. And you know what? I can guarantee Mrs. Falco will give you extra time on the project if you tell her what's going on. You need to do that."

"I will," I say, while thinking, *Here I go again, the girl who gets special allowances from the teachers.*

"Promise," she says, and I nod. "And promise you'll call me anytime you need to talk." I nod again.

Just thinking about Priya's words as I walk home brings on another round of sobbing, but luckily I've armed myself with napkins. I need to have all this crying out of my system before facing Mom and Dad. They don't need the added stress.

I've gone home to change and wash my face, so I can pass for a semblance of a happy human being who can help lift

Dad's spirits. I Uber over to the hospital and head straight to the cardiac intensive care unit, where I know it won't be visiting hours, but they'll let me in anyhow. Dad's so pale, and with all those wires sprouting out of him and all those machines beeping above him, it's a wonder he's as cheerful as he is. But that's Dad. His spirit is uncrushable. I shoo Mom out of the room after making her promise not to return for two hours, but she can't stay away and comes back after only forty-five minutes. Dad is in and out of sleep, and Mom is too—she has the good fortune of being able to sleep sitting up, probably from all those years she and Dad have spent side by side in their recliner chairs. Whenever they're asleep, I'm doing homework.

Dad's eyes flutter open and he looks up at me. Mom's asleep in the corner of the room where Dad can't see without turning his entire body. "Is Mommy still sleeping?" he asks in a hoarse whisper. I nod and walk over to kiss him on the forehead, which feels clammy against my lips. He lifts an arm full of protruding IV needles and weakly pats the back of my hand. It kills me to see him like this. At that moment, the nurse comes in and gives me a sympathetic look, which I know has a double meaning. I probably need to leave, although I'm sure they'll let Mom stay. I walk over to where Mom's sleeping and kiss her on the cheek. She startles awake.

"I have to go now," I say. "I just got *the look*."

"Can you fend for yourself for dinner?" she asks, which of course she knows I can. I take this to mean I shouldn't be expecting her for a while, maybe not until after I've gone to bed. And she'll be gone before I wake up tomorrow morning, if the past few days are an indicator.

I pick up my phone to order an Uber home, but my heart and head are so filled with everything that's been going on, it's borderline unmanageable. I wonder if Dr. Sokol is working and decide to go by the emergency room on my way out. If she thinks I'm crazy, she didn't let on the last time we talked. And I'm out of options. There are things I can share with Priya, but I can't tell her about Tati. Not about the incident in the cafeteria. And obviously, I'm not sharing anything with my parents right now. They're in survival mode.

At the admitting station for the emergency room, the guy asks me why I need to see the doctor. I explain that I don't, I'm just here to visit Dr. Sokol if she's working and has a break coming up.

"Are you her daughter?" he asks, eyeing me with interest now that he knows I'm not someone who needs immediate assistance.

"No," I answer and then ponder what I am. "A friend," I decide, even though we're not. I don't think any other answer will get my message through to her.

He picks up the phone and calls someone in the back and I hear him relaying my message. *Friend of Dr. Sokol. Wondering if she's on break.* And then a long answer I can't hear that probably involves being put on hold while someone goes to find her.

"What's your name?" he asks, and then repeats. Then he hangs up, and there's another long wait.

In the meantime, a young woman with a small boy is standing behind me so I step to the side. Although I turn my back and try not to listen, she's nervous and speaking loudly. Her son has put a pea up his nose and she can't get it out. Just then the phone rings and the receptionist says a few words into the receiver and then looks up at me. The young mother is busy filling out paperwork.

"If you can wait, she'll be out in fifteen minutes," he says, and I nod and take a seat.

No sooner do I sit than the door swings open and Dr. Sokol steps out. Her eyes scan the room and, as I stand, they land on me and she walks toward me.

"I'm so glad you stopped by," she says, taking my hand in hers in a semi-handshake that feels warmer than Priya's hug. "Do you have time for a cup of coffee in the cafeteria? I was just stepping out for a break so it's perfect timing."

But somehow, I have the feeling she wasn't just about to take a break. Somehow, I have a feeling she wanted to see me as much as I wanted to see her. Perhaps even more, although I'm not sure why.

"Is this okay for you?" She puts a hand over mine once we're seated in the cafeteria. She's purposely led us to a table as far away from the site of my unsettling vision as possible, but I can still feel some of the pure panic and adrenaline I felt at the time.

"It's fine," I say. I'm going to have to get over it if this hospital is to be my temporary second home.

"Your father," she says. "I've been keeping an eye on him . . . on his chart. If you have any questions you'd like to ask that haven't been fully explained, please ask away and I'll attempt to answer them as best I can, although it's not my field."

But I know enough about Dad's prognosis. I don't need to know more at this juncture because we're playing a waiting game and no new information is going to help that. Unless it's news of a donor's heart.

I shake my head. "I don't have any questions," I say. "About Dad."

"You know this is a transplant hospital, one of the few in the state. So, it's a fortunate thing for your family," she says. The soft, almost undetectable lilt of her accent is comforting somehow.

I nod my head, yes. "I heard that."

"Ana . . ." She ducks her head the way Priya did earlier to look into my eyes. To try to decipher a message that might be hidden inside of them. "Why did you come to see me tonight?"

"There's more I wanted to talk about," I say. "The . . . stuff . . . that's been happening to me. I don't know anyone else I can talk to about it." My throat's suddenly gone dry and it feels like I'm speaking cotton balls. I've brought a bottled water to the table, so I unscrew the cap and swallow a few sips.

"Mm-hmm," she murmurs before taking a sip of her own drink—black coffee, scalding hot. "And by *stuff* do you mean the vision you had last time we spoke? Something similar?"

"That's it exactly," I say, trying my best to sound confident, businesslike almost. Not crazy. "But not the same as last time. It's an ongoing thing. A nightly occurrence, or at least it has been recently."

"Go on." Dr. Sokol stares unblinkingly over her cup of coffee. A faint puff of steam tickles her nose, which twitches before she takes another sip.

"There's something I didn't tell you last time," I say, "because I wasn't actually sure of it until just yesterday. But the girl—the one I saw in the cafeteria—I think she was me."

"*You?*" Dr. Sokol arches her eyebrows high.

"Yes, me." I take a deep breath. "And I would never have come to that conclusion if it hadn't been for the other stuff . . . the other *events* that have been happening at night."

She's going to think I'm severely in need of a reality check, but she's probably chalking it up to post-seizure stress. Post *me-zures*. And the fact that my father is barely clinging to life. Who wouldn't think that, in absence of a concussion that may or may not have explained our last conversation? And maybe she'd be right if that's what she's thinking, but I don't think so. She simply nods, so I go on.

"There's another girl who comes to me every night, but not in my dreams. Her name is Tati and . . . she's real. In fact, she's me, but she's not me. You see, we're different in some ways but we're more alike than we're different. The same people are in both our lives but . . ." I pause, not wanting to get into the thing with Priya. "But we've made different choices."

"Tati . . . your full name is Tatiana, isn't it?"

I nod and swallow hard, imagining she must be following the lump of doubt as it travels down my throat. Now's when she puts it all together and comes to the conclusion that I've invented an imaginary friend—one whom I've bestowed with half my name. I didn't even do shit like that when I was in preschool and I'm not about to start doing it now, but how can I expect her to believe me?

"Do you believe in parallel universes, Dr. Sokol?" It's the first time I've said those words out loud to someone and I barely have the most basic concept of what they entail, even after all my recent online research. "That a version of you could be living out a similar life to the one you're living here and now, varying only in the decisions you've made along the way? That it could be playing out virtually right next to you at this very minute . . . or light years away. That there could be thousands, millions, trillions . . . an infinite number of parallel lives."

She nods, and her demeanor doesn't change in the slightest. I know now that's why I've come to talk to her. No matter what she might be thinking, she doesn't make me feel like I'm crazy.

"I'm actually quite familiar with that concept, which is part of the framework of what scientists call string theory. You say the same people inhabit both your worlds. Am *I* in Tati's world?" she asks. If she's about to burst my bubble, it doesn't seem like it.

"I . . . I don't think so. I mean, she never mentioned someone like you and I'm sure she would have."

So much for my theory that everyone is the same in both

worlds. Or maybe there is a Dr. Sokol and Tati just hasn't mentioned her. Nurse Pat is so important to me and yet Tati knows who he is but doesn't actually know him. Maybe it's the same with Dr. Sokol—she exists in Tati's world, but doesn't play a major role in her life.

"But . . ." There has to be a way of tying all these pieces together and yet I'm helpless to see how. "But, the girl in the cafeteria. The woman who was fighting for her, I think was you."

Dr. Sokol pushes her empty coffee cup to the side and leans across the table toward me.

"Yes, I remember your saying she looked like me," she says. "Has Tati told you why she comes to visit you?"

"Because she can," I say. "Because it's irresistible and she can't help but come. It is, you know?"

"Irresistible?"

I nod my head.

"How do you know that, Ana?"

"Because I feel the same thing. Whenever the tunnel opens for me, it's almost too much. Like having an addiction to a drug I don't have access to."

"So why haven't you gone into the tunnel, the way Tati has? Why haven't you been curious enough to see where it would lead?"

"Because something prevents me that doesn't stop Tati. And I think it can only be because I'm afraid and she's not."

"Or maybe it's right for her but not for you? Fear is something everyone should pay attention to because there are often valid reasons for our fears. I've made choices in my own life that were motivated by fear, and I think those choices have proven to be for the best. So, listen to your heart and choose deliberately and wisely. Succumbing to an urge without reason can lead to catastrophe."

"I'm not sure why I came to you tonight," I say. "Maybe it wasn't a deliberate or a wise choice. I don't know what you must think of me now. I don't know why I've even told you all this. You must think I'm a—"

"I think you're telling the truth, Ana," she says.

"You do?"

She nods slowly. "But we need to talk more. A lot more. There's so much I have to tell you that will help, I promise." She looks at her watch. "Can you meet me for dinner in an hour?" She pulls a pad of sticky notes out of one pocket of her doctor's smock and a pen out of another. She jots something down and hands it to me. "Here." She hands me the sticky note. "It's a small Italian restaurant, not too far from here—closer even to your home."

"I'll be there," I say, and Dr. Sokol rises from her chair and offers her hand across the table for a perfunctory shake. She wears a look of determination.

"One hour," she says.

I watch her exit through those same cafeteria doors that were only recently the site of a primal dance of life and death. I force my attention away from the awful memory as I try to decide whether to stay here and catch an Uber to the restaurant, or go home first, dump my backpack, and grab a warmer coat.

And then it dawns on me. *Closer even to your home,* she

said. How does she know where I live? I doubt she's memorized my address from Dad's file and, even if she had, he uses a post office box he's kept from when he was self-employed and preferred to keep work mail and bills separate from our home address. It's a habit he's kept up even since he retired.

In one hour, I can ask her for an answer to that question.

In the meantime, I make the decision to stop off at home. With Mom in control of our only car, I've been Ubering a lot recently and feel a little guilty about the cost. I think about calling Anthony for a ride, but our relationship has been so one-sided lately with him doing all the giving and me doing all the taking. Instead, I order another Uber and ask them to pick me up a half block from the hospital entrance, to avoid going through the boom barrier at the parking attendant's station. Dusk still comes early this time of year in Central California, but it's unusually warm, causing a chorus of confused frogs in the nearby creek to moan in anticipation of spring. A frisky breeze pushes skittering leaves across the road, like shaking maracas keeping the rhythm of the night.

I lean against a tree and remind myself, at least for this moment, the world is still a beautiful place. A gibbous moon veiled by a lacy cloud. Two owls taking turns in a duet high above my head. I have to cling to this beauty to preserve my sanity and give me the strength to move forward in the coming days.

"Did you drop this?" A low voice just behind me. I swivel, illogically expecting it to be Anthony teasing me about the man from whom I escaped to his house that day after school. But it's not Anthony. It's the same man.

I instinctively turn from him and try to run back toward the hospital. But other arms catch me, a cloth is forced over my nose and inside my mouth. My legs are useless, and then I just collapse.

CHAPTER 19

Pain is returning to my life. Pain in all its forms.
The memory of my mother lying on the floor
inside a crimson cloud of blood takes a sharp
and jagged bite from where my heart must
be if one still exists. The muscles of my feet,
squeezed into Mother's too-small boots, lock
up in spasm. Blisters are sprouting to protect
the places already rubbed raw inside my socks.
Mother's woolen scarf, which just an hour earlier preserved an olfactory memory of her, now
smells like the drenched stray dog I opened the
door to one day when Mother was at work. It
chafes against the back of my neck and provides
no protection from the cold, and no comfort
beyond its familiarity.

There is only this one last street left to
choose. The motorcycle is out there, although
its din has grown distant. It's still out there
hunting and prowling, and I know I'm its prey.
I thank the darkness of the street, unlit by gas
lamps, for giving me this one last chance. My
ankles turn precariously with each step over
potholes and gravel. One injury, one twist, could
spell the end of me, so I walk carefully to the
side where the mud is at least more predictable

T
A
N
Y
A

and forgiving. The titter of raindrops would be soothing under any other circumstances but now is just a reminder of my grave situation. My boots have soaked through and numbness from the cold is at least displacing the pain in my feet. My coat is waterlogged and useless. I move quickly to the first house with a light in the window and knock quietly on the door. When there's no answer, I knock again—this time a bit louder and longer.

"Who is it?" an older woman's voice calls from inside.

"I'm looking for Victor," I say, hoping against hope I've stumbled upon his home.

"Victor who?"

The question is not reassuring, and I realize for the first time I have no idea what Victor's last name is. It never seemed important before but now it seems like crucial information I should know.

When I don't answer, the woman speaks up. "I don't know any Victor," she says, and my heart feels as sodden as the coat on my back.

I want to beg her to grant me entry into her home. Beg her for refuge from the buzzing motorcycle. The merciless cold. The unknown friends of the murderer who I know will be coming for me.

"Describe him to me," she says to the other side of the door which, for all she knows, might be absent a person by now. I want to throw my arms around her in gratitude for not giving up on me.

"He's a boy," I say. A silent pause. "He's ten years old." Can she hear the desperation in my voice?

"You're not from here, are you?"

Should I admit this? She can probably tell by my accent. "No."

"Are you Russian?" The disembodied voice. Why should I trust her? What choice do I have?

"Yes, Russian."

I'm speaking to a door, which is somehow reassuring. A door can't kill me. But neither can it save me.

"There's a Russian family farther down the street," the voice says. "Last house."

"Thank you," I practically sob, so grateful for even this tiny semblance of human kindness.

"There's a boy who lives there," the voice says as I turn to make my way down the street, alert for the buzz of the motorcycle, should it grow closer.

The last house on the street is literally also my last chance. I knock on the door and it swings open almost immediately. A woman stands before me, perhaps my mother's age. She has blonde hair with silver streaks fighting for dominance. She's quite short and has a healthy girth. Her cheeks are red and her eyes twinkle blue. She looks at me as though she's seeing a ghost.

"Tanya!" Victor comes up from behind her. "Why are you here?" He's surprised but somehow delighted, as though it would be a happy event that brings me to his house in the dark of night. Me, the girl who stays hidden even during the day.

"Mama, this is—"

"Oh, dear God." She grasps my arm and pulls me inside,

shutting the door behind me. Holding me at arm's length she surveys me from head to toe. "Oh, dear God," she sighs, as though witness to a tragedy.

"Mama?" Victor's happy face and demeanor melt away with his mother's stunned reaction.

With the immediate danger out of the way, my mind is giving my body permission to fall into a state of shock. I can feel it dragging my soul down a well, and every inch of me with it.

"Your mother," Victor's mama drags me back into the world. "Where is she?"

"She's dead," I say, surprising myself with the indifference my words convey, even to myself. She'll think me a monster.

But she doesn't. She pulls me to her and wraps me in a tight embrace, rocking back and forth, side to side. I'm an infant in a cradle and I don't resist. I would stay here forever in this broad, strong woman's arms. Rocking. Swaying. Forgetting.

"I would know you anywhere, Tatyana," she says, calling me by the name I haven't heard in years. Regretfully I'm released from her arms, and with my eyes now open I see Victor, seated on the floor, his mouth agape as though he can't believe what he's witnessing. A girl sits beside him, her eyes huge with wonder. Victor's sister, I think, realizing I know nothing about her. I know nothing about their mother or even much about Victor, for that matter. So how is it Victor's mother knows so much about me—that she would know me anywhere? That she knows my name?

"Come." She leads me by the hand to the kitchen and seats me at the table. Victor and his sister follow. Their unfinished dinner is on the table and Victor fetches a plate, which he sets before me. His mother spoons out a stew so thick it doesn't require a bowl. Only an hour earlier, I was sitting down to my own dinner of mutton and chard, but now I can't eat. She pours me a glass of thick, red port. She pauses but then decides to pour a little more. She pushes the glass toward me. "Drink," she says, and I do. It's strong and bitter and makes me gag, but it unfreezes my heart and allows me to shed its weight through my tears. I cradle my face in my upturned palms and weep as softly as I can, so as not to alarm the children.

"It's all right." I feel Victor's small hand on the back of my shoulder. "It will be okay." But I don't see how things could ever be okay again, and I weep some more.

"Tatyana," Victor's mama says softly from across the small table. "My name is Klara." She gestures toward the young girl. "And Victor's sister—we call her *Kotehok* . . . kitten." Kotehok hasn't spoken once, except through her wide-eyed stare.

Klara's voice is rich and comforting. Although she must be similar in age to my own mother—deceased mother, I think morosely—she seems years younger. Not because of the bend in her back or the roughness of her hands, but through the brightness that projects from her eyes. She doesn't ask how Mother died—it's as if she already knows.

"I'm so glad you found us, Tatyana," she says, pulling her chair next to mine and wrapping her arm around my waist.

"I'll lay out some clean clothes of mine for you to wear while yours are drying. They'll be a bit short and a bit wide, but they should do until the morning. You'll stay with us tonight and then we'll talk in the morning when you're ready."

I nod.

"A nice hot bath now, perhaps?" She raises her eyebrows in question and I nod again.

Spontaneous tears roll down my cheeks, completely beyond my control. "Don't worry," Victor comes to my side again and whispers in my ear. "Your tears will dislodge the splinter in your eye, just like in *The Snow Queen*. Then you'll never cry again."

"Yes," I say. "Perhaps they will."

I envy Victor's happiness and innocence.

CHAPTER 20

It's been many years since I've been to the nearest village, although it's only five kilometers from our home. There's no reason to go there because we normally stock the house with products from Moscow. Everything we need, we have, including internet and satellite television. The village is poor and of no consequence to Papa except when he needs to find temporary help for minor work like mending a fence or fixing a leak in the roof. Everything else is tended to by workers from Moscow, many of whom also do work on our city home.

"One can't expect a pool of talent in a country village," Papa has said. "The people are ignorant for the most part and can only be counted on to perform the menial tasks they would do in their own homes."

Papa has contempt for the uneducated, although he is from humble origins himself. This I learned from Tyotya Irina because Papa never spoke to me of his childhood. Life was difficult for them growing up, she told me in private. Their father was a mean drunk who was often unemployed, and their mother so beaten into submission she never stood up for her children.

TATYANA

It's a miracle we not only survived but thrived, she told me. *A testament to the human will to persevere,* which, she hoped, I'd never forget. *All things are possible,* she often says. And although I can't be sure whether to love her or to hate her after what I've seen in the photograph, I try to embrace the will to persevere as I walk along the snowy embankment toward the village.

Magda came to us from the village. It was serendipity that brought her to our door the very next day after our housekeeper, Rosie, announced she would be leaving. Rosie was advanced in her pregnancy and her husband lived two villages away. They decided, she said, to return to their native Hungary, where they had friends and extended family. Irina and Papa were discussing between themselves the difficulty of attracting a full-time housekeeper to the country property, a place so remote that loneliness and isolation would discourage most job applicants. There was a loud knock on the door, and when Irina went to see who it was, she was surprised to find a woman who looked even older than she probably was. The woman said she'd heard about an opening for the position of permanent housekeeper. When Irina asked who had told her, she mentioned Rosie's name, someone she'd seen on occasion in the village—a fellow expatriate from Hungary and one of the few villagers she spoke with because she had no affinity for most of the other "slow-witted fools." That appealed to Papa, who also had no affinity for country people and privately described them in similar terms. The fact that Magda was old wasn't ideal, but she was still strong—after all, hadn't she walked five kilometers through the snow simply to apply for the position? She promised she'd be a tireless worker and wouldn't talk much or demand a large compensation, and she kept those promises—although five years later she would ask to keep a puppy with her for company. My father hired her on the spot.

But now as I trudge through the icy sludge on the road, I realize there's much more to Magda's story if she was telling the truth last night. It doesn't seem likely she just happened to hear of the position from someone in passing. It doesn't seem likely her unexpected appearance at our door was simply providence.

Where did you go, Magda? Why did you leave before I had the answers to my questions?

We keep a satellite phone in our country home and now I wish I'd brought it with me. There's no such thing as cell phone reception out here, but the satellite phone is heavy, and I barely have the strength to walk unencumbered. I wish I'd paid more attention to my physical fitness, but Papa and Tyotya discouraged me except for the occasional stroll through the woods. I try to estimate the distance I've covered by the amount of time I've been walking. I've calculated it will take me about ninety minutes if I keep to the hard surface of the road and walk briskly. Once I arrive, I'll have very little time to ask questions about Magda's whereabouts and, if I manage to find her, I'll have even less time to question her. I'm not even sure what I would ask her or where I would begin.

The sun sets early and, if I'm tired, it could take me

another two hours to walk the distance back to my home. I hope I have the strength to do what I need to do. I know I must. Two things worry me: the possibility of a seizure, and dehydration. Even an old lady like Magda wouldn't worry as much as I do about walking this relatively short distance. I consider the possibility she may have walked in the dark last night with Pepper at her side. There's no other explanation for why I don't see their tracks. Seldom does a car come by, and I know the main reason this short stretch of road is kept plowed is for our family's easy access in the event we need anything from the village. I wish I knew more about the village and its inhabitants. It never seemed relevant to my life until now. There are so many things I wish I'd paid attention to that only now seem meaningful. There's an entire world that could be mine. Why did I listen to Papa? Why did I let him make me so afraid?

The village is as I remember it, although it's been some time since I visited. Time appears to stand still in this community where there's a single main street boasting only a handful of small shops. A butcher. A tiny hardware store. A grocery store which is where I'll make my first enquiries.

The only employee in the grocery store is a young woman behind the counter. Her hair is tied back with a headscarf. Although there are a few other people in the store, she only looks at me. I know I must be a strange sight to her, my clothes finer than the others but disheveled from the long walk. My hair has come loose, and I tuck it behind my ears before approaching her.

"I'm looking for an older lady," I say. "I think she might live in this village."

"We have many older ladies who live in this village," the woman says brusquely.

"Her name is Magda." I realize I'm panting a little from my physical exertion and also from my nerves. I try to control my breath because the woman's manner leads me to believe she regards me with suspicion.

"I don't know any Magda," she says and turns to assist a customer who's purchasing a bottle of inexpensive vodka. "Do you know an old woman named Magda, Sergei?" she asks the customer, a man with a grizzled growth of facial hair, wearing a white apron smeared with what looks like blood.

Sergei grunts and shakes his head. She hands him a few coins in change and then he exits the market. The cashier looks at me triumphantly as though she's just proved her point. I can see another customer farther down the aisle, where personal care items are displayed for sale. She's peering intently at something on the shelf I can't see from this distance. I turn away from the cashier and begin to walk toward her, but the cashier stops me in my tracks.

"She doesn't know anyone named Magda either," she says.

It's obvious I'm not welcome in the store so I decide to go elsewhere. "I'm sorry to have disturbed you," I say.

Outside the sun is still bright, and it dazzles on rooftops iced with a thick, new layer of snow. My options for getting information are limited in this village. I notice another door in the same building that houses the market. It's a bank but the sign says it's closed. I'm not sure if it's closed for the day or just for a lunch break. For all I know, it might be permanently closed.

I double back to the butcher and, through the window, I can see Sergei carving up a cut of meat on a wooden chopping block. I should have known Sergei was the butcher from his blood-spattered apron. The brown bag, which I know contains the bottle of vodka he just bought, is on the counter next to him. I stand before the plate-glass window until he looks up and notices me, but he just shakes his head and returns to his work.

I don't have any better luck at the hardware store, which is so small that only two people can shop there at the same time. The man who runs the store looks me up and down as though I just arrived from the planet Mars, then shakes his head *no* to my inquiry about Magda.

Down a narrow lane, I see several large pigs in a pen joyfully rooting through a trough of slop. I turn down the lane until I come to the cottage to which the pig pen belongs. An old lady is coming out the front, holding a pail in her hand, and for a moment my heart catches, thinking I've found Magda. But it's not Magda—just someone with her general shape and appearance from a distance. When I get close enough she pauses, and I can see she has more slops to add to the pigs' trough.

"Excuse me," I say. "I'm looking for a woman about your age. Her name is Magda."

"About my age?" She snorts. "You mean she's old, don't you?"

"Yes, I suppose I do mean that." She's raised my hopes with just this meager response to my query.

"Well then why not say what you mean?" The silver bucket dangles from her bony arm and catches a glint of sun that reflects in my eye. I angle my head slightly away from it.

"Do you know . . . an *old* lady named Magda?" I ask timidly.

"What are you so afraid of, girl?" she asks. "You're not from here, so where are you from?"

This isn't going as I hoped it would. "I'm from . . . that way." I point, not wishing to identify myself as the occupant of the luxurious villa to the west. I know it won't do me any good.

"That way, that way. I know where you're from so just say what you mean. And no, I don't know any Magda."

"I'm sorry for disturbing you," I say.

"And don't be so sorry," she says. "Are you thirsty?" I nod my head. "You look thirsty. Give this to the pigs and I'll get a glass of water for you," she says, handing off the metal bucket, which has a mildly nauseating odor.

I walk to the fence and stand on the first rung, so I can tip the contents of the bucket into the trough. When I turn, the old lady is standing in front of me, holding out a large glass of water. I gulp it down so quickly, I lapse into a coughing fit from sending it down the wrong way. Once I've composed myself, I still have a little hope that the woman is holding something back simply because she doesn't like me, or my father, or any of the ruling wealthy class in this country who live extravagantly while so many people go without. But I can't leave without trying one last thing.

"Please," I say. "If you know *anything*. I can pay you. I have some money with me."

This was an enormous miscalculation on my part. The old lady turns her head to the side and spits. The warm liquid burrows a hole through the snow. She snatches the glass from my hand and strides into her home, slamming the door behind her.

I've been very stupid, and my time is running out.

Other roads spider out from the place where I'm standing, so I begin to walk. The houses are cottages, and the plots are small. I hear chickens and pigs and see a cow or two. I pass a man using a pitchfork to move hay from a covered stall to inside a barn where a cow is lowing. The thread of his shirt is so thin, I can make out the dark, coiled hair on his back. In spite of the cold, there are patches of sweat visible under his arms. I stop to ask him the same question, but he simply shakes his head before thrusting his pitchfork into the haystack once again. This man is my last hope. This village doesn't want me. Even if its people know where Magda is, they won't tell me.

My legs ache from the effort of walking through snow and sludge. My muscles aren't accustomed to this much walking and I still have to get home. I'm concerned that Papa or Tyotya might call to check in and I won't be there. If I get home and find they've called, I'll lie and tell them I was napping. Magda never answers the phone so that won't arouse their suspicion. In the background of these thoughts, I hear a dog barking. It's not the first dog I've heard barking since I've been in this village, but it's a bark I know well. It's Pepper, I'm certain of it. I stop in my tracks and turn down a lane toward the sound, when a streak of black and white comes rocketing toward me.

"Pepper!" I call out gleefully. I've never been so happy to see anyone or anything in my life. He jumps up on me, but I've braced myself so I don't fall over. At my home it's our fun game, but here I must maintain a serious poise and demeanor. "Where have you been, my friend?"

An extremely tall and thin young man wearing a cap and an old, tweedy overcoat follows slowly behind Pepper. The ends of his scarf barely cover his sternum, whereas in a normal-sized person they would hang to the waist. When he reaches me, he stoops to take Pepper by the collar and pulls him back.

"Are you the girl from the Andropov manor?" I shudder to hear my mother's maiden name.

"Yes," I say. "I'm looking for Magda. This is her dog, Pepper. Is she here?"

He shakes his head languidly. Everything is slow about this young man. Stringy, dark curls spill out from underneath his cap. I notice with astonishment the length of his ears, which are at least twice the size of mine.

"The old lady left with her daughter's family. She gave me the dog and I'll train him to be a hunting dog," he says with audible pride. "And her name isn't Magda, it's Maria . . . Hungarian, you know?"

"Yes, I know." This news is devastating. All this way I've come, for what? And how could Magda or Maria or whatever her name is just leave and abandon Pepper to this stranger? I would take him home with me, but I know the man would never relinquish him.

"Thank you," I say barely above a whisper. "I must go now."

"Wait," he says reaching into his pocket. "This is for you. Maria's daughter said if ever you should come to the village, I should give it to you and only to you. And I should do so privately so no one else sees." He hands me an envelope with my name neatly printed on the outside. "So now we're in agreement, I've fulfilled my obligation?" he asks.

"Yes, of course." *This must be in payment for Pepper*, I think. "And if I never came?"

"Then my obligation would be fulfilled as well."

I scratch Pepper behind his ears the way he likes and somehow, I know this will be the last time I'll ever see him. "Please. He's very dear to me," I say. "If he ever needs anything . . . if you tire of him or find he's not the hunting dog you had hoped for—"

"I have a good instinct for animals," he says, stooping to stroke Pepper's throat and muzzle. "I would offer you a ride but the alternator's gone out on my car."

"Thank you," I say. "For everything. I walked here, and I can walk back. It's not far."

We part and I turn to watch him amble off. Pepper never leaves his side, seemingly trained overnight. The man throws a stick off in the distance, and Pepper runs to retrieve it, happily returning it to his open hand. I watch for a few minutes until I can no longer see them. Pepper will be happy with this man—*is* happy. A dog is forgiving of abandonment and deceit as long as it's delivered to a happy home.

I look for a warm place to sit where I can open the envelope and read its contents. I suppose it's from Magda, although I don't think of her as the type to put words into a letter, or really anywhere at all. There's an old bench just off the road underneath a tree that's probably delightful in the spring but is now devoid of leaves. I sit down and wrap the scarf tightly around my neck, and carefully tear the edge of the envelope with the tip of my finger.

My dearest Tatyana,

If this letter finds its way into your hands I hope it finds you safe and healthy. You may have figured out by now that the woman you've known for the past ten years as Magda is my mother Maria. I hope you don't judge us for the secrets we've kept from you over the years, but the secrets were necessary to protect our lives. Since your mother died, my mother and I have taken turns watching over you as best as we could. In our hearts, we were fulfilling a promise to your dear, sweet mother—my childhood friend, my sister, and a second daughter to my mother. You see, sweet Tatyana, my mother worked for Mrs. Andropov, a kind woman who gave us a comfortable life. The only life I knew was the home of the Andropovs, and it was a happy one for many years. Later, when we grew and your mother went off to university, I also left to seek employment but didn't move far, only a few hours' drive. My dear, sweet mother joined me soon after to live out her years comfortably making a home for us, even after I was married.

Much time went by before I saw your mother again, God rest her soul. One day she came to see me when she was on her way to becoming an important doctor—no surprise to those of us who knew her because she was so quick and we always knew she would make her parents proud. She had met a man, your father, and couldn't stop talking about him. It was clear to me she was deeply in love, and I was so happy for her because I had also met a man who would one day become my loving husband and father to my two children. We were like children together that day, and it was the last truly happy day I believe your mother had until the day you were born. Later I would learn your father was not a good man and his attempt to control your mother caused her much pain. Still, I believe she was in awe of his intellect and his forceful personality, because your mother was a sheltered and protected child without guile. She had no defenses against a man like your father, but she still had a pure heart and natural goodness.

I didn't see her again until after your birth, and that's when I learned of the horrible things your father did to you even before you were born. You—his own flesh and blood, who he used for his vile experimentation. And your poor, dear mother, God rest her soul, agreeing to allow your aunt to carry her child because her own womb was weak. I know your mother's force is strong inside you and overcomes the demon seed of your father and his slavish sister. I'm sorry, dear Tatyana, to speak to you this bluntly, but I feel I must.

I'm not sure it's right, but if it's not meant to be, then this letter will never find its way into your hands.

When your mother discovered what your father had done to you, her beloved child, she could take it no longer. She came to me again and asked that I take you, the baby, and deliver you to a private adoption center outside of Moscow where an American family had been approved to adopt a child in need. Everything was arranged for your transfer to the Americans. Your mother had researched their character and found them to be loving and decent. The woman who facilitated the adoption had been paid off to accept the story that I was an unwed mother who couldn't afford the child and wished only to drop her off anonymously. People were compensated under the table. Papers were forged.

How much must a mother love her child that she could send you into the arms of strangers to protect you from the ongoing evil intentions of your wicked father? It's a thought I can't myself imagine, but your mother, God rest her soul, would stop at nothing to keep you safe. Mr. and Mrs. Andropov despised your father and tried to intervene before your mother married him. Unfortunately, the man they selected for your mother was someone she did not love, so she defied their wishes and went ahead with the marriage to your father. He never forgave the Andropovs and they no longer had the power to keep you safe. Only in another country, out of the long reach of your father's important contacts, did your dear mother feel her daughter could be safe.

That day, we arranged a meeting for the following week, but your mother never made it. I know you have been told your mother died from pneumonia, but she died in an automobile accident with her parents the day before we were to meet. The accident was never investigated by the police, but there is no question in the minds of those of us who knew her that this was more than an accident. This was planned and, dare I say it—planned by your father. So many times over the years I have thought what could have been if only we'd carried out our plan sooner, even by a day. I know your mother would have found a way to reunite with you in America. If only it could have been.

My dearest Tatyana, you're a woman now and I have young children of my own. My mother took my place in your life when I had my first child, Victor. But if your father ever learns who we are and what we know, we would meet with the same fate as your mother and I must protect my children. It's our time to go now, and we wish you Godspeed. No one will know where we have gone, but I can tell you it's back to my homeland of Hungary. You must destroy this letter now that you've read it. Do not take it to your home. The people in the village can be trusted—they will never give up any information to anyone associated with your father.

My mother overheard the angry words you exchanged with your father, so I know you now know what he's done to you.

Please take my advice, dear Tatyana, and run. I know not where, and I know not how, but you must get away from the monstrous and murderous man who is your father. You are smart like your mother and you are good. Someone will help you somewhere. Maybe even Irina will help you if she has a better nature than I suspect.

And if I've done wrong by telling you what I know, then may God strike me dead. If He means for you to know, He will deliver this letter into your hands.

God bless, my dear Tatyana.

Your Rosie (Klara)

Rosie. Klara. Rosie and Magda. Klara and Maria. All those years I avoided the woman I knew as Magda because her appearance was frightening to me and her demeanor was gruff. All those years, she was watching over me while I felt uncomfortable in her presence. She was fulfilling an unspoken pledge to my dead mother. And I loved Rosie, who I now know is Klara, who was always kind to me. Perhaps love is too strong a word because I can see, looking back, that she never let me get too close. Keeping her distance was what kept her identity a secret from Papa, so how can I blame her? But I liked Klara very much and missed her when she left. And now I've never felt more alone in my life. I know I must destroy the letter, but first I have to read it one last time, savoring every word about the mother I never knew and committing them to memory. And about the two guardian angels I never knew were watching over me until this moment.

After I've read it two more times, I tear the letter and envelope into thin shreds and rip the shreds into even smaller pieces. Then I let them drizzle from my hand into the wet snow at my feet. With the heel of my boot, I crush the tiny scraps, each one a precious gem, watching the words smudge and leach into one another, a tiny fleck of blue ink escaping into the snow. It's late and I should be heading home.

As I walk along the street that only a few hours ago held promise of leading me *toward* something instead of away from something, I go over in my mind what I'll do for the rest of the day. Tyotya won't be coming for me until around midday tomorrow. Will I tell her about Magda right away, or should I pretend she's just gone into town for a few hours, giving her more time to get as far away as possible from Papa, should he become suspicious for any reason? And what of the list I created this morning? I remember exactly what I wrote down, *Things I Must Do.* I've accomplished two of the three tasks, stalling Tyotya and walking to the village. The third won't be so easy—possibly exposing myself to more seizures in order to find the girl. I know from experience there's no way to bring on the seizures that have led me to her in the past. I also know I must find her again. If my finding her was important to Papa, then it must be even more important to me.

I feel the sting of snow burn on my cheeks and on my nose. With my skin so pale and the sun so bright, I'm vulnerable to its rays. The snow is melting rapidly, and the sludge permeates the edges of my boots. A chill creeps into the sides of my feet and I wish I'd worn heavier boots, although the walk would have been that much more difficult. A vulture circles off in the distance and is soon joined by another. Something has died out there and the vultures have been waiting for the sun to do its job—melting away the camouflage of frost to reveal a carcass, its odor ripening as the day grows warmer until it's detectable even from where they circle. I shudder at the thought of my mother and my grandparents, their blood spilled, perhaps on a snowy bank just like this one. There's so little that separates humankind from nature's savagery—sometimes, nothing at all. Did Papa pretend to be surprised when he got news of their "accident"? Distraught? Perhaps he was distraught, even if he was the architect of their destruction. Perhaps he viewed their deaths as a necessary but unpleasant casualty of the war between what he wanted and decency, humanity. What about Tyotya? Did she know? Does she know now?

I hear a car engine far off in the distance before I see it. It will be the first car I've seen on this road today and it's approaching from the direction opposite to what I'm walking. When it rounds the corner and comes into view I can make out a black limousine like ours and, of course, there can't be another one out here, can there? My heart jumps and a wave of acid washes over my stomach. I feel like I'm going to be sick. Tyotya must have come early and my mind races to come up with a story for why I'm walking home alone from the village. All sorts of foolish lies pop into my head but none of them seem credible.

The car is just ahead of me and then it stops. The driver's window rolls down and I'm face to face with Igor. I walk over to his window and peer in the back but he's alone.

"They sent me," he says gruffly. "Please get in."

It's just then I notice my list of *Things I Want* and *Things I Must Do* is on the seat beside him.

CHAPTER 21

TATI

It's gray and drizzling outside, so already I'm not a happy camper. Add to that the fact that Priya's doing something with extended family visiting from India, and that they'll be here for two more weeks, and I'm *really* not a happy camper. On the camper happiness scale, I'm about ready to pack up my tent and go home.

Dad's sitting across the table from me and, in contrast, he's in his element. He's radiating cheerfulness as he munches down on a breakfast consisting of four fried eggs, four strips of bacon, two sausages, and plenty of buttered white toast. A tiny glass of fresh-squeezed orange juice is supposed to miraculously turn this into a healthy meal. He's got the Sunday paper spread out on the table, and I wonder how many people still read an actual paper newspaper like Dad.

But the memory of my last visit with Ana is still fresh in my mind and I can't take it anymore. Someone needs to save Dad from himself and it's not going to be Mom, who indulges him like a child. So, it has to be me.

"Ahem." I clear my throat loudly to get his attention.

Dad makes a big fuss of turning the page and refolding the paper in half and then looks up at me. "What is it, honey? Or was that an actual mucous-clearing throat maneuver I'm politely supposed to ignore?"

"Dad, *really*? Look what you're putting in your body."

He halts and stares at the forkful that's just seconds away from making it into his mouth. He looks up at me. "This?" He raises his eyebrows.

"Yes, that. Why don't you just take a hypodermic needle and inject fat directly into your heart because that's basically what you're doing."

He pops the forkful into his mouth and chews thoughtfully. "Because that would hurt," he says. He pats at his mouth with a paper napkin and then looks up at me. "And it wouldn't be anywhere near as tasty as this. And to think, I was so happy just a few seconds ago, and now a black cloud is raining down upon me." He squeezes the sausage against his plate with the side of his fork until a plump, juicy bite separates, which he spears with his fork. I can hear Mom's sewing machine running in the next room.

"I'm not kidding, Dad," I say. My bowl of oatmeal with fresh blueberries is nearly empty.

"Okay," Dad says. "Let me get this straight. You want *me*"—he points to himself with the sausage-tipped fork—"to eat *that*." He swings the fork around until it's pointed at my bowl of oatmeal. "And I suppose the next thing you'll be saying is I should go buy some spandex shorts and join a gym."

"Dad," I say. "It's not funny."

"Don't worry, honey. Heart disease doesn't run in our family." The sausage is making its way to his stomach.

"Dad . . . all this worrying you do about *my* health. What about yours? When's the last time you've even seen a doctor? Do you even know what your cholesterol numbers are?"

"High cholesterol doesn't run—"

"Stop, Dad. Just please stop for a minute. What would happen if you keeled over? What would Mom and I do without you?" I know there's a tremble in my voice even though I'm trying to maintain emotional neutrality to argue my point effectively.

"You and your mom have nothing to worry about, Tati. I have a good life insurance policy and you'll never have to worry about money. I've been making payments on it for twenty years." He's dropped the usual Dad joking-around style.

"That's. Not. The. Point!" I slam my hand against the table hard enough to make the cutlery jingle. Mom comes to the kitchen door, drawn by my raised voice. "It's not your money we need. It's *you!*" Mom sighs deeply. "It's you," I repeat and the tremble in my voice grows a little more pronounced.

Dad pushes his half-filled plate to the side. "I guess it wouldn't be a bad thing for me to get a check-up," he says. "Maybe some bloodwork to see what's what. It's probably been at least five years since the last one," he adds.

"Ten years," Mom says. "At least."

"Okay, maybe closer to ten," Dad says, and reaches over

to put his hand on mine. "And if everything comes back a-okay, you'll let me eat in peace?"

"You could stand to lose some weight," I mumble. "And maybe get some fresh air every once in a while."

"You really could, George," Mom says. "And so could I. Maybe we could do it together as a family and make it fun."

"Fun," Dad grumbles. "I don't see the fun in going to the doctor and getting too much fresh air. You know, back in the old days people kept their windows closed to keep the fresh air out. They were convinced it was the root of all illness. Miasma, they called it. Maybe they were on to something."

"History Channel?" I ask, and Dad nods his head. "Ancient history, Dad. They haven't believed in miasma for, like, hundreds of years. We believe in germs now."

"Is that so?" Dad smiles and winks at me. "Germs, you say? It isn't easy at my advanced age to keep up with these newfangled notions. I was born in the Bronze Age, as you know."

"Let's go for a walk right now," Mom says. "Leave the dishes, we can clean up when we get back."

"It's raining?" Dad asks more than says. "And I might catch my death of cold."

"I'll go get umbrellas," I say, "while you guys get your jackets on."

Maybe Dad hears the determination in my voice or maybe he sees the steel in Mom's gaze. Either way, he's moved. At least enough to get out of his chair, grumbling all the while.

"Thanks, Mom," I whisper as I walk past her. She squeezes my hand in silent affirmation.

My mood has just gone from a *three* to a *ten*. I hope the version of Dad in Ana's world is okay.

Mom and Dad return all jacketed up and I arm us with individual umbrellas. We're ready to face the rain in our first-ever family trek.

"Just think, Dad. Your decision today could be the start of a new life for you." This only merits a grunt in return.

"Tati?" comes the timid voice on the other end of the line from a number that isn't in my contacts. "It's Olga . . . the person your parents hired to do research for you."

"Oh my gosh, yeah. Sorry, it took me a second." I'm back in my room after the walk, kicking off wet shoes and peeling off wet pants, which weren't much protected by either my umbrella or my jacket. The rain was as cold as it could get without being snow, which never happens in what's supposed to be sunny California. The tops of my thighs are numb and bright pink from where my pants were clinging to them. I jump in bed and pull the covers up over me, hoping I haven't completely alienated Dad from exercise before we had a chance to establish a routine. Dad made a beeline for a hot shower the minute we walked through the door.

"I have some good news," Olga says. "Well, I don't know if it's good or not, but it's news."

"Fantastic. What's up?" I wiggle my toes under the comforter and realize I can't feel them.

"I spoke to my father's first cousin's husband, who's high up in the government in Russia. I don't want to say exactly who he is or what he does because that's probably not appropriate, you know. But he's kind of important, so I thought I'd start with him because he has contacts and resources. Shoot, I should've cleared it with you first that it's okay to call rather than email, because I know your parents said—"

"It's fine," I say. This girl can talk. And I get the feeling it's nervous talk, which surprises me for someone as accomplished as she is at such a young age.

"Oh, okay. Good . . . good. Anyway, I found out the orphanage doesn't exist anymore. The one where your parents went to adopt you. It's been shut down for a long time, and all the files were transferred to the Ministry of Internal Affairs, where they keep records like that—so that makes the search a little more difficult. But actually, because of my contacts, it turns out it's easier for me to—"

My dad found Olga through a friend of a friend who teaches at the university where Olga's getting her PhD. He said she's earnest and hard-working. She probably feels the need to justify the money my parents are paying her, but I wish she'd just relax and get to the point.

"So did you get to see the records? Or did your dad's cousin or whoever get to see them?"

"Oh, I wouldn't ask him to do that, but he did know someone who could access the file and—hurray! It was still there. But you have to be really careful if you're snooping around over there because—I mean, there's nothing about your case in particular that would set off alarm bells, but—"

"So, what did they find in my file?" I've heard of people spontaneously combusting, but is it possible for a person to literally explode? Because I feel like I'm just about to if she doesn't get to the point. But I take a deep breath because she does have some pretty awesome contacts.

"Yeah, the file. You're right about the file and the woman they found holding you when you were a baby. And . . . I'm so sorry, please stop me if any of this is triggering you. But anyway, she had—they initially reported that she had shot herself and that some good Samaritan came along and took you to the hospital that was literally right there, lucky for you. Although, now that I think about it, I wonder why they didn't take you to the police. But maybe that's not so unusual, because a lot of people don't necessarily trust the police over there and might have wanted to avoid being dragged into something. So luckily, that woman, your birth mom, was right in front of the hospital when it happened, and it turns out the people at the hospital *did* call the police."

"And?"

"And here's the thing: There was a missing person report filed after your birth mother was killed, but it took the bureaucracy almost a year to match it to her. Eventually some clerk going through cold cases matched the description on the missing person report to your mom's physical description and the date she went missing. The person who originally filed the report was a Hungarian woman, the mother of your birth mother."

"My grandmother," I say.

"Yes, your grandmother. Her name was Maria Magyary and, like I said, she was Hungarian. An immigrant."

"I'm Hungarian," I say, more to myself than for confirmation from Olga. Why this should make a difference, I don't know. But all this time I thought I was Russian and now I'm reimagining myself. In my head, I'm already planning a trip to the library after school tomorrow to pick up a few books on Hungarian culture and history.

"Did she say anything about why my mother did this . . . shot herself?"

"That's the thing. I'm sorry to be telling you this all these years later, but I know you love your parents, so it's not like your life was changed for the worse. Sorry, I'm babbling. I'm nervous because this is my first job using my research skills and I want to come through for you."

"You *are* coming through for me. Really, you are. What were you just going to say?"

"So it seems there weren't any fingerprints on the gun, which is strange because your birth mother wasn't wearing gloves, so if she had shot herself, she would have left prints. In the absence of any other theory, the police decided it was a robbery gone bad. The robber was startled—maybe by the good Samaritan who wound up taking you to the hospital. They think the killer dropped the gun when he ran away . . . he or *she*. Maybe they didn't even mean to kill your mother but panicked, and . . . anyway, the gun was untraceable. I'm really sorry, Tati, but I know you wanted the truth. I hope I've been helpful."

"You've been more than helpful. And I do want the truth. My birth mother, did you find out her name?"

"Klara," Olga says. "Same last name as your grandmother. Unmarried with no other children according to the missing person report, so you don't have any siblings on your birth mother's side. So far, I've come to a dead end with your birth father. I'll keep trying, but for now it's a big zero because I don't even have a name to go on. Your grandmother probably left the country after learning what happened to her daughter. She hasn't been heard from since. If she went back to Hungary, you might be able to hire an investigator over there and see if they can get any leads."

"Olga, you don't know how much I appreciate this. Thanks so much for everything you've done. And please email my mom or me whatever we owe you and I'll make sure you get paid right away."

"Oh, before you go . . . two things. Sorry, but I don't want to leave out any details. In the police report, your grandmother claimed your birth mother had been depressed ever since her best friend died in a car accident. But that really isn't relevant to the case. Still, it's a detail you might be interested in."

"That's so sad," I say, thinking immediately of Priya and how it would kill me to lose her in an accident. The thought is too disturbing, so I sweep it from my mind. "What was the second thing?"

"There was a description of the good Samaritan. A huge bear of a man. But that's not relevant either."

"Priya, guess what?" My parents are napping, and I can't wait to share the news with Priya. Over the phone I hear voices in the background speaking what I assume is Hindi. Her houseguests. "I finally know what I am."

"What you *are*?" She lowers her voice to a whisper. "Do I get three guesses? Beautiful. Wonderful. Perfect."

"Oh yeah, all those and more," I say. "But seriously, that girl we hired who's getting her PhD at UC . . . she just called, and it turns out I'm not Russian, after all. I'm Hungarian."

Soon Ana will also know what I know. We're Hungarian, not Russian.

CHAPTER 22

ANA

Our birth mother was really Hungarian, Tati is saying. *Killed during a robbery gone bad . . . Grandmother . . . missing person report . . . She was depressed . . . Best friend died in a car crash . . . Klara . . . Maria.*

And then *whoosh* . . . Tati's gone and I'm in the back of a van. Whose van? What time is it? What day is it? Why did Tati leave so quickly, and does she know where I am?

How cliché is it to be kidnapped and thrown in the back of a van and yet here I am. My head is pounding from the inside, like the time Dad bought a coconut and tried to open it in our backyard by beating it against a rock. *Bam! Bam!* If it doesn't stop, my skull's going to meet with the same fate as the coconut, and it won't be pretty.

Something tells me I'm not alone! I can vaguely make out a dark shape leaning against the side of this windowless van, by the exit door. I can smell another body in here with me—not a bad smell. Aftershave. Sweat. Coconut? That last one's probably just me projecting. Being as stealthy as I can, I slide my phone out of my pocket and, unfortunately, the screen glows to life. What kind of a kidnapper is this who hasn't bound my hands and feet or taken away my phone?

Amateurs, I decide.

"Power that down, okay? Otherwise I'll have to take it away from you."

The dark shape speaks and now it's all coming back to me—the guy who picked up the bag of grapes near the bus stop. The guy who asked me if I dropped something when I was waiting for Dr. Sokol, right before I lost consciousness.

"Why does my head hurt?" I power off my phone and slide it back into my pocket. "And who are you and where are you taking me?"

"I'm just here looking after you, ma'am," he says. He has the slightest hint of a Southern accent, which I remember from my past encounters with him. "To protect you."

"Protect me?" I try to raise myself up on my elbows and I know the room would be spinning if I could actually see anything in this darkness. "From what? You have a pretty strange idea of how to protect a person." I flop back down and . . . *ouch.* "Okay, you've had your fun and you've done an admirable job of protecting me. Now can I please go home?" My boldness surprises me. Is it Tati? Is it because I feel that somehow she'll come to my rescue?

Tati, please come find me.

"No, ma'am," he says, and . . . okay, he's not the talkative type. I'll try again.

"Why does my head hurt?"

"Just the—just something we had to give you to help you relax. So you wouldn't cause a scene. It'll be out of your system in a few hours. Don't worry, there's a doc waiting who can check you out when we get there."

"Help me relax? You've got to be kidding, right?" This is too much for me to take and I sit up in one sudden movement. Too fast! I empty my guts on the floor of the van and then brace myself on my two hands before crawling to the corner where I sprawl out again.

Mr. Dark Shape says nothing.

"Sorry," I say reflexively, but then. "No, I'm not sorry, I hope you step in it. I hope it makes you as sick as I feel."

"It don't bother me," he says. "I've seen worse."

Apparently, Mr. Dark Shape is the master of understatement.

"Okay, help me out here, please. Can you at least tell me what you're protecting me from?"

"No ma'am," he says. "It's on a need-to-know basis, and I don't need to know."

The van is making a series of pretty dramatic turns, which have the effect of making my stomach turn in opposing directions. It's taking every bit of my willpower to keep from puking again, although I'm pretty sure there's nothing left in my stomach to puke.

Suddenly, I remember the scene that played out in the cafeteria. The girl who was me. Who was Tati. The guy. The knife. The gun. The blood. And the more that I come to my senses, the more terrified I become.

"Please," I sob. "Please don't kill me or rape me. Please let me go. My parents will pay anything."

"*Kill? Rape?*" comes the disembodied voice, and to be

honest he sounds as alarmed as I feel at this moment. "I told you I'm here to *protect* you. There's not gonna be any killing or raping as long as I'm around."

There's something about the authentic outrage in his voice that reassures me for the moment. He's not going to tell me anything, I've already figured that out. Unless I can trick him into unwittingly giving up some information. But I'm not feeling particularly tricky right now, with my pounding head and the taste of vomit in my mouth, the scent of it in my nostrils.

I make a mental list of the facts so far:

Things I Want to Know	*Things He Won't Tell Me*
Who is he?	*Who is he?*
Where are they taking me?	*Where are they taking me?*
Why have they kidnapped me?	*Why have they kidnapped me?*
How long have we been traveling?	
How much longer before we get there?	

"How long have we been driving?" I ask. "I mean, it seems like about an hour."

It's a gambit. I have no idea how long we've been traveling. Either some of the time or much of the time, I've been out cold. There's no light or dark in here. No windows. No clue. This is me being tricky.

"Can't say," he says without hesitation.

"Can't say or won't say?" I ask.

"Won't say."

Well so much for that. If I don't know how long we've been traveling, then it doesn't really matter how long before we get there. But it does matter, at least to my sanity.

"How long before we get to wherever it is we're going?" I ask, expecting nothing at this point. Things are so bleak it's everything I can do to keep from crying out for my mommy because that's all I really want to do right now.

"Not long," he says, and I detect a note of compassion in his voice. "Thirty minutes max. You wanna drink of water?"

"Yes please."

He scoots over next to me in the dark and I hear him swear softly under his breath. He's probably just landed a knee or a hand in my puddle of vomit.

"Here," he wraps my fingers around a plastic water bottle. "Took the cap off for you." At this close distance I can make out the features of the guy with the bag of grapes. He scoots back to his position in the far corner—away from me and close to the rear exit door.

I take a swig of water and swish it around inside my mouth before spitting it as far away from me as I can because, why the hell not? It's a mess in here already and I'm a mess. Then I drizzle a little across my face before downing the rest.

"What's your name?" I ask. There's nothing he's going to volunteer that will help me one iota.

He pauses a few seconds before answering. "Paul."

"Is that your real name?"

"No."

"Then why did you say it is?"

"So, you'd have something to call me. Maybe make it a little less scary for you."

It's a silly thing. A really small thing. A barely-there evidence of humanity. But it's enough to make me weep, which I do silently for about a minute or two before squeezing my eyes dry.

"Well, Paul," I say. "If you really are here to protect me, I sure as hell hope you do."

"Yes, ma'am" is his response.

When the van finally comes to a stop, it's after about ten minutes of driving down a gravelly-sounding, pothole-filled road.

"I'll take you to the door," Paul says. "I won't be inside with you, but I'll be right out here if you need anything. Keeping you safe. Protecting you."

Ah yes, keeping me safe. Totally.

"I need to put a blindfold on you," he says. "For your own protection because you really don't want to remember where you've been, just in case."

"Just in case *what*?"

"Just in case," he says, while he loops a scarf across my eyes and ties it tightly at the back of my head. I don't even try to see if I can peek through the edges but I've no doubt he's done his job well. I must be trembling because he adds softly, "Don't be afraid. Really. Nothing's gonna happen to you. Oh, and give me your phone, okay? I'll give it back to you when you're done."

Paul leads me across the uneven surface, holding tightly on to my elbow in case I trip.

"Is it light or dark?" I ask, and then add. "You know, this would almost be funny if it didn't suck so much."

"It's dark," Paul says, and I can almost feel the heat a house gives off as we approach it. "What do you mean, *funny*?"

"I mean . . . the back of a van, the blindfold—it's so corny. Like a really bad B movie."

"It works," Paul says. "Maybe that's why you keep seeing it in the movies." We come to a halt and he kind of hoists me up by the elbow . . . one step . . . two steps. Then we stop again. "Okay, we're here. There's a lady standing right in front of us and I'm gonna hand you off to her. She'll take it from here. Take *you* from here."

But now I don't want to part from Paul. Have I already fallen victim to Stockholm syndrome by identifying with my kidnapper? It's just that I kind of know Paul now, and I believe him when he says he's here to protect me. I mean, I know he's not exactly protecting me, but he didn't harm me either, and he was nice. I believe him when he says nothing bad will happen while he's around, and I have no idea who this lady is who's standing in front of me. I grab his arm tightly, but he gently unpeels my fingers and I feel a different hand slide over mine.

"Come in, Ana. I'll take the blindfold off as soon as we're inside and the door is shut." Her voice isn't unkind, and I have no choice but to switch my allegiance to her now. She's my new caretaker and I'm no better than a helpless child.

Tati, please come back tonight. Are you so excited about Olga's discoveries that you're not even thinking about me right now?

True to her word, when the door clicks behind me, the

woman removes my blindfold. The pupils of my eyes rally to contract so I can make sense of the brightly lit room and its inhabitants, but initially it's just visual nonsense.

Then I hear it . . . the voice in all its familiarity, "Tatiana, dear. What have you given her? She looks awful."

It's Dr. Sokol and she's peering into my face from about six inches away. I take a reflexive step backward and step on someone's foot. The lady who brought me inside sucks in a sharp breath of pain, as I crush her toe with the heel of my shoe. She puts her hands on my shoulders to steady me as she moves me off her foot.

My first thought is, *Thank God, Dr. Sokol's here!* My second and third thoughts are, *I look awful? How awful? And why the hell is Dr. Sokol here?*

"Sit down, Ana," the unidentified woman says, and Dr. Sokol takes me by the hand and leads me to a sofa that's definitely seen better days. I dodge a spring that's jutting out from the back rest but Dr. Sokol wedges a pillow over it for my protection.

"Let me examine her, please," Dr. Sokol says. "Before you say one more word to her. I had your promise."

"Be our guest," says a man's voice, and I'm only now aware of a man hovering in the doorway behind me. He's a few decades older than me—maybe Dr. Sokol's age, maybe a bit younger. He wears glasses that aren't exactly stylish, but neither are his clothes: khaki slacks with a collared shirt and running shoes, not a great look even to my unqualified fashion eye. Add to that the wrinkles in the kind of shirt that isn't supposed to be wrinkled, an unruly mop of hair, and a pen sticking out of his shirt pocket, and he looks like the type of guy who spends a lot of time behind a computer screen. But he's tall and lanky and when he walks in the room to take a seat in an armchair opposite us, I can tell he possesses an athletic grace.

His armchair companion is the woman who led me in. And now with Dr. Sokol poring over every inch of my body and questioning every scratch and freckle, I have a chance to size her up as well. She's already seated in a chair that looks somewhat similar to the one the guy's sitting in but it's obvious this isn't a matching set. None of this furniture matches, in fact. It looks as though someone was told to go out and get the bare essentials to furnish a house and they cobbled together a collection after visiting about ten different thrift shops. The floor is bare of carpet and the hardwood floors, which were probably really nice about fifty years ago, are warped and discolored.

"What is this place?" I ask. "And why are you here?" I turn to Dr. Sokol, who seizes the opportunity to shine a flashlight in my eyes, which just makes me wince.

"Ana, I apologize we had to do this to you," the woman says. "But we needed to get you here and we couldn't afford to have anyone see you leaving. Obviously, you wouldn't have come on your own if we'd asked."

"You could've tried," I say. "I might have come, especially if Dr. Sokol asked me, and you would've saved me a lot of trauma in the process."

The man clears his throat. "Dr. Sokol came the same way

you did," he says. "She just had a better driver who didn't get lost on the way here. Again, our apologies to both of you."

"Who *are* you?" I ask.

The woman looks a bit younger than the man. She has blond hair pulled back in a ponytail and is wearing athletic gear and looks fit. "You can call me Jane," she says. "And you can call him Paul." She gestures toward the man.

"Paul like the guy who brought me here?" I'm totally confused. Is this *my* Paul? Back-of-the-van Paul? Dark-silhouette Paul who crawled through vomit to give me a bottle of water? It doesn't sound like his voice.

"Is that what he said his name is?" Jane asks. "Okay, then you can call him Steve." She nods at the guy facing me.

"Are those even your names?"

"No, truthfully, it's just so you have something to call us."

"So, you know our names, but we have no idea who you are." I look over at Dr. Sokol to see whether she knows who they are, and she shrugs as if to say she's as lost as I am.

Dr. Sokol is apparently satisfied that I'm well enough because she turns to face our hosts while keeping my hand protectively enclosed in hers. "I know something of why we're here, Tatiana," she says. "I've already been briefed, and this is what I was hoping to discuss with you over dinner."

I pull my hand gently from her clasp. "Well, then anyone care to fill me in?" I ask. My heart is pounding—no longer out of fear for my safety now that Dr. Sokol is here—more from what I'm about to hear and how it will affect my life.

"Let me get right to the point," Jane says. "Steve and I work for the United States government but we're not going to get into specifics about which department, and it's better if you don't know. Your birth father has been granted political asylum and he's entered the country."

"My *birth father*? What birth father? I didn't even know he was alive."

Dr. Sokol makes another grab at my hand and this time she's trembling. This time I don't pull away from her.

Steve tosses a file on the table between us so it's facing me. *String Pulsation in Interuniverse Travel* is printed boldly on the cover. "You're welcome to peruse what I've gathered here. Just for your information and not to be shared, mind you. It stays with us when you leave."

I reach forward and pick it up, setting it down in my lap. "Can you give me the Cliffs Notes version?"

"In a nutshell," Jane says, "your father is spearheading a multinational conglomerate of morally questionable scientists and their financial backers, who we believe are developing technology that will allow operatives of rogue governments to commit political acts of terrorism and then escape into different dimensions . . . parallel universes, if you will."

"In other words," Steve says. "Bad guys working with bad governments, doing what they will and getting away with it by escaping to where no one can ever catch them."

"So why did you let my . . . *father* . . . into the country if he's a terrorist?"

"Good question, Ana," Jane says. She leans forward in her seat as though sitting is not natural behavior for her and she'd much rather be running or doing jumping jacks or something. "The various divisions of government don't always see eye to eye, and in this case, we disagree with the decision to grant him asylum, although it might be better to keep your father close where he can be watched. He says he's had a change of heart and wishes to work with our government to stop further progress of S.P.I.T., as it's referred to. But we think he has ulterior motives. We think he's come here to claim you."

"*Me*? Why would he want me after all these years?" Dr. Sokol squeezes my hand.

"Because he's just finally found you," Steve says. "As have we."

"And why am I important to him? I already have a mom and dad, and I would never go back to him."

"Do you mind?" Dr. Sokol looks at Steve and he nods. "Tatiana," she says. "Your father did a very bad thing. He committed an unpardonable sin. Before you were born, he altered the genetic code of your DNA to provide entryways, portals, to three other parallel universes. Four separate versions of how your life plays out in the multiverse. There are an infinite number of versions of your life, but in the best-case scenario—or worst, depending on how you look at it—you only have access to three. The way your father did this is explained in the file you're holding, so you can access that information when we're done speaking. But the result for you was a lifetime of what you were told were seizures. And now, probably because of your physical maturity, they're transforming into what your father originally intended."

"Tati. And the girl I saw in the cafeteria," I say.

"Precisely," Dr. Sokol says. She slides the extra few inches to close the gap between us, and I can feel her warmth against my side. Her grip on my hand has loosened, so I pull my hand away, not comfortable with all this sudden closeness.

"And this is why my DNA tests came back as animal DNA?"

"A standard test wouldn't recognize your DNA as human. Therefore, they'd default to animal, not knowing what else to make of it," she says. She leans forward and turns her head to bring her eyes into direct contact with mine.

"How do you know about all of this? Why are you involved?" I rotate my hips on the sofa, putting a little distance between us without breaking our eye contact, but whatever it is she's about to say causes her to look away, dropping her gaze to the ground before looking back up at me. She reaches out as if to make another grab at my hand but then thinks better of it and settles both hands in her lap.

"Because I'm your mother," she says softly. "Your birth mother."

Steve and Jane are quiet, but the room feels like it's closing in on me. The overload of information is too much, although everything feels like it makes sense for the first time in my life. But . . .

"My birth mother? But my birth mother was short and blonde and heavy. And she died when I was a baby. Shot in the head while she was holding me, during a robbery gone bad. At least in Tati's life. That's how Tati came to the orphanage, although I have no idea how that happened in my life. But Tati and I would have the same mother, wouldn't we?"

"What else did Tati tell you?" Dr. Sokol asked. "About her mother?"

I think back to an hour ago when Tati came to me while I was sprawled in the back of the van, my head throbbing like a stubbed toe. Had they used chloroform on me? Do they still use that stuff in the spy world? What was it Tati had said she'd learned from Olga?

"Just that Tati's grandmother spoke to the police afterward and told them my mom was Hungarian, and she'd been depressed after the death of her best friend in a car accident. And that my mother's name was Klara."

"Dear God." Dr. Sokol goes white. "I can see it's best not to know the alternative outcomes of one's life. Klara was my childhood friend, like a sister to me. This means I'm already dead in at least one other universe, the one where Tati lives. And Klara is too."

"Two universes," I mumble.

"What?" Dr. Sokol looks up, shaken from her own dark thoughts.

"You're dead in at least two of the universes I have access to. Remember the girl in the cafeteria? The woman who looked like you?"

"Oh, dear God." Dr. Sokol shakes her head.

"I'm sorry," Jane says. "I know this is a lot for both of you to take in. I wish there was another way, but we feel your lives may be in jeopardy. We also feel you may be able to help us, Ana. To help the world."

"How can I do that?"

"Your mother has filled us in on the experiences you've had with at least two different versions of your life."

"*Birth* mother," I say, and look apologetically at Dr. Sokol. "I'm sorry, but I have a mother. I hardly even know you."

"Of course," she murmurs, and is it my imagination, or are her eyes glistening with unshed tears?

"Birth mother," Jane corrects herself. "We need you, Ana, to help us access your other parallel lives. Any information you can give us about your birth father might help us stop him—at least in this world. Anything. Even if it doesn't seem obvious to you—or even to us—right now."

"But Tati—"

Jane rises from her seat and begins to pace. This room seems too small for her, and I understand that feeling because I have an almost uncontrollable urge to go through that door and run as far as I can, as fast as I can. "Based on everything you've told us, it seems that your father in Tati's world hasn't made an effort to find her," Jane says. "We can't be sure why, but for now it's the other two we're interested in. The Tatiana in the cafeteria whose life seems to be in danger, and the Tatiana we don't know. Dr. Sokol said there were four parallel lives, including yours, Ana."

A sickening thought comes over me. "Tati hired someone to track down her mother, someone with connections in the government. What if her inquiries get back to people who know her dad?"

Jane looks at Steve and arches an eyebrow.

"I'm sorry, but we can't do anything to protect anyone

outside of the world we inhabit," Steve says. "You might warn her, though. Perhaps without unduly alarming her."

"How did you find me?" I ask.

"We found you through your mo—through Dr. Sokol," Steve says. "She disappeared shortly after you were born. We learned she moved to Poland after securing your private adoption and transfer to the US. She forged a new identity and eventually emigrated to the US to be near you. It took years, but we pieced together all the clues until we found her. And then it was a simple matter to find you."

"I'm sorry, Tatiana," Dr. Sokol's eyes are moist and her lower lip is trembling. "Saving you from your father was my sole purpose in life once he admitted what he did. He was conducting tests on you, even as an infant—as if you were one of the animals in his laboratory. I knew I'd be reunited with you one day, but I had to immediately put as much distance as possible between you and him. I knew the names of your adoptive parents, and they kept your first name out of respect for me."

"Sit with the notes," Jane says. "Take your time. Ask us questions if you have any and we'll answer them if it's appropriate. Then we'll take you home."

"Her father is very ill," Dr. Sokol says.

"Yes, we know. We'll get both of you back to your homes ASAP," Jane says.

"Contact," Steve says before getting up from his chair to leave me alone with my reading. "Establish contact, Ana. Ask questions. Get us whatever you can, even if it doesn't seem important to you. Find the other two girls. The other Anas."

"I don't know what I can do," I say. "I don't have control over what happens to me the way Tati does. I don't know if I'll ever see the other Tatiana again, and I've never even seen a fourth one."

This isn't anything I would have voluntarily signed up for, and in fact I'm a lot more hostage than I am volunteer. But strangely, at this moment I feel like I'm a disappointment, and I wish I could do better for them.

"You've already been a help to us, Ana," Steve says gently. "Just do whatever you can. If the opportunity presents itself again, ask questions. Find out anything about your father's existence in the other worlds. What he's doing. The other girls may know something, and anything they tell you could potentially help us, even if it doesn't seem important to you. Can you do that?" he asks.

I nod. "How will I get in touch with you?"

"We'll be in touch," Jane says. "Paul will never be far from your side."

CHAPTER 23

When I wake the next morning, my prospects seem bleak. Klara has explained things about my father's wickedness that seem more fanciful than the dark fairytales Victor hungers for. But I don't doubt her word. I only have to think of the beautiful Tanya who lives in a castle of ice to know she speaks the truth. Victor and Kotehok were sent outside to play while she spoke frankly, their small faces appearing at regular intervals, pressed against a window frosted with their breath. But now Victor has been sent to the rail station to purchase a ticket for me. I'll be put on a train to Hungary where Klara's mother will hide and care for me until Klara and the children can safely join us. I've never been out of the house on my own before, and now I'm about to embark on a journey that will take most of one day and pass through four different countries.

"You've never had a moment of peace in your short life, have you?" Klara's chair is pulled up next to mine, and little Kotehok sits in her lap with one arm slung around her mother's neck. I'm wearing my own clothes again, which have been cleaned and dried. I had an uneasy

TANYA

night, punctuated only by a few feverish hours of sleep, but Klara promises me I'll sleep on the train. I don't believe I will. "All the different towns and countries your mother fled to, but she was always right here in my heart." Klara presses her flat palm to her chest, and Kotehok puts her small hand on top of her mother's as though adding her own dose of love. "Your mother, God rest her soul, knew this day would come, as certain as a person could ever be, but she wanted to give you time. Give you a chance to grow into a woman."

"You were her friend." The thought of my mother having a real friend is surprising. I never imagined her beyond the bitter woman who showed up at the end of each work day, riddled with resentment for life. But to have a friend like Klara . . . that means something.

"Her *sister*," Klara rests her hand on mine. Her brows dip to cast shadows over her twinkling eyes, like a cloud passing over the sun. "Your grandfather, Mr. Andropov, imposed himself on my mother when she was employed as his maid. I know this is difficult for you to hear, Tanya. It was very difficult for me to hear, too, when my mother first told me. She was young and felt she had nowhere to go. In those times she had few options and no recourse against her employer. And although it happened only once, she found herself with child. Mr. Andropov was not a good man, but your grandmother forgave him and kept my mother on as the housekeeper, although many others would have thrown both of us out on the street. She didn't. Instead, she raised your mother and me as sisters. She was a decent enough woman, and she could have treated us much worse."

"Why didn't my—"

"Why didn't your mother tell you about me? When she escaped from your father, I accepted money from him to find her and bring her home. I thought he loved you and your mother was emotionally disturbed by the sudden loss of her parents. I didn't believe the things she'd said about your father. I thought I was doing the right thing, but all along, I was betraying my sister." A tear rolls down Klara's cheek and she wipes it away with her sleeve. "Thank God I didn't find her until after your aunt Irina told me the truth. When I finally managed to get word to your mother and admit what I'd done, she wrote back, saying I was dead to her forever, but I didn't give up. After years of searching, I finally found you right here in Nordhaven. I sent Victor to your house when I knew your mother was gone. I clung to the hope of reconciliation, but I knew if I could find you, it was only a matter of time before your father's people found you too. I confronted your mother one day after work, but she refused to speak to me. And now I live with regrets." She buries her face in one hand and Kotehok runs tiny fingers through her mother's hair.

I think of the motorcycle droning like a hornet through gaslit streets and wonder when Victor will be home, and when I'll begin my journey.

Victor returns with my ticket. He's seen no motorcycles nor any strangers near his house. Klara has packed a lunch and some additional snacks for my trip. She presses a roll of small-billed Euros into my palm and a cool, dry kiss upon my cheek. I haven't told Klara about the ruby ring and the pearl necklace and earrings. I've left them on the pillow of Victor's bed, where I slept last night. I hope Klara will sell them and come to me quickly once I've arrived safely in Hungary.

"I'm sorry it has to be second-class, Tatyana," she says. "But you'll be noticed less in a crowded car. Remember not to speak to anyone except to present your ticket when the conductor comes by. And, if possible, try not to speak even then. There's no reason to arouse suspicion with your accent."

"I speak badly, I know," I say. "I've had nowhere to practice my accent."

"You speak beautifully, my dear." She hugs me for the fourth or fifth time since we began our goodbyes. "If anyone gives you trouble, find the conductor and ask for help. He'll understand—your German is perfect."

Another hug, another kiss, and then Victor and I are off to the train station.

"I know the back way," he says. "We won't be seen until we arrive, and then I'll wait with you until you get on board."

It's a marvel to me that someone so young can have such a command of his surroundings. Can be so brave and yet compassionate. Victor shows no fear of moving through the streets and back alleys. He isn't alarmed at the sight of a stranger. He's innocent and wise. Vulnerable and strong. Victor's my cousin, which makes me so proud and happy that my heart swells to a size that feels as if it can't be contained.

Impulsively, I reach for his hand and force him to a stop.

"I can't leave without telling you something," I say. I feel tongue-tied and unable to adequately express what I want him to know. What he *must* know if I'm to leave. "You're like Gerda from *The Snow Queen*, and I'm like Kai," I say, and I hope he'll understand. "So much of my life, I felt trapped inside a winter that would never end. But the day you arrived at my door, you brought springtime with you. You brought the sun in your pure heart, like Gerda."

Victor looks up at me, his eyes huge and solemn, and I know in that instant he understands.

"We have to go." He tugs at my hand. "The train arrives soon."

When we arrive at the station, the train has just pulled in. There's no time for anything more than a quick hug and a kiss on the cheek. Victor helps me up the steps and hands me the small bag of food which he's been carrying. Another few words and another quick goodbye. I'm glad I spoke to Victor in private before arriving at the bustling station. I find a seat by the window and look out for him, but he's already gone.

I've been on trains and buses before, many of them, but always with Mother, who decided everything and guided my every move. Now, simply choosing a seat seems like an enormous responsibility. I naturally sit in the one closest to the door where I can see out the window, but perhaps it's not the best choice because it's a rear-facing double seat facing two others. I'd have done better to choose the single forward-facing seats, where there's only one person who might try to engage me in conversation. I look around, but the seats are filling fast, and I don't want to risk losing the one I have. There are other cars in front of me and I know one can walk between cars, even if the train is moving, but I don't want to risk it and the idea frankly frightens me.

There's a woman with her young son who looks to be about Kotehok's age in the seats facing me, and the two seem safe and familiar. The mother is busy trying to keep the child entertained with various electronic devices alien to my world. The boy scrambles from his seat and plugs one end of an electrical cord into an outlet just beneath the seat. The other end is plugged into his device. How much I have to learn about the world this child navigates so easily. The mother looks up at me and smiles apologetically, perhaps thinking I'm bothered by the sounds coming from the box that transfixes him.

I reach inside my pocket to feel for the reassurance of the paper where Klara has recorded the stop immediately before each one where I'll disembark. She's also written the platform number and train number for each leg of my journey. My trip requires two transfers, which causes me great anxiety. In one instance, the platform number isn't available, so Klara explained how to locate the train number and destination on the big board, and then wait until the platform number is posted. If anything goes wrong, and *only* if anything goes wrong, Klara has given me a phone that will connect me with a man in Hungary whom she hasn't named—all I have to do is press and hold the number 5 and tell him who I am. After I've arrived safely at her mother's house, I'm to destroy the phone with a hammer. Klara says it isn't expensive and I should make sure to do this before disposing of it in the trash. All of this seems simple enough, as long as nothing goes wrong.

At the first stop, the mother and her young son get off and a man with a long trench coat takes her place in the window seat opposite mine. He's not old, but already balding and his stomach protrudes over his belt by a few inches. Men in general make me nervous, and this one looks directly at me in a way I find just short of rude. He nods curtly and then pulls a newspaper from his briefcase and begins to read. I look out the window and then toward the aisle—anywhere except at him. From the corner of my eye, I catch him staring at me from time to time. The conductor makes his way down the aisle toward us. His uniform is smart and gives him an air of authority, which is somehow reassuring. A leather pouch is slung around his neck. His manner of walking is somewhat of a waddle, which I suppose prevents him from tipping over into the passengers on either side of him. I reach for my ticket and have it ready in my hand when he pauses at my seat. He looks at it. Looks at me. Gives it back. Then he reaches for the ticket the man is holding out for him. After examining the ticket without any words being exchanged he moves on, and once again I'm left alone with the man.

He's tall and I am too, so our knees are practically touching. I pray he'll get out at the next stop, but that's still thirty minutes away. I don't have anything to read so I have no way to divert my attention from him except to look out the window or close my eyes and pretend I'm asleep. The lady across the aisle suddenly stands and takes the seat beside me, which is somewhat reassuring—at least now I'm not alone with the man in the trench coat. I smile gratefully at her and, although she couldn't possibly know my smile is one of gratitude, she smiles back. I assume the man she was previously seated next to is distasteful in some way, thus explaining her motive for moving across the aisle. To distract myself, I try to imagine what could have caused a confident woman like her to switch seats—bad breath, body odor, flatulence, unwanted advances, a distracting tic. She pulls a paperback novel from her purse and settles in to read. She kicks off her shoes and angles her bare feet into the corner of the empty seat opposite her, closest to the aisle. The man in the trench coat glances at her feet and allows his gaze to slide up to her lap. I'm frankly a bit shocked at her brazenness. I pull Mother's unbuttoned coat tightly around my chest.

The sound of the train gliding over the tracks is soothing and somewhat hypnotic, and I struggle to stay alert. The man's newspaper is in his lap and his head dangles forward, chin resting on his chest. Even the lady next to me has her hand inside the book, marking the spot where she's left off. Her gaze is unfocused and drifting.

Unexpectedly, the train jerks sideways and a colossal wall of light replaces the window to my left. My muscles go rigid, starting with the smallest ones in my hands and feet, then moving like a wave to encompass my entire body. My neck snaps back and I feel my eyes roll into my head until all is black. Once I can see again, it happens slowly until I'm observing a brightly lit room with pale-green walls. Before me is the girl I've come to think of as my better self. Her head is shaved but I know it's her. She's laid out on a metal table, arms and legs secured by leather straps. Bags of clear liquids hanging from poles connect to her arms through needles and tubes. Wires connect her chest and bare scalp to computer screens that are constantly shuffling numbers and graphs. She looks like an angel, clothed in a white gown. Four adults surround the table, one bent so close to her face he seems poised to either give or receive a kiss from her. But he's not. His fingers are lifting her closed eyelid, a tiny point of light beams from a tube in his hand and is aimed straight into her unresponsive eye.

Is she dead?

My mouth opens wide as if to scream but I make no sound. I want to get to her, to help her, but a clear membrane blocks my entry into the room. Nobody looks at me. Nobody can see me. Apparently, nobody can even hear me. And then there's a sudden explosive flash, and I fall forward into the green room. Everyone turns. The girl opens her eyes and finds me. She looks through me, a tale of horror scrawled across her face. With no hair on her head, her dark eyes seem enormous.

Watch out for that man! she screams. *Get away from him!*

I tumble backward into the train, with all its accompanying sounds. When I open my eyes, my seatmates are leaning over me. Across the aisle, I see necks craned in my direction, some passengers are on their feet trying to see what the commotion is about. Everyone is trying to get a good look at the strange girl.

"Are you okay?" the woman asks. Her book has fallen on the ground. Her hand is on the sleeve of my coat.

The man in the trench coat sets his newspaper on the empty seat beside him and leans forward. "I think she's had a seizure," he says, and I press against the back of my seat to put as much distance as possible between me and him.

The woman pats me on the back, "You're okay," she says soothingly. "It's okay."

But it's not okay. The girl, the other Tanya. She saw this man and told me to be careful of him. She must know he's one of them, like the man who killed my mother. He's been sent by my father to capture me and I have to get away, but how? I rise from my seat, but he pulls me back down. "Don't stand," he says firmly. "Rest first." He hands me a bottle of water, but I swat it away and it lands on the ground and rolls under my seat.

"Leave me alone." I want to back into the aisle, but the woman is resting her legs on the seat opposite again, and she's blocking my exit.

"Leave her," the woman says sharply to the man in the trench coat. "Can't you see the girl is frightened and you're making it worse?"

"She shouldn't stand up right now," he mumbles. "That's all I'm saying."

Someone must have alerted the conductor because he's rushing down the aisle, a worried look on his face. A few rows ahead, a finger points my way—one of the concerned faces perched on top of a craned neck. Once the conductor reaches us, the woman lowers her legs but now the conductor is blocking my exit. This is the worst possible scenario. I've called attention to myself and will be forced to speak. And the man seated only inches away from me is probably trying to kill me.

I remember what Klara told me: *If anyone gives you trouble, find the conductor and ask for help.*

I have no choice and he's here right now, standing in front of me. The train is coming to a stop, so I could get off and run but this isn't my transfer station and the man would get off and follow me. Outrun me. And where would I run to? I don't even recognize the name of the stop.

"Please," I say. "Please help me. I can't be left alone with him." I stare accusingly at the man in the trench coat. I can feel the train beginning to slow in speed as we approach the station.

"What has this man done to you?" the conductor asks.

"What have *I* done? Bloody hell," the man exclaims indignantly. "I've done nothing except try to be a good Samaritan. This girl is sick and needs help."

The conductor turns to look at me and repeats his question. "What has he done?"

"He wants to kill me," I say. "His friend has already killed my mother."

At this the man stands to his full height, which is imposing and intimidating. "I'm not going to sit here and listen to these outrageous accusations," he says. "Let me pass.

This is my stop." He picks up his briefcase and stuffs the newspaper inside.

"Your identification, please," the conductor says to the man. "Yours too," he says to me.

Now I'm done for. My identification is back at my house in Nordhaven, where my mother's dead body is most likely still lying undiscovered in a gruesome dance of death with her murderer.

"Nobody's done anything," the woman says. "Can't we let calmer heads prevail? I've been sitting here the entire time and seen no evidence of wrongdoing, so why not let the gentleman get off at his stop. The girl has obviously suffered a minor seizure and will be thinking more clearly once she's had a chance to collect herself."

If the man gets off at this station, I've misjudged him. Perhaps the other Tanya can't be completely trusted.

The man in the trench coat passes his ID card to the conductor. "Yours too, please, miss," the conductor says to me. The train lurches to a stop and the conductor widens his stance to keep from falling forward. Passengers begin to mill toward the doors at either end of the car and I merit a good look as they pass, but then they're on their way. This will be a good story to tell when they get home tonight. For me, it's anything but a good story.

"This is ridiculous," the woman says. "You're traumatizing a child who's already been traumatized. You're behaving like a bully."

"Madam," the conductor flashes her a warning look.

"Either take your seat or disembark. You're hindering the performance of an official—"

The man across the aisle gets up and stands behind the conductor. He's slender with a brush cut of iron-gray hair and a startling thin, black moustache in contrast. He's the man who was seated next to the woman before she changed her seat. "Step away," he says softly with a distinct Russian accent. "Do what the lady says, and no one will get hurt." When I hear his Russian accent, I wonder why I didn't pick up on the faint trace of it in the woman's voice until just now.

The man in the trench coat falls down on his seat, his face a ghastly pale shade. He's seen something I haven't seen, and he holds his hands up, like in the cowboy movies—only not straight up in the air, just a little above his shoulders. Now the conductor is doing the same thing and I glimpse a flash of steel in the Russian man's hand buried between the shoulder blades of the conductor's blue woolen jacket. The doors hiss open and passengers stream out, unaware of what's playing out right behind them.

"Let's all leave together," the Russian says. "Nice and easy. *You* . . . stay in your seat until the next stop." The man in the trench coat nods grimly.

Then with one hard blow across the head with the butt of the pistol, the conductor is knocked unconscious. The woman pushes him onto the seat I've just vacated. The man in the trench coat takes in a sharp breath and closes his eyes, as if he's feeling the blow of the gun on his own skull. He sits perfectly still, his hands still raised and visibly trembling.

"Let's go, Tatyana," the woman says, and we move as

one toward the exit, the Russian man on one side of me, the woman on the other, the gun jabbed against my ribs.

CHAPTER 24

Igor and I don't speak for the entire two-hour journey back to my home in Moscow. At this point, what would we even have to say to each other? The minute he pulls up to our house, I get out before he's had a chance to open my door. I rush up the stairs to my room, where the bedroom door has been removed. My desktop computer is missing from my desk. I still have my laptop in the suitcase Igor allowed me to pack, under his supervision, before we left the countryside. I power it up but there's no Wi-Fi connection.

I charge downstairs and follow the murmur of voices to the private sitting area where Papa prefers to relax. He has company—my Uncle Vadim, although he's a longtime associate of Papa's and not an uncle by blood. They each have a snifter of brandy close at hand. Uncle Vadim is raising his to his lips. The mismatch of color between his gray hair and black moustache always used to put a smile on my face. Now nothing will put a smile on my face, and I can't even bring myself to acknowledge his presence.

"The Wi-Fi is down," I say and then turn

TATYANA

on my heel and walk out of the room in spite of my father's voice calling after me to come say hello to Uncle Vadim.

Back in my room, I retrieve my cell phone from my purse. There's no cell phone service. Nothing. I have nowhere to go and nothing I can do to immediately change my circumstances. I want to scream but am aware enough to realize I must harness all my available resources—both emotional and physical. I must come up with a plan, but I don't know where to begin. I lie back on my bed in a room with absolutely no privacy. I'm in a room with a missing door. I have a father with a missing heart. The only person who feels true, honest, and safe is the missing girl, but I don't know how to find her.

I slept so poorly the night before that I fall asleep against my will. When I wake, my father is sitting on the side of my bed with his back turned to me. The room is dark, but I have no idea what time it is, and I don't want to look at the clock for fear of alerting Papa that I'm awake. But he doesn't need alerting, he's sensed it somehow.

"You betrayed my trust, Tatyana. That's why I've done the things I have. If I can't trust you, then you must be monitored, which means the door will stay off and you'll have no access to the internet or use of your phone."

"Who would I call?" I slide back so I can lean against the headboard of my bed. I don't attempt to turn on a light because the darkness fits perfectly with my reality, and I don't want to look at my father's face. "You've made sure

I have no friends. The only people I know besides you and Tyotya are the servants you pay and the minions who worship your scientific achievements. If they only knew the truth."

"That's uncalled for," he says, and I wonder if he truly feels indignant about what I've just said. How could he? How has he managed to alter the truth of the facts until they make perfect moral sense to him? But maybe we all do the same in our own way—his facts are just so much more heinous than most.

"Your Uncle Vadim and I were just discussing your . . . case," he says.

"He's not my uncle. He's just another one of your sycophants."

There's a cloud cover tonight so I can't see the moon. Not even a star. I would like to see one of the heavenly bodies just now. In this way, at least, I could connect to the girl—the other Tatyana. She would look at the same sky, wouldn't she? Or is her sky different from mine?

"I wish you would make an effort, Tatyana. Try to reach out to the others . . . while you can."

While I can? Why does Papa sound so defeated?

"Don't you think I would if I could? If only to get away from you?" His shoulders heave and a deep sigh escapes from his lips. His back is still turned, as if shame won't allow him to face me, but I know it's not that. I know it's more likely I repulse him. His creation. I'm the monster to his Dr. Frankenstein. "Maybe you did a bad job of designing me," I say, because I think that will hurt him the most.

But if it does hurt him he doesn't let on. "As I said, Vadim and I were going over your DNA test results from the time you were born to the present day."

"All that blood and spit you stole from me," I interrupt. "All those years I thought you were trying to find a cure, when in fact you were looking for a way to make it worse."

"You don't know what this has cost me. My reputation . . . everything I lived for."

"I know about S.P.I.T.," I interrupt. "I know everything. How Tyotya was the surrogate who carried me. I suppose she knows everything too. And Vadim. Who else? They all must know. All these people who come to visit you and worship at your fallen alter. I know how Mother found out what you did to me and tried to send me to America, but you had her killed, along with my grandparents."

"That was never meant to be!" My father's voice explodes like a gunshot in the still of night. I've never seen emotion from him like this, and I wonder if the servants can hear since I no longer have a door. He quickly lowers his voice. "That was never supposed to happen. I had word from Igor who had driven your mother to our country house—"

"You mean the Andropovs' house," I say. "I know that too."

"The Andropovs," Papa says as though trying to rid himself of a bitter taste. "Your grandparents never allowed me to set foot in their home because I didn't come from a background they'd envisioned for their daughter. None of my accomplishments made any difference to them, not even my wealth. So when Igor overheard them making plans to leave and take your mother with them, I asked him to disable the car to prevent them from leaving until I got there, until I could reason with your mother. Beg her. Do whatever it took to make her stay and love me the way she'd promised to love me."

"So Igor killed my mother, then, with your permission. And, how was she supposed to love you after what you did to me? Did you have a way to design her love the same way you designed me?"

"It was a terrible, tragic mistake," Papa says. "The car started when it shouldn't have. There wasn't any brake fluid." He sobs into his open palms and then pulls a cloth handkerchief from his pocket and wipes away tears. "I loved your mother," he says. "More than anything."

"Not more than yourself," I say. "You weren't poor, and you didn't do the in vitro fertilization in a government lab because it was free. That was all a lie. You did it because of S.P.I.T. And you're still trying to keep S.P.I.T. going because your legacy means more to you than I do."

Maybe I'm still clinging to a shred of hope that Papa will deny this, but he doesn't. He paces silently around my room in thought, stopping at the window, where the curtains have yet to be drawn. He stares into the darkness. Thick, gray clouds part for just a moment, and the moon I was hoping to see is there, and then it's not. I hope Klara and Maria are far away in Hungary before Papa thinks to ask how I've come to learn so much.

Maybe there's a better life for me in another world. In *her* world. Maybe I can find more freedom, a better family. Friends. At least one friend . . . the girl, the other me. Can

I live in her world? Can we exist at the same time? All I know is that what I have now is no life at all. Better to be dead than live like one of the rats in my father's laboratory.

"Papa," I say, resigned. "I don't believe anything you say anymore. But I want what you want, which is to be reunited with the other Tatyana. I only know one, though you say there are three. So tell me what I need to do to get there and I'll do it. Tell me what you and Vadim have concluded."

"Yes," he says turning away from the window. "Yes, I suppose it's true we want the same thing. Perhaps for different reasons, but what does it matter now? All that matters is the science. The science and the possibilities."

Papa and I have become unlikely allies. If there's a way to escape from my world and help my other self, I'm ready to take that chance.

"For the past two days, Vadim and I have gone over the results of years of testing, and we've both come to the same conclusion, which is at once troubling and motivating."

"Which is?"

"The breakthroughs you've recently experienced, I attributed to your finally reaching physical maturity, and that seems to be the case. But what I'd hoped was the beginning now appears to be the end. We think your DNA is repairing itself, and during this process, there have been opportunities which most likely will vanish altogether once it's complete."

I bite down hard on my lower lip without being aware I'm doing it until I taste blood. My body is healing. This is what I've always wanted, isn't it? But once my body has completely repaired itself, I'll never be free of this life—Papa.

Tyotya. Igor. Stories of my mother. No one will be left who understands except people I can never trust. If my body heals and Papa no longer needs me, how could I continue to live with him? And yet I don't know how to live without him—he's seen to that. I am a freak. An oddity. The girl no one could possibly understand. Even Klara and Maria are lost to me forever. With time running out, only with my father's help do I have any hope of escaping my prison.

"Why is this happening?"

"No matter what men do, nature will always insist on having the last word. The only thing imperfect about nature is her perfection." Papa says this sadly, as if it were something to be mourned instead of rejoiced.

Isn't it wonderful, I should cry out in happiness. But I don't. I'm as sorry as Papa is.

"Your superior from when you began the project before I was born . . . It was Vadim, wasn't it? Not someone who died, like you claimed."

All pretense is gone between us and Papa nods his head to confirm. "What began as a small, top-secret government project has evolved into an international conglomerate of interested investors."

"And Tyotya? She carried me in her womb? Does she know everything now? Did she know back then?" I need an answer to my question because Irina is my last hope for this world.

"I did, Tanyusha." Irina has been hovering in the open doorway for how long, I'm not sure. "Your father rescued me from our father's beatings and abuse. He got me into medical school when no one else believed I had what it took. He's always taken care of me." Her voice trembles with emotion. "Everything we've done since we escaped our wretched childhood, we've done together, and I would never betray your father. Never."

They say the truth will set you free, and now it has. Now I know for certain that nothing is left in this life for me. Not even Irina.

"When do we start?" I ask. "What do you need from me?"

Once we've finished talking and Papa and Irina have left me alone, Igor appears carrying the door to my bedroom and wearing a carpenter's belt of tools strapped around his waist. Ten minutes later I have a door again, and I lock it uselessly against uncertainty. They know I won't leave—our fates are too intertwined. They know I have nowhere else to go.

For reasons Papa can't explain, one of the genetic modifications differs greatly from the others, which is the reason I only have access to one Tatyana instead of three. Perhaps the others are functional in different worlds, but not mine. The one pathway that exists for me is closing every day as it repairs itself. Papa sees evidence of it when he looks through the electron microscope.

An induced coma followed by drilling a tiny hole in my skull through which an electrode is inserted isn't something most people would volunteer for . . . but I have. There was no guarantee of success, but with time running out there was no question I'd take the risk. The electrode was inserted to stimulate the area of my brain most likely to align with the genetic alteration. I literally have put myself in Papa and Vadim's hands, hoping their brilliance will set me free.

When Papa said I'd be put into an induced coma, I imagined waking up when everything was over and being presented with the facts: success or failure, although I wasn't sure what either one would look like. But this isn't the case. Somehow, I can hear everything, feel everything, see everything. Monitors that beep in time with my heart. The jagged cold of drip, drip, drip as the IV bag runs into my veins. Murmured voices muffled by surgical masks. Focused. Deliberate. Concerned? Blood swooshing up my throat, roaring when it passes my ears. And then a jolt like a lightning bolt through my skull. A black moment followed by another jolt. It's like the opening tunnel of my seizures but multiplied exponentially.

"This level of brain wave activity can't possibly be maintained." It's Vadim's voice. "I recommend we stop immediately. We need to bring her vitals down now," he says. "*Now!*" he repeats, this time forcefully. I want to scream out against his decision, but I'm powerless to speak.

"We proceed," Papa says calmly, and I've never been so grateful to him as I am right now.

"She may not survive it," Vadim says. "And if she does, who knows with what damage in the long term."

There is no long term, I think.

"There is no long term," Papa says.

Thank you, Papa.

A third jolt, which feels like the end. But then the other

Tatyana tumbles through the membrane separating our worlds—a membrane imperceptible but impenetrable in the past has now been breached, and with it comes the loss of my sense of self, my sense of individuality. An overpowering urge connects me to her so undeniably, I can't imagine life on my own hereafter. Death would be preferable.

She sees me as clearly as I see her. She's traveling by train with a man and a woman who I know aren't her parents. Who are these people, and why is she with them? Where is she going?

Tatyana, my soulmate and sister in the truest sense, don't be frightened by what you see before you. This horrifying scene . . . the surgical table . . . the bright lights . . . my head shaved to the bare skin of my scalp. It's all so I can come to you. Please be brave and wait for me. Please.

Across the aisle, I spy a man with his nose buried in a book. It's only when his head angles up and looks in my direction that I recognize Uncle Vadim. And it's only then I know Tatyana is headed for disaster, regardless of where her train is going.

I scream.

"It worked," I say once they've brought me out of the induced coma. "I saw her as clear as day and I'm certain she saw me."

Papa is thrilled as I've never before seen him. "Tell me

everything," he says. Vadim is there and Tyotya Irina too. Only their eyes are visible above their surgical masks. There's another doctor assisting, but I don't know her well. She dims the lights to reduce the blinding glare in my face.

"The girl—"

"The same girl?" Papa asks.

"Yes, the same girl. She was on a train."

"A train? Going where?"

Uncle Vadim places a gloved hand on Papa's sleeve. "Let her speak," he says softly.

"I don't know where she was going, but—"

"Did she see you?" Papa, unable to control himself.

"She saw me. Yes, I'm sure."

"Did she speak to you?"

"No, no . . . I think she was surprised. She seemed to be frightened when she saw me."

"As she would be, quite naturally," Tyotya says.

"She was with a man and a woman, but I didn't recognize them."

"Tatyana," Vadim says. "You called out a warning to her. You said, *Get away from that man.*"

"I did?" Although I know perfectly well that I did.

"What man were you talking about?" he asks.

"I . . . I don't know. I don't remember. Perhaps the man who was with her, although I'd never seen him before."

My skull throbs where the flap of scalp has been sutured to protect the hole in my head. I want to sit up, but my restraints are still on and I know enough to realize that sitting up wouldn't be wise at this time. I feel nauseous and dizzy. Even the dim lights are disorienting, as are the faces peering down at me.

"It's not important," Papa says. "The important thing is our success. We've achieved what no one ever thought possible. We've had our doubters and our detractors. But in time, we'll learn how to make the modifications permanent, and this procedure will one day be as commonplace as routine surgery. And to think you're a part of history, Tanyusha! Every one of us here today has witnessed a miracle, and we can all hold our heads up and be proud of what we've accomplished at last."

But Uncle Vadim's eyes narrow in suspicion, and I suspect he believes I'm holding something back. I'll never tell him the truth of what I saw. I won't tell him I now know I can pass into Tatyana's world as easily as she can pass into mine. I did it for the briefest moment before they brought me out of the coma. I stood behind the crowd that had gathered, all eyes on Tatyana. I saw the woman seated next to her, expressive brown eyes like the doctor who's assisting Papa right now. I saw Uncle Vadim reach into his jacket and curl his fingers around the butt of a gun. Next time I'll make my move before they have a chance to call me back.

If a tree falls in the forest and no one is there to see or hear it, has it really fallen? If I leave this world behind, will it cease to exist? If I enter the other Tatyana's world, will one of us have to die?

"When can I go again?" I ask, knowing time isn't on my side.

"You need to recover," Tyotya says. "You can't withstand the strain too soon, if at all."

"Do you . . . would you like to go again, Tatyana?" Papa asks hesitantly. "Irina is correct; it would be extremely dangerous for you."

"I'm ready to go," I say. "As soon as possible."

Papa's eyes light up. They radiate something that, if I didn't know any better, I would mistake for love.

CHAPTER 25

T
A
T
I

Ana has news. Life-changing news. Mind-bending news. She fills me in on everything that's happened since I last saw her. Kidnapped like in a spy movie. I'd been worried sick about her since our last visit when she was in a state of semi-consciousness. Thrown in the back of a van and then asked to help the government by getting information to stop her father—*our* birth father—who turns out to be an evil scientist from, of all places, Russia. In the meantime, her *real* father is getting sicker by the day and is no longer considered a candidate for a heart transplant. He'd never survive the surgery, the doctors say. I can't stand seeing Ana like this, not to mention hearing about Dad's dire condition. I want to be there for her in any way I can.

"But we're Hungarian," I say. "At least our mother was. Olga—"

"Listen to me, Tati," she says. "Our birth mother wasn't Hungarian, she's Russian. I know her . . . I've known her for a while without realizing who she was. She's a doctor at the hospital where my dad's being treated. And the woman you think was your mother, Klara . . . she was our birth mother's best friend. They were raised together as sisters and most likely Klara was trying to get you away from our father when she was killed."

"Hang on, back up." It's like a truck just pulled up and dumped a load of marbles on my driveway. Out of control information overload. "Our birth mother . . . who is she and how do you know her?"

Ana tells me about our birth mother being a doctor and escaping to Poland where she changed her identity and then waited years before she could get a visa to come to the US. My heart kind of hurts to think about what it would be like to have Mom and also to have a birth mother who loved me enough to make all those sacrifices for me. What would it be like to know that the person who gave birth to me was still alive and wanted to be a part of my life?

"Maybe our birth mother is out there somewhere in *my* world watching over *me*," I say.

"Tati," she picks up my hand and holds it between her own, and I realize this is the first time we've ever touched. My hand gets warm and then hot and it tingles like when your foot falls asleep. I look down at our hands and they're a blur, like they're trying to melt into each other. We both pull away quickly. "Woah!" Ana says. "What just happened?"

"Dunno," I say. "But maybe we should keep hands to ourselves." I rub my hands briskly to bring back the feeling.

"Our birth mother probably never survived in your world, Tati. Olga told you Klara was depressed in your world be-cause her best friend died? That best friend was most likely our birth mom. And Klara was probably trying to get you away from our father."

It's a gut punch to find your birth mother and then lose her within the space of two minutes. "Okay, and our birth father—the mad evil genius—what's his problem? What did he do?"

"Get ready, because this is the hardest part," Ana says, and the dark circles under her eyes tell me everything's been the hardest part for her lately. "He made us this way, Tati." She explains the me-zures and their significance. How our father used us as guinea pigs in the name of science, but when big money came pouring in, he sold our souls to the highest bidder for the most disgusting of nefarious purposes. Straight out of an evil genius movie—if only it were.

Just hearing this makes me want to get back to Mom and Dad and Priya. To love and be loved by the people who matter. To count my multitude of blessings. I feel the tunnel materializing as if, like a genie, my wish is its command.

"It literally makes me sick to my stomach to think that half my genes come from a man who would sell his soul for a few bucks."

"It probably won't make you feel any better, but our birth mom—Dr. Sokol is her name in my world—she says our birth father's a megalomaniac. He's not in it for the money, he's in it for the glory. To feed his own delusions of grandeur."

I feel the warmth of the tunnel. Its approaching glow.

"You're right, it doesn't make me feel better. In fact, it makes me feel worse."

"Tati," Ana says. "We're not condemned by our DNA. We can choose our own paths, and I want to stop our birth father if I can. I think Dad would want me to. I think he'd be proud of me. But I need to get to the Tatiana I saw in the cafeteria that day. But I don't know how."

I want to help Ana do that, but how do you explain to someone how to breathe? How to sleep? I don't know why I can only access Ana, and Ana can see a different version of us that I can't see. Her bravery makes me sad because of where it might lead. I don't want to lose her, but how can I ask her not to do what she's determined to do?

It's time for me to go home. "Did you ever see *The Wizard of Oz*?" I ask.

"Of course, a million times. It's one of my favorite movies."

I should have known because it's one of my favorite movies too.

"You know how Dorothy always had it in her to go home? I can't explain it, but once you stop fighting it, you'll realize it was always within your power."

She looks at me helplessly as if I've just handed her an unsolvable riddle, and it breaks my heart. She reaches out for me but then withdraws her hand, perhaps remembering our earlier physical encounter. "I'll tell you our birth father's name," she says, "so you can ask Olga to find out where he is in your world. You need to protect yourself from him."

She speaks his name just before the tunnel pulls me away. The journey back through the tunnel is less pleasurable and more difficult than in the past. When I arrive home, I'm physically exhausted and emotionally drained.

Something is changing.

CHAPTER 26

ANA

My life is basically a sad version of Tati's. Dad is dying. I don't have anyone to love the way Tati and Priya love each other. It's true I have Dr. Sokol in my life, but when she *wasn't* there I didn't miss her because you don't miss what you don't know. And if it wasn't for Dr. Sokol, my father would never know where I was, and I wouldn't need Paul's constant protection. On the other hand, if it wasn't for Dr. Sokol's selflessness seventeen years ago, I'd still be in Russia under my birth father's control.

There have been unexpected gifts, mainly the friendship of Anthony and Priya, who are always there for me these days when I get caught up in a late-night ugly-cry session. I can always count on one or the other to come through with class notes for all the school days I'm missing or take me to the hospital whenever Mom's already there with the car. I know I could count on Paul for a ride because he's always around, but I prefer to live my life pretending as much as possible that he doesn't exist.

Armed with our birth father's name, Olga comes through once again for Tati, delivering the news of our birth father's fate in Tati's world. After losing his wife and daughter, he took to drinking too much and wandering the streets alone at night talking to himself. Everyone knew him as the mad but brilliant and tormented scientist. People were afraid of him, and if they saw him coming, they gave him a wide berth. One morning, after a night of heavy drinking, he was found face down on the street, his nose buried in a rain-filled pothole where he'd face-planted and knocked himself out. He drowned in water no more than two inches deep, a puddle that would have evaporated by that afternoon. I expect that if he hadn't devolved into alcoholism, he might have tracked down Tati one day, just as he's tracked me down in my world.

Tati's safe, thank God. Nobody connected with our birth father's work knows where she went, and the Hungarian woman, Maria, made sure to cover Tati's tracks by claiming her as Klara's child on the police report. Even if anyone succeeded in tracking her down, her father is long since dead and S.P.I.T. most likely died with him. Only I'm left as a reminder of Tati's past, and soon that might not even be true. Tati says it's been harder for her to get to me. Who knows what's happening to us?

So Tati's safe, but the other me is in danger. Since the day in the cafeteria, I've seen her only one time, in the mirror as I was brushing my hair. She was climbing the steps to a small jet plane. There was a woman in front of her and a man close behind her. He had gray hair and a strange small, black moustache. When she got to the top of the stairs, just before entering the plane, she turned around and looked right at me before the man nudged her inside. In a multiverse of infinite lives, why do I care so much about this version of me?

Because I know her, and we care most about what we know most about.

Anthony's face pops up on the screen of my ringing phone. I've been home from school long enough to grab a snack and change into more comfortable shoes.

"'Sup?" he says. "Just calling to see if you need a ride to see your dad. Oh, and also my mom made dinner for you guys. I was going to bring it by anyway, so it's no problem to take you to the hospital."

One thing I've learned from everything that's happened: two really good friends are all anyone needs. It's easy to descend into self-pity, and I can't deny I've given in to it. I just try to hold my head above water by remembering the blessings I do have.

"That'd be great," I say. "Honestly, I owe you so much I don't think I could ever begin to repay you."

"Shush!" he says. "When your dad's all better and home again, maybe just let me win a few games off of you next time you come over."

I know Dad won't ever be better, but I let it go.

"Hope you like homemade tamales," he says.

I do.

I have twenty minutes before Anthony will be over, so I text Mom to let her know I'll be there soon. I flop down on my bed, thinking I'll close my eyes for a few minutes, but I'm so swamped with thoughts, no way is a nap happening. The me-zures have been few and far between lately, which is surprising considering all that's been going on in my life, although there never has been a link to stress. There never was a link to anything—just scary randomness. The tunnel I used to see is basically gone, or at least it's been a while since I've seen it. I think about what Tati said about letting go and not fighting it, but it's not even there anymore as a tantalizing possibility. But the times I've seen the other Tatiana have been different from Tati's visits. Those times I was able to look into her world. In the cafeteria, I was actually a part of it. Thinking about the last glimpse I had of her, I get out of bed and stand before the mirror where I saw her boarding the plane.

If you're there, I think, *come to me now.*

I close my eyes and hold on to the edge of my dresser, breathing deeply and methodically. I glance at the clock, which shows 4:03 p.m. Good. I still have some time before Anthony comes.

Come to me.

In my mind, I say it over and over like a mantra until an image of her face replaces my words. I'm in a zone. Finally, I open my eyes and her face is peering back at me. I close my eyes to make sure I'm not in some kind of meditative trance and then I open them again. She's still there, staring back at me through the mirror, and I swear my heart nearly stops.

I raise my hand to touch the mirror and she raises hers to touch back. We're in such perfect unison that for a second, I think I'm looking at my mirror image. But her clothes and hair are nothing like mine. Even her skin tone is nothing like mine—paler, slightly blotchy, she's a little broken out. I raise my other hand and so does she, and now I feel her warmth and nearness and know it's within my reach. It's what I want, isn't it? I can go to her, but if I go, will I find my way back? But it isn't a choice, so I push harder against the mirror until the cool, hard surface bows under the pressure of my hands. It becomes pliant, supple, almost rubbery. I push harder until I plunge through to the other side.

I'm here but, where am I? In a room, an office. It's dark, lit only by a desk lamp. The green glass lamp shade casts an eerie pall over the windowless room. The desk is cluttered with papers, books—a language I don't recognize in an alphabet I don't recognize. The mirror girl is here, standing close to me. Another girl sits on the floor, leaning against the wall. Her head is completely shaved, and an angry red circle stands out in contrast to the whiteness of her scalp. It looks disturbingly like a hole, but I don't look too closely. She's wearing a white gown, like the hospital kind that ties in the back. She stares at me and I know she's me. The three of us take each other in for a minute before I speak.

"I'm Ana," I say.

"Tanya," says the mirror girl me.

The girl on the floor pulls her knees to her chest and wraps her arms around her legs. She's shivering. "Tatyana," she says.

Then another few seconds of silence while we all come to terms with what's in front of us.

"You speak English?" Tanya asks. Her accent is very thick.

"Yes, I'm American. And you?"

"Russian," she says and points to Tatyana. "Russian also." Tatyana nods and manages a feeble smile.

"Where are we?" I ask. "What is"—I wave my hand around the office—"this place?"

Tanya says something to Tatyana, who replies in Russian. Tanya turns to me.

"This is our father's office," she says. "Tatyana . . . she come to me . . . from her life . . . through that door." She points to the only door, which is shut. "She open the door, which is locked. *Was* locked."

So, the door was locked and since Tatyana was the one to unlock it from the other side, I make the safe assumption that Tanya was previously locked inside.

"Where's our father?" I ask.

"He's a very bad man," Tanya answers. Tatyana asks something in Russian and Tanya answers her.

Tatyana nods in agreement. "Bad man," she says, mimicking Tanya's words to me.

"But, where *is* he?" I ask. I already know he's a bad man.

"Gone, but . . . maybe not for so long," Tanya says.

"Then we have to get out of here," I say. "Before he comes back."

Tatyana asks Tanya something and Tanya answers. Then Tatyana slowly lifts herself up from a sitting position, keeping her hands on the wall to steady herself. When she teeters to one side, Tanya and I rush over to lend support, each of us holding on to one of her arms. I feel that same heat and tingling that happened before, with Tati. Our hands blur where they touch Tatyana's body. Tanya and I pull our hands away from her, alarmed by the mingling of our flesh.

"Oh yeah," I say. "Don't do that. No touching." But I can see Tatyana is extremely weak and I still don't know what caused that hole in her head. I don't think she can make it far without help from one of us. "So . . . shall we get out of here?" I point to the door.

Tatyana says something to Tanya who turns to me. "She says there is a man out there. A bad man. Protecting. *Guarding.*"

Oh. I didn't consider that possibility. I look around for a chair that could be used as a barricade under the doorknob and carry it next to the door. Then I turn the knob as quietly as I can and open the door slowly, wincing at a barely audible squeak. When there's just enough space to stick my head out for a peek around, I look down a dimly lit hall in one direction and see nothing but wood-paneled walls and a closed elevator door. I look in the other direction and see a stairwell with a man sitting in a wooden chair at the top of the stairs. His chair is angled away from us. I close the door quickly and quietly, my hands shaking more than I thought possible. Tatyana and Tanya stare at me.

"There's a man out there," I say, stupidly confirming what they already know. I shove the back of the chair under the doorknob, not really knowing what good that could possibly do us, except maybe buy a little time. "What do you know?" I ask and sit down on the chair. These two obviously know a whole hell of a lot more than I do.

Tanya says something to Tatyana who, in turn, speaks for two or three minutes straight. Tanya nods occasionally and I'm dying to know what she's saying. When Tatyana stops I can see just the act of speaking has pushed the limits of her endurance. She holds on to the side of the desk and Tanya and I watch her carefully, but we don't move to touch her.

"Our father has done to us before we were born—"

"I know that," I say. "My mother . . . *our* mother told me what he did." No need to go into the rest of it—Paul and Steve and Jane—when time is running so short.

Tanya raises her eyebrows and says something to Tatyana who raises the ridges of where her eyebrows were before they were shaved off.

"Our mother . . . you know her?" Tanya asks.

I nod my head. "I know her. She's alive in my world."

"And Klara?" she asks.

"Klara," Tatyana says, followed by what I know is a question because her voice comes up at the end. Tanya says something and Tatyana moans, obviously surprised.

"What did you say?" I ask. "About Klara?"

"Our mother's sister," she says. "Our aunt."

"Like a sister," I nod in agreement. I only know about Klara through Tati.

"No. *Sister*. Real sister."

What?

And then Tatyana says something that generates the same amount of surprise in Tanya's eyes. Perhaps even more.

"What?" I say, knowing by Tanya's reaction it's something big. *Really* big. "What did she say?"

"She says our DNA, our genes, are . . . fixing themselves. Our father allowed to visit . . . for four of us. Here we are, three of us, but there is another somewhere. Soon, we won't see." She points from Tatyana to me to her. "We won't see the other," she concludes.

This explains Tati's increasing difficulty passing through the tunnel. But how long can the three of us coexist in the same world?

I nod. "I've seen the other. Her name is Tati and she lives in America. We're kind of . . . friends."

Tanya speaks to Tatyana, whose eyes open wide, and she murmurs in approval. "Good," she says in thickly accented English.

What do we do now? Jane and Steve told me to get information to stop our father. Proof of what he's up to. There must be something in this office, but could I even take it back with me? I can't read Russian, and even if I could, I doubt I'd understand scientific details enough to commit them to memory.

Tatyana says something to Tanya and motions toward the door.

"What did she say?"

"She says we must, how you say . . . murder . . . *kill* the man outside. Bad man."

Wha-what?!

"Umm, I don't know if I can do that," I say.

"You . . . No, it's not necessary. You talk to the bad man. I will kill."

And then I remember she did at least try to kill the guy in the cafeteria. Or did I kill him after she passed me the knife? In any case, Tatyana says something, and I turn to Tanya for the translation.

"She says hurry. Laboratory is downstairs."

"Why are we going to the laboratory?" I ask. "Shouldn't we try to get out of this place and get some help?" But my question sounds dumb even to me. How would the three of us be able to escape anywhere? If I leave this office, will I ever make it back to my world? These girls seem to know what they're doing, so I figure I'd better stick with them, especially since my question is ignored.

Tatyana shuffles to the corner of the office as though she's been here many times before, which I suppose she has. Each step she takes registers as pain on her face. She grasps a wooden club leaning against the wall. It's ornately carved and looks heavy like a bat, maybe some type of a weapon, but Tatyana uses it to support her weight. She maneuvers toward the door and I'm glad to see she moves more easily while leaning on it. Tanya removes the chair and Tatyana gives her the club. It's magnificent now that I can see it close up.

"What is that?" I ask.

"She says our father receive this gift from very important man. He brings back from trip to thank you . . . thank *him*."

"Beautiful," I say as she quietly pulls the door open.

"You go say hello," Tanya says. "To bad man. Go fast." And she kind of nudges, kind of shoves me out the door.

I'm out there bare and it dawns on me that she wants me to distract him. Then it further dawns on me that I might just confuse him because of the similarity in our looks. And furthermore, he probably won't kill me because I'm pretty sure our father wants me . . . *us* . . . alive. So, in a wide arc, I sprint down the hall on tippy-toes and no shoes until I'm facing him. I shrug my shoulders and give him the goofy grin, and I can literally see his brain working overtime to make sense of the strange and unexpected sight before him. Hopefully, he won't look behind him, which will give Tanya and Tatyana the opportunity to escape without any more foolish talk about killing and murder. I don't mind being the diversion because when I play everything out in my mind, the guy throws me back in the office and locks the door and that's when I say goodbye and go home like Alice through the looking glass. Not much help to Jane and Steve, but at least I can help out Tatyana and Tanya.

Then, just when he rises from his chair to grab me, Tanya runs up behind him. She's holding the club in her hands just as though it was a Louisville Slugger. She takes a swing that would make any MLB player proud and connects with a force and a fury I didn't think possible in her. I hear a sickening *crunch* and the guy falls to the ground. His eyelids flutter briefly and then drift downward, stopping halfway as though he was just about to nod off for a nap. The beautiful club is tinged red with his blood at the point of impact. Tatyana reclaims it as her walking stick. She motions us toward the elevator while I try to pick my jaw up from the ground where it's fallen in astonishment.

It's a quiet and sober ride down to the basement in that rickety elevator. When it lurches to a stop, we follow Tatyana out the door and through a hall, making first a left and then a right until we come to a set of double doors which, I assume, must be the entrance to the laboratory. The three of us enter together and a man in surgical scrubs takes one look at us and his mouth drops open. But Tanya doesn't need the pole anymore because she's holding a gun, which she co-opted from the bad man and is now pointing at this new man. Behind him I see an empty room that looks like a surgical room in a hospital, complete with metal bed, IV poles, all kinds of monitors and big old lights beaming down on the table. It looks like this guy was getting the room ready for someone. Maybe Tanya?

Tanya shoves the gun into his ribs and Tatyana says something in Russian. He leads the way into another room that really does look like a laboratory, and I hope he doesn't try anything. I know Tanya isn't fooling around, so I hope he realizes that too. The walls are lined with cages filled mainly with little white mice, but also some bigger mice that look suspiciously like rats. Tatyana takes her pole and shatters the glass of the largest window. We're in the basement, so there's only a tiny bit of outside world visible just at the top of the window. She starts pulling cages off the shelves and, one by one, she liberates the mice and rats through the hole in the window to the outside world. The man watches on in horror, but Tanya's gun is pointed right at his head, so he doesn't say a word.

Then Tanya and Tatyana say some stuff back and forth

and I'm not sure what my purpose is until Tanya hands me the gun. I keep pointing it at the man even though I can't stand the feel of this thing in my hand. Still, I reason, I'm with Tanya and Tatyana. After all, they're me, aren't they? Me brought up in a decidedly unfriendly and violent world.

"What?" I ask. "What are you guys saying?"

"My father's research," Tanya says. "We take . . . someone will help us. Cure us. Stop our father."

Tatyana seems to know exactly what she's looking for as she pulls out drawers and flips through files, tucking some under her arm, passing others to Tanya, throwing most on the floor. The man, who I now recognize as the man who got on the plane with Tanya, looks positively apoplectic. His jet-black moustache quivers with what I assume is either fear or rage, but it doesn't much matter at this point. After a few minutes of this, Tatyana hollers something at Tanya, who turns to me and says, "We go now." She trades an armful of papers for the gun and I'm grateful to be rid of the vile thing.

I'm so distracted by everything that's happening, I don't see him when he enters the room. But I see the look on Tatyana's face and I follow her gaze to a man standing in the doorway. He's handsome for an older guy. Well dressed. He looks like a man used to being in charge. And he looks unnaturally calm. After glancing at me and Tanya, he makes his move toward Tatyana. For every step he takes toward her, she takes a half-step back. He says her name, almost in disbelief. Almost as if he were expecting her.

Soothingly. Calmly. Lovingly.

I'm looking at my biological father, and he's the very face of evil.

Tanya is still pointing the gun at the man with the moustache but now she slowly moves its barrel in the direction of our father. He doesn't seem to fear the gun. It doesn't distract him in any way or stop his forward motion. He glances first at me and then at Tanya, and the smile he wears is so smug I want to slap him. But he just keeps moving toward Tatyana, who now seems to be in a trance—under the spell of this man, our father. He moves toward her as though she's some kind of miracle he's witnessing.

He murmurs. Soothingly. Calmly. Lovingly.

Without shifting his gaze, his hand motions for Tanya to give him the gun, and for one horrible second I think she's going to do it. If he gets the gun, I have no hope of escape, so I start to back up toward the exit. Nobody seems too interested in me even though I'm holding a pile of what I imagine are very important papers. They must be thinking I'll be the easy one to deal with once Tanya has been disarmed. But Tanya sees what I'm doing and begins to follow, calling out to Tatyana while keeping the gun trained alternately between our father and the man with the moustache. Her voice seems to snap Tatyana out of the trancelike state, and the words that come out of her mouth—well, I have no idea what they are, but I know I wouldn't want to be on the receiving end of them like her father is. Tanya continues to slowly make her way toward me and the exit while Tatyana continues to unleash a fierce tirade against her father.

I'm now standing in the open doorway leading to a set of stairs to the upper floors.

Tanya is within a few yards of me. And at that moment, the man with the moustache badly misjudges Tanya's resolve and makes a run for her. I hear the shot at the same time I see the bullet, meant for him, hit instead a large tank a few feet behind him. On the tank, written in English—*methane*. There are four more just like it and one after the other, they explode, morphing into a giant fireball.

The heat is unbearable even from where I'm standing. Fire sweeps through the lab until Tatyana and the two men are mere silhouettes in a sea of orange. Even Tanya, who's closer to the firestorm than I am, hasn't escaped the devastation. Her hair and clothing sprout flames. Her exposed skin quickly blackens, and she screams in pain. I throw down the armful of papers and lunge at her to smother the flames with my body, but when I grab her arm, I feel her skin slough off in my hand. She pulls away with surprising strength and with one last look at me, she turns and screams Tatyana's name before stumbling toward what I know is only charred remains.

I don't need Google Translate to understand the parting message in Tanya's eyes. She wasn't leaving without Tatyana, so she wasn't leaving. Why she so willingly entered this funeral pyre, I'll never fully understand. What I do understand is the connection they must have—like the one I have with Tati.

It would be easier to rip your soul from your body.

I could die here today but I don't want to die. Not without

saying goodbye to Mom and Dad. Not without saying good-bye to Dr. Sokol and Anthony and Priya. Not without saying goodbye to Tati. Not here, not now, not at all. I want to live, so I run up the stairs through a stairwell that's become a funnel for billowing clouds of black smoke. I duck low and run blind, my shirt pulled up over my nose. My lungs are cooking from the inside out, and as filled as they are with smoke, there's not much room left for air. But somehow, I make it past the man with the bashed-in skull to the office where my birth father, or a version of him, cooked up his evil plan to carve out a legacy of deceit and disgrace. Somehow, I make it to the mirror, and with no effort or thought—just like Tati said, simply by thinking it—I'm transported back to my home with nothing to show for everything that just happened except a deep longing for parts of me I will never have again.

Nothing but one person's decision and good luck has led me to the life I've been granted, a life so different from Tanya and Tatyana's. Everything could have been different for me and now I've seen how. I've witnessed all my better qualities, the ones that would have been nurtured under different circumstances of extreme duress. I've witnessed unbelievable bravery and sacrifice. Could I have done that? Risen to that level of nobility? I did in another world.

I could have.

I *would* have.

My loss feels too profound to bear.

"Ana?" Anthony's anxious face is peering down at me. "You okay?"

I sit up in bed and am flattened by a fit of coughing. Anthony hands me a bottle of water from my bedside table. I glance at the clock, which shows 4:09 p.m.

"Did you have a . . . ?"

"I'm fine," I say, although I feel far from it. "I must have fallen asleep. How long've you been here?"

"A few minutes."

"How'd you get in?"

"I was ringing the doorbell, but nobody answered. I remembered where you left your key from the last time we brought dinner, so I let myself in. Don't worry, I yelled before I came up and made a lot of noise so I wouldn't catch you . . . changing your clothes or anything." His cheeks flush pinkish and it's a little charming.

"So do you need time, or are you ready to go?" he asks.

"I'm ready." I run my fingers through my hair and slip on my sandals.

I cough a few more deep, hoarse, phlegmy coughs and pray I haven't done permanent damage to my lungs. I think about Tanya and Tatyana, dead now in their fiery grave. Ashes to ashes—I know that's their fate. But what of their worlds? Do they go on, or did they cease to exist the moment the girls traded their lives for what they knew was right?

My life feels diminished without them.

Never send to know for whom the bell tolls, we read in English lit. *It tolls for thee.*

"I left dinner on the kitchen counter," Anthony says.

I pull him into a deep hug and then step back and look straight into his eyes. "Have I ever told you what an amazing, incredible, kind, and wonderful human being you are? And how grateful I am that we got to be friends this year? Truly, from the bottom of my heart?"

He blinks slowly, bewildered by my inexplicable flood of emotion, just short of tears. "Maybe you mentioned it once or twice," he says. "But, nah, I don't think so." He wrinkles his nose. "Your hair smells like smoke."

When I walk through the front door of the hospital, I have an urgent need to get to Dad as soon as possible. The elevator takes an eternity to arrive, and once I'm on and staring at my shoes instead of the impassive faces around me, the floor numbers light up and then go dark at a maddeningly slow speed. Each time the elevator stops to let someone off, I feel precious moments ticking away. When I finally reach my floor and move quickly toward the nurse's station I could reach blindfolded by now, I already know I'm too late.

"I'm so sorry. He's gone." A kind nurse I've gotten to know steps out from behind the desk to wrap a comforting arm around my shoulder. "Your mom's in there with him. I was just calling you."

But it doesn't register, although I can see the curtain pulled across the glass cubicle, giving Mom the privacy she needs to accept this truth and prepare for the rest of her life without Dad. It can't be real. This beautiful man who traveled halfway across the world to give me the second chance that separated me from Tanya or Tatyana. Who built the foundation of my life with the security of his unconditional love. Who never failed to bring a smile to my face no matter how bad I thought my day was going. How can Dad be gone?

Hours later, when Mom's distracted with paperwork that she clings to like a lifeline, I wander out to the waiting room where somehow Priya and Anthony know to be there and are waiting for me. But Dr. Sokol is also there and asks for a moment, inviting me into a small doctor's consultation area nearby.

"I'm so sorry," she says as she wraps me in her arms. "So very sorry."

I'm numb and nothing feels real yet. Will it? Can I handle it?

"I was with them," I tell her. "Two of them. In Russia. They're both dead now. I tried to bring back papers . . . proof . . . but nothing made it back with me, so I have nothing to give you. Nothing." My flat monotone must convey the same sense of unreality I feel about my father's passing, my real father—the one who loved me. "You should probably know that Klara was your biological sister, and that my genes are repairing themselves. Naturally. Soon, I'll be done with the me-zures. Tati and I won't be able to reach each other anymore. And now that it's happening, I don't know whether to be happy or sad."

If she's surprised about Klara, she doesn't show it, but then we've never really talked about Klara before. "Ana," she says. "I've loved you from a distance for your whole life, and I wish it could go on forever. We all live with the decisions we make. We can't go back and change what's propelled us forward, but you've had the chance to at least see some of what your life might have been. And what has that brought you? Unhappiness? Perhaps we're never meant to know what might have been, because then we cease to cherish what is. You say your doors are closing, so now's the time to choose which life you want. Tati's life is safe and happy. I've never wanted anything for you but to be safe and happy. Paul will protect you for now, but he can't always be there. I don't want you to spend a lifetime looking over your shoulder the way I have."

"I . . . I'm not sure what you mean," I say, although I have a sense.

"*Tvoi otets bil zamechatel'nyi chelovek,*" she says.

"It's true, Dad *was* a great man," I answer. "I was blessed."

How did I understand what she just said in Russian? Are Tanya and Tatyana already a part of me?

Dr. Sokol is pensive. She's sad and so am I. "Someday we may never see each other again," she says. "You will make the best decision for yourself." And at that moment I wonder whether I've been helped or hurt to know there was any other way than the only way I knew.

That night Mom and I sleep in the same bed together. We fall asleep weeping in each other's arms. Mom sleeps deeply for the first time in a long time, and I pray that if she's having any dreams at all, they're good dreams about Dad and the happy times we shared.

When Tati comes, I sense she already knows about Dad. I also feel she might be coming to say goodbye.

"Our dad?" she whispers so as not to wake Mom who's sleeping only a few feet away from us.

I nod my head.

"I'm so sorry, Ana." She leans over to hug me and that feeling of heat, tingling and melting into each other happens everywhere our bodies meet.

I jerk out of her embrace and take in a sharp breath, triggering the cough that's still roiling my half-baked lungs. With one hand over my mouth to muffle the sound, I motion her into the hallway with the other.

"Are you here to say goodbye?" I ask, and this time she nods.

"I almost didn't make it," she says. "Maybe I'm losing my touch."

I can't bear the thought of saying goodbye to her. This is going to be the hardest of all. There will be no more Tati in my world. No Tanya or Tatyana. "It's not that," I say. "I was with the others . . . both of them. Our DNA is repairing itself. Soon we won't have the me-zures, but we won't have each other, either."

Tati looks like she's about to cry. "Come with me, Ana," she blurts out. "Our lives aren't so different. We have the same parents, the same friends. Do you remember when we touched hands and they kind of melted together? Maybe we *can* be the same person. Maybe we're *supposed* to be."

I think about the time when Tanya, Tatyana, and I had the same experience of melting, merging into each other. And now they're within me; I've been certain of that since Dr. Sokol spoke to me in Russian and I understood every word. Maybe we *are* supposed to be one person, and nature is finally catching up to us. Prevailing in the end like it always does.

I think about Mom in bed right now, sleeping peacefully and then waking to the new sad reality of her life. What if I wasn't there when she woke? Would she be losing a husband and a daughter? They say if a tree falls in a forest and no one's there to hear it, it doesn't make a sound. If I'm removed from my life, does my life continue to exist or are we all seeing a different version of a multi-layered life through our own eyes—a life that ends with us?

Tati says no time passes when she visits me in my world. No time passed when I was with Tanya and Tatyana either. Doesn't that mean our world stops when we're not in it?

"Even if I wanted to, how would we do it?"

"Hold onto me and don't let go this time. Try to come back through the tunnel with me."

"How long could I exist in your world? We don't know the answer to that question."

"How long will you exist in yours? We don't know the answer to that or anything else. But for now, my life is safe and yours isn't. Our father is alive and well. Our mother is happy. Nobody knows what's going to happen tomorrow or the next day, so let's see what happens. Let's see if—"

"If I can become you?"

"If we can become each other," Tati says. "Before it's too late."

CHAPTER 27

"Here you go, girls," Dad says. "I think I've finally perfected it. Spaghetti à la George. Spiralized zucchini noodles. No meat, no dairy, just plenty of veggies in the sauce. Hope you like it." Dad ladles out a generous helping of sauce over the noodles.

"Oh my gosh, George." Priya chuckles. "You've become Mr. Super Healthy. And such an amazing chef, too."

"Why thank you, my dear," he says as he ladles out a serving of sauce onto Mom's plate. "Maggie, will you be ready for our walk after dinner?"

"Anytime." Mom winks. "Just say the word and I'll follow you anywhere."

"You guys both look . . . amazing," Priya says, and I have to agree. Mom and Dad have both dropped twenty pounds and replaced it with a healthy glow.

"Care to join us for a walk afterward?" Dad asks.

"Next time, Dad. We have to get to work."

TATIANA

Back in my room, after dinner, Priya sets up her laptop on my desk and I lay out everything on my bed. We're working on college applications, which seem to be more fun when we're doing them together or at least doing them in the same room. We're applying to the same places and keeping our fingers crossed that they want us both. Afterward, we'll tackle homework.

"I had one of those dreams again," I say. "Where I was speaking Russian."

Priya swivels around on the chair and looks at me. "How do you even know it's Russian? What if it's . . . I don't know, something else?"

"Because the second I wake up, I google the few words that are still stuck in my mind. And it's Russian, trust me."

"So, what're you saying in your dreams? In Russian." She launches off with her right foot until the chair is spinning with her on it.

"Stop it, you're making me dizzy just looking at you. Anyway, I have no idea. Just random words."

Priya plants her foot on the ground and the chair comes to a halt. "Okay, back to our essays. What are you going to write for the last one?"

"Actually, I was thinking of writing about Nurse Pat."

"Nurse Pat, as in . . . ?"

"He was the school nurse just before we got there. Anyway, I was thinking that being a school nurse is something everyone takes for granted but they probably make a huge difference in the lives of some students."

"But how would he have made a difference in yours?

Remember, this is a person who's made a difference in *your* life, not someone else's. And why him? Why not Nurse Whoever-it-is right-now? Do you even know?"

"No, but . . ." I trail off.

"So, anyway, I was thinking of writing about—"

"Priya, let's text Anthony right now and see if he wants to come over. I overheard him today saying he's working on his applications tonight too."

"Anthony?" Priya doesn't even swivel the chair this time. She just twists her neck to look back at me and then returns to her screen as though waiting for it to give her inspiration.

"I mean . . . I feel kind of sorry for him, being new and all. It must be lonely to work on applications all by yourself."

"If you want," Priya says. "I mean, it's kind of random, but sure, why not? Do you even have his number?"

"I'll see if he's in the directory."

Priya gets up from her chair and plops herself down on the bed beside me. "Now that you've totally distracted me from working, have I told you lately that I love you?"

"Yes, ma'am." I plant a kiss on her lips. "But you're lying on top of my homework."

She pulls the sheets of paper from underneath her and hands them to me. "Tatiana, I've come to a decision. Now I'm being serious."

"Uh oh." I close the lid of my laptop and set it behind me. I lean forward, propping my elbows on my folded legs. "What's up?"

"I'm going to tell my parents about me. About *us*."

This is totally unexpected and kind of mind-blowing.

"O . . . kay. I can't deny that I'm thrilled, but what brought this on?"

Priya's lying on her back facing the ceiling and its universe of glow-in-the-dark stars. Her lips are slightly parted, and I have the ridiculous and fleeting thought that if a star fell down right now, it could land in her mouth.

"I realized that if I wait to tell them until I've gone off to college, they'll think it's college that changed me, and I don't ever want them to think that. I want them to know this is me. Who I really am and who I've always been."

Tears come to my eyes, but I don't want Priya to see them. I don't want her to feel anything but my pride in her, and I'm worried she might mistake my tears for something else. I squeeze them tight and when I open them again, I'm back in control. Sort of.

"I'm so proud of you," I say. "And your parents will be too, once they have the chance to process everything."

"I hope so." She reaches for my hand and squeezes it. "But either way, it doesn't change what's right. What's *me*."

I can't remember the last time I've felt so content. Life seems to be falling into place in all the right ways and I'm excited about my future. I have the greatest parents and am in love with the greatest girl in the world. And she loves me back. I almost want to pinch myself to make sure I'm not dreaming.

"Oh, I forgot to tell you my results came back. Third time's a charm, I guess, because it finally worked."

"The DNA?" Priya sits up and looks at me expectantly. "What'd it say?"

"Like we expected. Northwestern Russian, some Eastern European. No big surprises."

"Glad they finally got their act together," she says. She glances at her laptop and then back to me, her expression thoughtful, and I can tell she has something on her mind. "Tatiana, remember when you dropped the pencil that day and we both leaned over to pick it up at the same time and our hands touched?"

"Of course." The memory makes my heart warm. "How could I ever forget?"

"The random things that drive our lives . . . the decisions we make based on those things. What do you think would have happened to us if that pencil hadn't dropped? Do you think you still would have approached me? Would we still have gotten together?"

There are so many variables that run through my mind. The obstacles that stood in our way, like the disapproval of her family. My general reticent manner and tendency to introversion. The courage I got from the way she smiled at me.

"Without a doubt," I say.

ACKNOWLEDGMENTS

Thank you to Caroline Larsen, Mari Kesselring, and the staff of Flux and North Star Editions for falling in love with my story and giving me the platform and the support to tell it.

Ricochet is a work of science fiction, and in no way should events in the story be construed as a representation of the very real condition of epilepsy. Thankfully, organizations such as the Epilepsy Foundation and others like it are available to provide support and information to those who suffer from seizure disorders.

The multiverse has long been a tantalizing concept, bewitching me ever since my first college physics class. Who among us has never paused to reflect on how a decision or a chance encounter has altered our life path? Much of the science in this book is already here. The rest is, of course, the fiction part of science fiction, limited only by our imaginations. Lucky for me I had a crack team of physicians and scientists who didn't mind (or if they did, didn't let on) being pestered with odd texts from me at odd times of the day and night, asking the most improbable questions. So, to Joseph F. Antognini, MD; Joseph M. Antognini, PhD; Lucas A. Berla, PhD; and Mark Lewin, MD . . . thank you! I promise to never bother you again (okay, my fingers were actually crossed just then).

To Igor Charsov and Alla Volkova, thank you so much for giving me a peek into the beautiful Russian language.